SISTERS IN LAW

FRAT PARTY

JOHN ELLSWORTH

PENNY LAWN PRESS

For the People of Mexico
Gracias Por Su Bienvenida

1

Theta Kappa Alpha had a party. It was homecoming weekend, which was reason enough to throw a toga party, an affair where the pledges and brothers dressed in sheets and Greco-Roman garb and sandals. Lots of young, eager sorority sisters arrived and crowded the room.

The TKA fraternity house occupied a half block near the university. It was a sleek longboat of a house, occupying three floors. It also had a basement, largely unfurnished except for the handcart of folding tables and the five handcarts of folding chairs. With all the tubular furniture unfolded, the 35 x 40 foot room easily accommodated three long rows of multiple tables each.

At the head of the tables, on the north end, were a dais and a tub. On the dais sat the homecoming king, a brother in the fraternity, and his date, a Kappa, who was prettier than the homecoming queen although she wasn't the homecoming queen. In the tub were a bed of crushed ice and a keg of beer. There were four other tubs and kegs scattered strategically around the cavern. The rule among the brothers was that if you were too inebriated to make it to the keg and back to your table, you were shut off. It was a simple rule; everyone understood it. By eleven o'clock more than a dozen of the forty-two members were shut off. Most of these had been carried upstairs to the pledge dorm and the brothers' rooms. Herculean vomiting had erupted upstairs and it reeked of illness. But that was upstairs.

Downstairs the party was under full sail. A reggae band came and set up. Why a reggae band at a Roman party? Why not? replied the brothers.

The girls wore sheets belted around the waist and pulled over one shoulder and tucked down in the waist on the back. The belts were red and black and white. Like the men of the fraternity, they also wore sandals and woven crowns of twigs in their hair.

Large red plastic cups of beer were swilled and swigged and spilled and abandoned on the tables while the partygoers made merry on the dance floor.

At midnight a Theta Kappa Alpha tradition was honored. Everyone filed past the king's dais and kissed his class ring. It was traditional, required, and even those too intoxicated to care were assisted into the queue.

The king was Noah Adams and he was from Anchorage, Alaska, where he had starred on the high school basketball team and taken them to state in his senior year. A basketball scholarship at the Big 10 University had brought him to the Midwest, where he thrived. His team had made the Sweet Sixteen two Marches in a row, but had lost out to the competition both times. Noah was mindful of that fact-- and it was the one regret that he had so far in life, that he hadn't advanced with his team to the Elite Eight, much less the Final Four.

As the final pledge filed past and kissed the ruby ring, Noah's cell phone chirped (carried in his pocket Tee beneath his toga).

"Upstairs, Franklin's room. We've got one ready."

"Coming," said Noah, and he told his date to find someone to dance with, that he was needed outside.

He ran up the four flights of stairs.

Franklin's room was the largest on the floor because he was a senior and in charge of room assignments. Noah opened the door and went inside.

There were two brothers and two pledges and one young girl.

Near the single bed stood Steve Emel, a junior from Piscataway majoring in computer science. Emel was a partygoer from day one, and was usually so intoxicated by 10 p.m. that he had to be helped upstairs to his room, next door to Franklin's. But tonight Steve had come upstairs with his date, the young girl lying on the bed unconscious.

Proudly, Emel said to Noah, "I cherry methed her." Meaning, in campus lingo, he had slipped her what was known to the fraternity brothers as cherry meth, which was known to pharmacists as gamma hydroxybutyrate, a CNS depressant. Easily acquired, it was used to facilitate sexual intercourse with one's date for the evening, commonly known as date rape.

A second brother in the room was Hanley Miscont III, the son of a tire manufacturer in Ohio. Hanley was the coolest of all the brothers, driving his own Rolls Royce and sending stand-ins to appear for his classes and take lecture notes. Hanley was short and always attempting to utter profundities which, to most listeners, were often more idiotic than profound. "Heaven is today; hell is tomorrow," he would say. Or, "Labor builds character; sleep builds healthy bodies. Take your pick, because you don't need both." Stuff like that. Hanley was also the student who ordered and paid for the beer kegs, as he was twenty-two and could purchase alcohol legally. In his sixth year at the university, he was a second term junior.

When Noah came into the room, Hanley was examining the nude girl's vagina. As he went about his adventure, he would snap pictures with his cellphone. Even as Noah watched, Hanley turned the girl onto her stomach, balanced her on her knees and shoulders and splayed arms, and snapped several pictures of her naked buttocks and vaginal area, making sure her face was turned so that identification of the victim was easy. He had no particular dislike of the girl; it was just how date rape was done. Pictures, posted to the Internet, just because.

A third brother in the room was a pledge, Jordan Weeks. Jordan was from Tupelo, Mississippi, the birthplace of Elvis Presley, and his claim to fame was that his grandmother had once spent a week with

Elvis in Paris, where they had ridden motorcycles and spent long afternoons making love in a room that overlooked the Seine. No one bothered to ask Jordan how he knew this about his grandmother. He would have lied if they had, because Jordan was one of those people with the ability to conceive and toss out a lie without missing a beat. Jordan was nude and touching himself--stroking, actually--as he watched Hanley's arrangement of the girl in her various poses. A freshman pledge, Jordan knew he would be last in line, so his stroking was moderated by his known limitations. He didn't want to over-extend before his turn came to "ride the pony," as they called it.

A fourth brother was Parks N. Swansong, a sophomore pledge from Nutley, Virginia, majoring in communications. He was handsome by TV standards and planned to make a living behind the TV anchor desk. Parks was also very bright and burdened with an unrelenting conscience. He knew that what was about to happen was morally wrong, ethically contrary to his true self, and highly illegal. Still, he had to go along if he wanted to ever be sworn into the fraternity as a brother with full rights and privileges. The fraternity was known for its post-graduation ties and recommendations that worked behind the scenes for members making job applications or seeking contacts for their businesses or professions. In the present economy a guy couldn't have too many resources. Watching the nude girl being handled and probed, Parks shuddered. He had already decided that he would appear to participate but he wouldn't actually effect penetration. Smoke and mirrors, like TV programming--he was all up in that. No, he would look like he was taking her, but he wouldn't actually do it.

Franklin. Although it was Franklin's room and Franklin's bed, Franklin wasn't present.

The fifth brother was Noah, the president, newly arrived on the scene of the crime. As the chapter president, it was his job to settle the lineup.

"I go first," he told the group. "Then Steve, Hanley, and Jordan. Parks, you're last unless you jump in ahead of someone. You're the wild card and you can play anytime. Except ahead of me."

Just then the door opened behind them, a head appeared, and Noah back-kicked the door shut without turning around. "Out!" he shouted. Jordan leapt around and locked the door. Noah nodded.

Pounding on the door ensued; someone was outside and demanding to be let in. "What the hell are you guys doing in my room?" demanded the voice. It was recognized as belonging to Franklin.

But he was ignored.

Noah continued. "Hanley, you're doing the snaps. That's great. Have them posted by morning."

"Where do you want them?"

"Usual websites, ex-fiancée this and ex-wife that. You know the drill."

Parks, his conscience biting, asked, "Why would you do that? No need to put her picture anywhere, is there?"

"Well, duh," said Adams. "We ruin her, we own this bitch. We can have her anytime we want 'cause no one else will want her."

"So we're creating a sex slave? Is that what we're doing here?"

"Hey, Parks," someone else said. "Don't go all righteous, brother. Pull it out and stroke it. We need to see you boff this bitch."

Noah asked, "Any other dumb questions?"

Nobody had any questions. This wasn't their first time out in the boat.

By now Hanley had the girl on her back again and was spreading her legs. He looked up and shouted at the door, assuming it was Franklin, whose room it was, "Got any Vaseline?"

"What are you guys doing in my room?" came through the door. Then he was ignored.

Her name was Bussie Speers. She was a Kappa and she'd never seen it coming.

2

Bussie Speers was eighteen years old, a freshman majoring in zoology with a plan to attend med school or vet school, depending on acceptances. She had always been a friendly but deep down private person. That was before the boys stole her life. By nine the next morning, nude pictures of her had migrated around the world. With the clicks of buttons by faceless haters, her life was over.

She was five-ten, with blue eyes and blonde, nearly white, hair that was bleached out during the six outdoor months she spent every year playing tennis. Even, white teeth and an easy smile had made her a top choice for the sororities during rush week two months earlier. She had finally pledged and was keeping a 3.8 on a 4.0, so life was looking good.

Until the TKA party.

Since that night, and since moving back home to Barrington the next day, she had remained indoors, in her room, peeking out the curtained window and watching fall slip into early winter. Upon withdrawal, she had received W's on her academic transcript.

The university called her daily. Would she consider returning? Would she accept university-paid counseling? Would she like to convert to online and finish her courses by computer? They had even offered to waive her tuition. All in all they couldn't have been friend-lier. Or less terrified by what might be coming next, knowing that her father was a high profile lawyer in the same county where their school produced graduates like Oreo produced black and white. Eventually the university completed its investigation. They had learned very little. No names were uncovered, no identities, no one was talking. "It might have been someone from the outside," they told Bussie's father. "Maybe party crashers."

The morning after the TKA toga party, Bussie had watched her nude body appear on her cellphone, courtesy of a friend's text that said, simply, "I know you'd want to know."

She was sitting in the student lounge at the student union when she received the text. One minute she was joking and laughing with five other sorority pledges like herself; the next minute her life was over. When she first saw it, she wasn't sure it was her. But then more texts followed: close-up of face, close-up of vaginal opening spread for all to see, close-up of semen-spattered breasts and pubis--and various poses where her body had been arranged into severe contor-tions, all of them exposing her sex organs, all of them revealing her face. Stunned, she stood up from her chair at the round table of laughing friends, and moaned a long, low moan that traveled up through her torso and out her mouth in a pained expression that ended, "Noooooooooo! It can't be! Oh, my God!" She lapsed into a stupor and her roommate took the phone from her. She viewed several of the pictures. Then she grabbed Bussie by the arm and led her from the building.

Outside on the sidewalk, the friend stood before Bussie and implored her to talk.

"Talk to me, Bus! Talk to me! We can handle this. I know there's something we can do. You have to call your dad."

Bussie, all but catatonic, simply stared ahead. Her future flashed in front of her.

Again taking control, the roommate steered Bussie back to their dorm. At 9 a.m. the halls were virtually empty, as only freshmen like

Bussie and her roomie were dumb enough to sign up for classes starting before 10 a.m.

They unlocked and went inside their room. The roomie's father, a carpet wholesaler, had sprung for wall-to-wall white shag. The girls were fixed, as they liked to say. The usual posters and idols looked down from each girl's wall and both room halves were equally cluttered with discarded clothes, books, plastic drink cups and bottles, snack food leftovers and all the detritus that goes with being eighteen, innocent, and in love with life.

Which was the moment it ended for Bussie.

Looking at their room, she knew she could never return here. The Internet made sure of that. By now, she had no doubt, her images were as available in Hong Kong as they were in Sydney, San Francisco or London. And definitely on the university campus in Chicago. She knew, all too well, what happened to girls who posed nude because some boyfriend had asked, only later on to watch their pictures flood the Internet when the boyfriend-girlfriend thing inevitably ended. There were even websites dedicated to nude photographs of ex-girlfriends, ex-fiancées, and even ex-wives. She shuddered and sank to the floor. Those carefree days of just hanging out and hoping to meet someone special--those days were done. Her life had changed irremediably. Then she turned her head and grievously threw up on her unmade bed. Her roomie rushed for the wastebasket.

Her father had warned her in the fourth grade, "Don't ever say or do anything on the Internet you don't want the whole world to see. The you that is you is available to everyone in the world if it's on the Internet. This is your reality. Don't be nasty, don't be coquettish, don't be sexual, don't be naked, don't be spiteful, don't be angry, and don't be mean--in fact, the best idea for what to put on the Internet at your age is to put nothing there at all. That would be my best advice to you."

What would he think? she thought with a gasp. Even her own father would see her nakedness before it was all over. And her mother? Don't even go there. She was ruined and she knew it.

"I have to move out. Today, Cindy."

Cindy didn't immediately respond. Then she said, "I think so. We can't sugarcoat this. Forgive me, but I'm not going to tell you it will be all right, 'cause it's not."

"Thanks for the hope, Cin."

"You always said you liked me because I tell it like it is."

"Still do. What do I tell my dad?"

Cindy shook her head. "The truth. Tell him you went to the TKA party. Tell him someone put something in your drink."

"I only had part of one beer. I don't even like alcohol. You know me."

"Miss Straight Arrow, I guess."

Cindy sat and thought long and hard. Then she said, "Okay, here's what I see happening. You withdraw from school. You take a year off. During that year you cut off all your hair and have plastic surgery. Wear contacts that make your eyes a different color. Go through a legal name change. Then enroll in a school in California. No one will know you. Everyone loves you here; everyone will love you out there."

"But I don't want to go to California! I live here! I love it here."

"Sorry, Bus, 'here' is no longer an option. That's done."

Bussie didn't reply. She had lapsed back into her stupor. She would later say she couldn't force a thought to form even though she was trying. She looked down. Her nails were light blue, except for the ring finger of her left hand. That nail was black with a white sparkly star. It was how it was done at that time and place. Just how it was done.

And she had done it all like it was supposed to be done. She had fit in. She had created a world outside her family and outside old friends. It was a new world of new faces, new places, and new ideas being hurled around in classrooms like confetti at those bashes whenever her dad won re-election. Except that world was gone. Cindy was right. "Here" was no longer an option.

In fact, maybe even life was no longer an option. She suddenly fell in on herself and began sinking into a deepening mire of depression. No matter where she went, East Coast or West, someone, somewhere, at some point, would spot her nude body and face and it would come right back on her. Having children was out. The possibility of her new Internet persona finding its way to her own kids made that avenue impassable. She couldn't and wouldn't journey down that road. So what was there for her? Was there nothing?

Her life was over.

She pressed speed-dial 1 and waited for her father to pick up his direct line.

3

Christine Susmann stood at the counsel table. "Give me one moment, Judge, please."

She tossed her head back and gazed at the ceiling. Quickly she weighed who should appear as the next witness. Her dark eyes took in the jury and she saw they had enough patience left in them for an important witness; no need to tread water the rest of the day. She ran a hand through her shag hairstyle, allowing the $400 cut to fall naturally back into a perfect frame for her face. She lowered her gaze to meet the eyes of the judge. She nodded and he raised a hand indicating she should proceed.

"Defense calls Mishabbi Currant to the stand," she said, and looked at the bailiff to indicate he should retrieve the witness from the hallway. He strode briskly up the aisle and opened the courtroom doors. The jury and judge and spectators and participants heard the bailiff call the witness.

She entered the courtroom wearing black tights, a plaid pleated skirt, a turtleneck sweater, and a gold chain around her neck with a crucifix pendant. Her face was very pale and her black hair was cropped close to her head and around her ears. Small coral studs adorned her ears, the only color on an otherwise white-on-white face. A small, friendly smile was offered to the jury as she walked past them on the way to the witness stand. She could have passed for twenty-three but she was actually thirty-three.

Christine nodded at the young woman once she was seated in the witness chair.

"State your name, please."

"Mishabbi Currant."

"Mishabbi, where do you live?"

"Here in Chicago. Do I have to give my street address? I'd rather not."

"No, the question doesn't call for your street address," said Christine. "City and state are enough."

"Thank you."

Christine checked the judge with a quick glance. She needed Judge Leamon Waters to really focus on the witness. It would be his job to decide whether Mishabbi Currant qualified as an expert witness. A responsible man who was known to be a fair and impartial jurist, he appeared that he didn't want to miss a word of it. He was hard of hearing in his left ear so he inclined his head sharply in the direction of the witness. His long white hair fell away from his head on the left side and he brushed it back into place.

Christine continued. "You are aware that this case today is a sexual assault case?"

"Yes."

"You are aware that my client, Evan Rushdie, claims that the sexual exchange between himself and the alleged victim was actually consensual?"

The witness looked at the young man sitting next to Christine. His name was Evan Rushdie, a sixteen-year-old boy who'd had his driver's license all of two months. He was tall and lanky and shaving his face was still down the road, although his upper lip was trying out light, immature whiskers. He wore black jeans and a white shirt with a cream tie. His hair was neatly trimmed and his shoes had been recently shined. He was making a concerted effort to sit up straight at the table, as Christine had directed.

Mishabbi looked from Evan back to Christine. "You told me that Evan said the sex was consensual. You told me that when we met. First time, I think."

Christine stood fully upright and looked at the jury. She was wearing a gray pinstripe suit with white shirt and red necktie. Her red lipstick was modest, applied sparingly--not too much, not too little-- as was the light eyeliner. She fastened her eyes on those jurors who were looking back and smiled. "How many times have we met, Mishabbi?"

"Twice."

"Where was that?"

"Once at Kathy's Kafe and once at your office."

"The first time we met, what was the topic of that meeting?"

The witness fingered the gold chain around her neck. "You asked me some questions about how I was doing, stuff like that. Then you said you'd heard that I was a witch, or had once been a witch."

"What did you tell me about being a witch?"

"I told you that I had once been a witch."

"What happened next?"

"We made a date to meet in your office. That was for the next day. So I came to your office and you explained to me about Evan's criminal case. You said the girlfriend was in high school and she was claiming that Evan had raped her. You said Evan was a freshman at Central High and that he had been seeing the girl for about one month."

"Did we discuss you becoming a witness here?"

The pale young woman nodded. "We did. You asked me if I would testify in this case about being a witch and about some of the practices of witchcraft."

"What did you say?"

The witness shrugged and looked at the jury. "I didn't really want to do it, but you explained to me the trouble Evan was in. You said he could go to prison. Then we talked about what happened in the girl-friend's bedroom."

"Now, let me ask about your practice of witchcraft."

"The black arts."

"Yes, the black arts. How long were you a witch?"

"Ten years, give or take."

"Are you a witch now?"

"No, I'm a Christian now."

"Tell us what it means to be a witch."

"Well, in my practice, I closely followed the ceremonies and practices of witchcraft. It all depended on what we were addressing."

"What do you mean, 'addressing'?"

"Say there was a girl after your boyfriend. We would have a ceremony where we would sacrifice her to Satan."

"Actual sacrifice?"

"No, it was always ritual. Never the real thing."

"What about sacrificing animals, drinking blood, the stuff some of us might have heard about?"

Mishabbi smiled and leaned back. "That's voodoo. That hasn't got anything to do with being a witch."

"Was some of your practice spiritual?"

"Yes. I exteriorized at times."

"What's that mean?"

"I went on journeys through the universe. By trancing."

"Trancing."

"Putting myself into a mental state where I could leave my body and travel through space and time."

Christine looked over at the jury out of the corner of her eye. Most, especially the women, were clearly skeptical. They had leaned away from the witness, arms folded across chests, not making eye contact with her. The lawyer knew she was not accomplishing what needed to be done. But she wasn't finished yet.

"When you and I spoke in my office, Mishabbi, do you remember me asking you about becoming an expert witness in this case?"

"Yes."

"I want to pursue that with you. You've told us you were a witch for ten years. This next question might strike you as odd, but this is how we qualify witnesses to be experts: we ask them about training, education, and experience. You've already told us about some of your experiences, so let me ask you about education. Is there any sort of training or education that a person would go through to become a witch?"

"Well, I started with the books. There are books about the pagan holidays and practices. Lots of meditation on the Goddess and God is required. I did mine on the coast of Oregon, where I had my first out-of-body flight."

"Where did you go? Rather, what happened?"

"I went into space. I looked at the planets, zoomed around stars, and got caught up in a thunderstorm. It drove me back to Oregon and back into my body."

"What else might one do to become a witch?"

"Learn herbal, crystal and candle magic."

"Did you learn these things?"

"I did. By joining a coven."

"You joined a group of witches?"

"Yes, we practiced our magic together. We had ceremonies, we celebrated pagan holidays, we chanted to the Goddess, everything necessary to practice our magic."

Christine paused and looked at the judge. He appeared rapt. She decided that she would attempt to qualify the witness as an expert at that point in the testimony.

"Have you ever testified before as a witch?"

"No."

"You have talked to other people about witches and what they do?"

"Yes."

"Are most people knowledgeable about witches and rituals?"

"Not yet. No, they aren't. They look at it like some kind of disease."

"Tell us what you know about what happened between Evan and Charlene Meier on the afternoon of the sexual exchange."

"You told me that they were in Charlene's bedroom in Niles. The police reports confirmed that. I read them all. Plus I read the witness statements, including the girl's statement and her father's statement.

Anyway, the girl and Evan got together in her bedroom every afternoon after school and listened to music together."

"What else did you learn they did together?"

"They practiced witchcraft."

"What and how did you learn about what happened sexually?"

"Like I said, I read the police reports and I read Charlene's statement. Then I listened to the recording, the confession Evan gave to the detectives."

"How old was Evan when this happened?"

"Almost fifteen."

"How old was Charlene?"

"Seventeen."

"Do you have an opinion based on a reasonable degree of certainty in the field of witchcraft about the sexual exchange that went on?"

Mishabbi nodded. "I do."

"What is that opinion?"

"Objection!"

Christine had known all along that Woody Smitts would object at that exact moment. Woody was the First Assistant District Attorney, and was heralded as one of the best prosecutors in the Cook County DA's office. He was known for being a hard-nose on sex crimes and had made this case one that was impossible to settle with a negotiated plea. He had demanded five years' imprisonment and not a minute less. Now, Woody launched into the basis for his objection: that there was no recognized science known as witchcraft and the witness wasn't an expert--couldn't be--in something that wasn't real.

Christine responded, pointing out that while everyone might agree that black magic was a fraud, the practice itself had been ritualized and it had its practitioners of its rituals, including the young couple around which this case was swirling.

Judge Waters listened intently, first to Woody, then to Christine. "Overruled," he quickly decided. "She may answer the question."

Christine began again. "Do you recall me asking whether you have an opinion about the sexual encounter?"

"I do."

"Please tell us that opinion about the sexual encounter."

"My opinion is that they were practicing the ritual known as the Maidenhead."

"What is the basis for your opinion?"

"First, they had been practicing black arts together ever since they met at a basketball dance a month before. He was heavy into *Dungeons and Dragons* and she was heavy into Wicca readings and even belonged to a coven. She drew him in."

"Tell us what facts you are relying on to determine that they were practicing a ritual of black magic?"

Mishabbi faced the jury. "First, they both had their clothes off. That was her idea, according to Evan. Then she lay back on her bed and told him to get on top of her. This is the typical Maidenhead routine. In the ritual, the male then penetrates the female and withdrawal prior to ejaculation follows. Candles are then lit and the couple sits up in bed, across from each other, and they lapse into chanting spells. That's what he said actually happened. Her story is different. She says there wasn't supposed to be penetration, that he forced himself on her."

"According to the witchcraft practice, however, you say the ritual actually requires penetration."

"It does. I believe she performed the ritual and used Evan, but then when her father came home, he walked in and caught them together. So she immediately cried rape."

Smitts again exploded out of his chair. "Objection! Calls for an opinion outside the scope of her so-called expertise."

"Overruled. She may tell the jury what facts she's relying on. The father catching them together has been established by Detective Salk. Please answer the question."

The judge nodded at Christine, who asked, "How did you know the father caught them together?"

"Evan said that to the police. It's in the police reports. That's how his jaw was broken and wired shut. The girl's father hit him and kicked him."

Christine looked over at the jury. Arms were no longer crossed on chests; the members were for the most part leaning forward, receptive and making eye contact with the witness.

"To summarize, it's your testimony that Evan and Charlene, a freshman and senior, were engaged in a Wiccan ritual until the father walked in?"

"Yes."

"Nothing further, Your Honor. I would ask that we break for the day now as it's almost five o'clock and it's Friday. I'm sure the jurors want to get right home."

"Very well. It's four-fifty. We'll resume at nine a.m. Monday with the district attorney's cross-examination. Please remember the admonition. Do not discuss the case with anyone, do not read about the case and do not watch TV reports or listen to radio reports about the case. You're excused."

Sitting next to Christine, Evan Rushdie was making a concerted effort to sit up straight at the table, and his hands were trying to remember to abstain from the customary fidget of a young boy brought up to the principal's office--or worse, into court for all the world to hear. While Christine stood and began stuffing books and papers into her roll-around briefcase, Evan remained frozen in place.

"Hey." She smiled at him. "It's okay. You can stand up now."

"I didn't know."

"I know you didn't. This is all very foreign, I'm sure."

"I'm so--so--"

"Let me guess. You're scared out of your wits."

The young man allowed a small smile. "Exactly. I had no idea they were going to go into all this--this private stuff."

She dropped a gray copy of *Illinois Evidence* into the briefcase. "Oh, yes. Nothing is off-limits inside a courtroom."

"Charlene--she got me to do it all, you know."

"I know. I'm sure she was responsible for much of what happened."

"I mean, I--I--"

"You weren't exactly taken away at gunpoint. I get it."

"Gunpoint?"

"Never mind. Let's get out of here."

They hurried up the aisle to the two main doors and headed left toward the elevators, stopping momentarily while Christine scanned the waiting crowd in order to be sure the jury had already been taken downstairs.

It was safe.

They joined the crowd awaiting the elevator, all eyes fastened on the blinking numbers above the doors.

SAFE inside her office where no one was watching, Christine kicked off her Givenchy pumps and sat back in her executive chair and wiggled her toes. "Such fine toes," she said to her feet. She smiled at her words. Law school graduation and the bar exam were almost a year in the rearview, and she was just now beginning to realize the world was, indeed, nuts and that the practice of law was making her nuts, too. At least the things people got themselves into and called her about--those things were nuts.

She pulled open the double drawer and retrieved her slingback sandals. They said "Prada" on the topside and still reeked of Barney's of New York, the scene of her last shopping spree. She had always been a very reserved woman when she had worked as a paralegal, one who more often than not dressed down. But since jumping into Chicago's mainstream of the practice of law and accepting that she not only had to act the part but look the part as well, she had taken to wearing designer brands not especially of her liking but definitely expected in the hallowed halls of justice around Chicago. In short, she had been warned by friendly female lawyers that the judges in Chicago put great stock in how lawyers not only comported them-selves and how well they were versed in the law and how prepared they sounded when they spoke out in court, but also in how they looked and what they wore. Chicago was a city and it was cosmopolitan and she was resigned to playing a new role. New to her, at least.

She opened the top drawer of her massive teak desk and plucked out a half-full pack of Salems. She spun the tiny wheel on the gold, engraved lighter and inhaled mightily. A coughing spell immediately overwhelmed her chest and lungs and she stabbed the cigarette out in the glass ashtray she hid inside the same drawer. It was a terrible habit, she thought, and she kept it hidden from Sonny and the kids. "Call it my nasty little secret," she told herself. "I'm entitled to at least one nasty little secret, after all." She drank a mouthful of the early morning coffee in the Starbucks venti cup on her desk. Anything to wash away the taste of the cigarette. Then she pressed the intercom switch and said, "Okay. Bring it in."

Billy A. Tattinger knocked once and entered. In his hands he clutched at least a dozen blue phone messages. Billy was a forty-year-old African-American paralegal whom Christine had stolen away from the law firm where she had once worked as a paralegal. They were longtime friends and knew everything about each other. On the day Christine got the letter from the IARDC informing her that she had passed the bar exam, the first person she had called was not Sonny, her husband. She had called Billy, and she had told him that from that moment on, he belonged to her. He was on the payroll. Then she called Thaddeus Murfee and told him she had stolen his chief paralegal. "I knew he would follow when this day came," Thaddeus laughed. "I'm just excited about the bar exam news. We'll have dinner tonight, you and me and Sonny and Katy. The celebration is on!"

And they did have dinner that night. Sonny and Christine made it home just before eleven. Christine had driven; it was Sonny's turn to have the family limit of three drinks, and he had enjoyed himself.

Now, ten months later, Billy Tattinger approached Christine's desk, his right hand clutching phone messages.

"Put the new ones on your right. Put the current ones on the left. Hold the whiners."

He dealt the messages into two hands as instructed, but withheld the third.

"Only one new one, Miss," said Billy. He pulled out a client chair and sat back. Three messages were held to his chest, like a poker player hiding his cards.

She gave him a suspicious look.

"Whiners," he said, waving the three messages at her.

"I'll call them first. Let me hold their hands and get it over with."

"No, call the newbie first. Some guy in Alaska."

"Really. Alaska? What's that one sound like?"

Billy shrugged. "I didn't get much out of him. He found you on the Internet and said he thought he'd better call. His house fell in some river."

"Why call me? The website makes it pretty clear I don't handle property law cases. Only cases involving real people with real problems."

"He fits the mold. Evidently when the house fell in the river, his wife drowned."

"How horrible. Poor guy."

"He needs to hear from you, Chris."

"Hold that one. I've got other cases ahead of new ones."

"As you say."

"Everything in time. First things first. And all that."

4

Monday morning found Christine back in court for the defense of Evan Rushdie, the high school sophomore. Something she almost never did--allowing the defendant himself to testify--was about to occur. Evan had insisted he "get to tell my story," and, for maybe the first time since beginning practice, Christine agreed. The young man was clean-cut, wholesome, and his childish innocence would come through. Or so she hoped.

"Your Honor," said Christine, "defense calls the defendant, Evan Rushdie."

After he told his name and address, Christine went straight to the heart of the case.

"You're a sophomore in high school now?"

"Yes."

"Where?"

"Page High School."

"But you were a freshman when the sex act occurred, correct?"

"Object, leading."

Judge Waters, his head inclined for enhanced auditory reception, nodded. "Harmless. Overruled."

"Again, you were a freshman when the sex act occurred, correct?"

"Correct."

"At that time, had you ever had sex with a girl before?"

"You mean--"

"I mean intercourse."

"No. Never."

Christine took her time with the next question. She looked as if she were innocently locating a reminder in her notes. Then she asked, "Were you a witch, a warlock?"

"Warlock is insulting to male witches. They're just called witches."

"Then were you a witch when you were a freshman?"

He rubbed his hands together. His blond hair was fastidiously combed and parted in a straight line, front to back, and Christine got the feeling he would look more at home behind a fast food counter than in some girl's bedroom a year ago.

"I don't know if I was a witch. I never mind-traveled. I didn't do spells. But I played roles. I was big in *Dungeons and Dragons*."

"Did you engage in witch rituals?"

"No. I mean, we were having a ritual when we had sex that time."

"Tell us about that, please."

He looked down, away from the jury. "It was after school."

"Recall the date?"

"No."

"Proceed."

"It was in the fall. I remember that because her mom had planted bulbs that weekend when I rode my bike over."

"What happened between you and Charlene?"

"No one was home. Both parents were at work. We were in her bedroom and we listened to Black Sabbath. Charlene had changed after school while I was actually in her bedroom."

"She changed her clothes in front of you?"

"Yes. She wore a short skirt to school. When we got to her house she changed into leotards and a T-shirt."

"In front of you."

"In front of me."

"So you saw her in her bra and panties."

"I did."

"How did that make you feel?"

Evan looked sheepishly at the ceiling. Clearly he was struggling for words that, as oftentimes happens with people describing an extraordinary event, were just out of grasp.

"I felt--turned on."

"You were aroused by seeing her in her underwear."

"Sure. I guess."

"Were you embarrassed?"

"No. She did it lots of times before."

"So this wasn't the first time she changed clothes in front of you?"

"It happened lots. Every day."

"Tell the jury what happened after she changed clothes."

"Like I said, we listened to Black Sabbath."

"Where were you and where was she?"

"We were sitting on her bed with our backs against the outside wall. We were listening to the words."

"Do you remember the song?"

"Sure. Our favorite. 'The Wizard.'"

"What's that song about?"

"About a guy who's a wizard. That's another name for a male witch. All the people are happy when the wizard walks by. Something like that."

"What happened?"

"Something in the song talks about a spell. Casting a spell or something. Charlene says, 'Do you want to cast a spell over me?'"

"What was your reply?"

"I told her that would be okay but I didn't know how to."

"What did she say?"

"She said there's all kinds of spells. She said there's one where the wizard mounts the witch and says some words. They say some words together. She said we should try that, but first I would have to take off my clothes."

"Did you? Take off your clothes?"

"We both did."

"Did you watch each other?"

"Yes."

"Describe what happened?"

"She pulled down the spread on her bed and sat down and rolled down her leotards. Then she unsnapped her bra and dangled it in one finger and smiled at me. Then she slid under the spread. She watched me take off my jeans and T-shirt. That left my shorts."

"What happened?"

"I took them off."

"What were you feeling?"

"Embarrassed beyond belief. And--" He stopped.

Christine gave it a minute, then she continued. "Were you feeling aroused in addition to embarrassed?"

"Yes."

"So you got under the spread with her?"

"I did. She whispered to me to take off my Jockeys. So I did."

"And next?"

"She told me to get on top of her. Which I did. Then I--I--"

"You told me in the office when we discussed this that you ejaculated onto her stomach when you got on her, correct?"

"Yes."

"Why did that happen?"

"I was too excited. It just happened."

"Okay, what happened after that?"

"She took me and put me inside of her."

"She took your penis and inserted it inside her vagina?"

"Yes. That's how it happened."

"Now, at any time during this were you holding her down?"

"No."

"Was she resisting?"

"No."

"Did she say 'No' or other words that meant you should stop what you were doing?"

"No."

"Did she resist in any way?"

"No."

"Did she try to hold her legs together so you couldn't enter her?"

"I don't think--no."

"So her participation in the intercourse was purely consensual?"

"Objection!" cried Woody Smitts. "Seeks to invade the province of the jury!"

Judge Waters nodded and a profound look came over his face. "Indeed it does. Sustained."

But Smitts wasn't finished. "Seeks to have the witness testify about a question of law."

Judge Waters leaned forward in his chair. "Mr. Smitts, you've already won. I've already sustained your objection. Counsel, please continue."

Christine looked at the judge. "Yes, Your Honor. Now, Evan, did Charlene ever give you any impression other than that her participation was consensual?"

Smitts shot to his feet. "Objection! Same objection!"

"Your Honor," said Christine, "it's a different question. I'm asking for his impressions, not whether the act was consensual on her part."

Judge Waters slowly nodded. "I have to agree. Counsel," he said, addressing the DA, "the question asks about the young man's impressions. I'm going to allow it."

"Let me repeat the question," said Christine, and she did.

"I thought it was okay with her," said Evan. "I never gave it much thought."

"What happened next?"

"All of a sudden the door banged open. We found out her dad had been knocking in the hallway but the music was so loud we didn't hear him. He came crashing inside."

"And he caught you with his daughter, nude, in her bed?"

"Yes."

"What happened next?"

"He grabbed my arm in one hand and my hair in the other. He pulled me out of the bed and got me down on the floor. He kicked my face and I guess I blacked out."

"What's the next thing you remember?"

"EMTs were there. It was all fuzzy. They put me on a stretcher and took me to the hospital."

"What happened next?"

"An oral surgeon fixed my jaw."

"Did the police come to the hospital to talk to you?"

"Yes. I couldn't talk to them 'cause my mouth was wired shut. So they asked me questions and told me I could either nod or shake my head and they'd write it down."

Christine backed away momentarily. She wanted to let that last response sink in with the jury, how unfair it was that the police would write down his statement based on nods and head shakes. Some of them made notes as she watched.

Then she said, "So let me be clear. It says in the so-called confession you gave the police that you had nonconsensual sex with Charlene. Do you recall that?"

"I recall they asked me about it."

"Did you actually tell them you had nonconsensual sex with her?"

"No. I shook my head. What I meant was, I didn't understand what nonconsensual sex meant. I'd never heard of that."

"You were a high school freshman then?"

"Yes."

"And you were asked if the sex was nonconsensual?"

"Yes."

"And this was when your jaw was wired shut?"

"Yes."

"And they took whatever response you made with your head and wrote that down to say you admitted it was nonconsensual?"

"I guess. Now that I know what it means, I never would have said that."

"Why is that?"

"Because for one thing it was supposed to be a ritual and it was her idea in the first place. Maybe if we hadn't been listening to Black Sabbath or something, she wouldn't even have thought of it--I don't know."

"It also says that you restrained her against her will. Do you recall that?"

"They asked me if I restrained her. I nodded my head."

"Why?"

"Because I was on top of her. I was definitely restraining her."

Christine again paused, this time looking at each individual juror, making sure they were getting the full benefit of the so-called confession.

Then she asked, "But the restraint--was it against her will?"

"It was supposed to be. The ritual said the witch on the bottom is to be violated by the witch on top."

"What does 'violated' mean to you?"

Evan looked down at the floor. "You know, it means you put your organ inside her organ."

"Does it mean nonconsensual?"

"I didn't get that. It just means you do it to her."

"So to you, that's violation?"

"The way we did it, yes. I mean she put me in her."

"Did you tell the police that?"

"No."

"Why not?"

"Because I couldn't. My jaw was wired shut."

"What else?"

"I decided not to talk to them anymore. They were smirking and winking at each other."

"How many cops were there when you nodded and shook your head?"

"Two. Dumpy and Dorky."

"Dumpy and Dorky. Why do you call them that?"

"Dumpy was wearing beige pants that hadn't been cleaned in a year. The bottom button of his shirt was unbuttoned so his gut was hanging over his belt and you could see stomach hair. Dorky was crew-cut with thick black glasses. He also had one of those pocket protector things and about a dozen ballpoints clipped to it. Weird."

"Dumpy and Dorky. Were they friendly?"

"Not really. They were acting all tough and something like they were piss--mad at me."

"Do you see either police officer here in court today?"

"Yes. Dumpy is here."

"You're referring to Detective Francisco?"

"Yes."

There was shuffling and a whisper at the DA's table. Detective Francisco could be seen glaring at the young man in a threatening manner.

"Evan, look at Detective Francisco. Is he giving you dirty looks while you talk today?"

"He's trying to scare me. But he's wasting his time."

"Why is that?"

Evan shrugged. "I told you. I didn't do anything wrong. If the girl was raped, it was self-inflicted."

A smile and murmurs erupted across the jury. *Bingo*, thought Christine. *Nicely done.* When she looked back at the DA's table, Detective Francisco had lowered his gaze and appeared to be making notes. Christine guessed he was doodling.

"When they came to the hospital, was your jaw hurting?"

"Yes. I was still on some kind of pain medicine. It was inserted in my hand through a tube."

"So you were somewhat out of it?"

"Lots out of it. It all felt like I was underwater and stupid. Like I was moving inside a dream."

"Did the father say anything when he kicked you in the face?"

"Yes. He said I was an asshole."

"Seriously? He called you that?"

"Yes."

"Have you and I discussed what you would like to do about his assault?"

"Yes. After this is all over I want to sue him."

A rustling and whispered commotion emanated from the first row in the courtroom, the row where the girl's parents were sitting. Evan returned their look; he even glared back at them.

"They're smirking at me right now."

"Objection, no question pending."

"Sustained. Please continue."

"Your Honor, I think those are all the questions I have for the witness."

"You may cross-examine, Mr. Smitts."

Woody Smitts came to his feet while Christine was settling back into her chair. She was attentive and watched him closely. He had every opportunity to get Evan to convict himself with one wrong misstep. She said a silent prayer the youngster wouldn't walk into something.

"Mr. Rushdie, did you climax inside Charlene?"

"I don't--her father came in before I could."

"Did you intend to?"

"I intended to, I guess. Yes, I did. At least it felt like it."

"All right. When she said for you to stop, did you stop at that time?"

"She didn't say stop."

"She testified she told you to stop once you entered her. She said penetration wasn't part of what she had agreed to."

"Maybe not. But she's the one who took me and put it in her."

"While you were lying on top of her."

"Yes."

"She was somehow able to reach around and take your penis and insert it?"

"I guess. It happened pretty fast."

"But you knew this was just a ritual, a game?"

"Yes. But I guess it became more than that."

"What made you think that?"

"Well, when she took off her bra, she dangled it on one finger and smiled at me."

"Smiled? How did she smile?"

"It's hard to describe. Kind of like teasing, I guess."

"So you felt like that gave you permission to rape her?"

"No. Not at all. I felt like that gave me permission to climb on and see what happened."

"Isn't it true she pushed you away with her hand when you tried to penetrate her?"

"It didn't feel like pushing away. It felt like pulling it in."

Smitts paused and went over his notes. Christine watched out of the corner of her eye then looked over at the jury. Several were paused with their pencils over their spiral notebooks, as if they had been taking notes and were waiting. She didn't feel good about that; she would have preferred folded arms across chests and lack of eye contact. But they weren't sitting like that. They looked involved, all in. She dropped her eyes and considered what she might ask on re-direct. Probably nothing. Smitts hadn't drawn blood. At least not yet.

"Do you recall telling Angelo Woodson that you raped your girlfriend?"

"I told Angelo that I had a wild time with Charlene. I don't remember if I said 'rape' or not."

"Is it possible you said 'rape'?"

Evan scratched his arm. He shuffled his feet.

"Possible, I guess. I don't remember."

"Well, Angelo testified you said you raped Charlene. Would he be lying?"

"Angelo doesn't lie. He tells the truth."

"So when he says you told him you raped your girlfriend, he would be telling the truth?"

"Objection!" Christine cried, on her feet in a flash. "Seeks state of mind."

"Sustained. Counsel, please rephrase."

Smitts looked at the judge and shrugged. "I can try."

"Please do."

"You said Angelo tells the truth."

"Yes."

"So if he said you told him you raped Charlene, you would accept that as the truth?"

"Probably. Yes."

Now Smitts busied himself with papers and notepads, allowing the admission to sink in. It was very damaging to the defense and Smitts knew it. Relished it, even, as he took almost three or four minutes--a long period of quiet air in a courtroom.

"And if you told Angelo you raped her, would that statement be closer in time to the rape than today's testimony?"

"Objection. Rape."

"Let me rephrase. Would that statement be closer in time to the event than today's testimony?"

"Yes."

"It would also be un-sandpapered, meaning your lawyer hadn't coached you."

"Objection! Improper comment on counsel!"

"Sustained. Mr. Smitts, were you about finished with your cross?"

"I am finished, Your Honor," said Smitts, and he took his seat.

Christine again stood up.

"Evan, were you talking face to face with Angelo when you told him what had happened between you and Charlene?"

"No."

"You specifically remember talking to him?"

"Not talking. Texting."

"Why was that?"

"My jaw was wired shut. I couldn't talk if I wanted to."

"So whatever it was you told him about you and Charlene, you told him by text?"

"Yes."

"Do you have that cell phone with you today?"

"Yes."

"Please get it out and check to see whether that message sequence is still in memory on the phone."

The young man withdrew his phone from his pants pocket and tapped its screen several times.

"Yes, I have it."

"Can you read us the part where you told Angelo what happened?"

"Yes. It says 'Dude, me and my lady got it on.'"

"What else?"

"He texted back."

"What did he say?"

"He texted me 'WTF!'"

"What does that mean?"

"You want me to say it? In here?"

"Yes, please."

"It means 'what the fuck.'"

"And when you read this, what did you think?"

"I thought he was surprised. I was a virgin up to then. So was he."

"Was he also a freshman?"

"Yes."

"What did you say in response to WTF?"

"I said, 'Seriously, Dude. It was gr8.'"

"You told him the sex was great?"

"Yes."

"Anything else?"

"Not really. He jokes about me needing a penicillin shot because everyone was hitting that."

"Hitting that? Translate, please."

"It means everyone was having sex with Charlene."

"Did you believe him?"

Evan looked at DA Smitts and a small look passed between them.

"Like I told the DA, Angelo doesn't lie. If he says everyone was having sex with her, I believe him."

"That is all."

There was no attempt at re-direct. The judge announced they would recess for the day and Evan left the witness stand.

TRIAL CONTINUED with jury instructions and closing arguments. The case was then given to the jury to deliberate.

Once the courtroom was cleared, Christine turned to Evan.

"Good luck, Evan. I've got my fingers crossed."

"Me too. I think you won, though."

"Why is that?"

"Closing arguments. The jury made notes while you were talking. The jury didn't make any notes while Mr. Smitts was talking."

"That's definitely a good sign."

Four hours later, the judge called both attorneys into his chambers and indicated to them he had a note from the jury.

"May I read it into the record?"

Both attorneys assented.

"Okay, here it is. 'Question 1: Can we find Charlene guilty of statutory rape?' And question 2, 'Can we award damages to Evan and against the father for kicking him?'"

Christine smiled. "And I suppose the court is inclined to answer affirmatively to both questions?"

Smitts scowled. "Obviously the answer is negative to both."

"Obviously," said the judge. "But I think we're very close to a defense verdict, counsel."

And they were. Thirty minutes later, the jury reported a Not Guilty verdict.

"Now the work begins," Christine told Evan and his parents when they gathered at the counsel table. Now we're going to sue the father. For physical and mental damages."

"We'd like that," said Evan's mother.

"Go for it," said Evan's father. "Hit it hard."

Christine looked at the father and grinned.

"I intend to do just that. I'm going to hit it hard."

Evan needed a hug and Christine obliged him. Then she hugged his parents.

Smitts and Officer Francisco left the courtroom in a huff, right after asking for a Judgment Notwithstanding the Verdict, which was denied.

On the way back to her office, Christine phoned Billy Tattinger. "Prepare a complaint alleging aggravated assault and battery against

Charlene's father. Seek punitive damages of five hundred thousand dollars."

"Done."

She slid back the sunroof and tilted her head toward the bright afternoon sunshine.

It was beautiful being free.

She hoped Evan was enjoying every single minute of it.

Then she laughed. What the hell was a senior doing with a freshman, anyway? Had things changed all that much since she was in school?

Doubtful, she decided. Maybe Charlene should be included in the lawsuit.

Statutory rape: he was underage, she wasn't.

Calling Billy again, she updated him. "Add the daughter as a defendant. Allegations of the civil equivalent of statutory rape."

"Serious?" said Billy.

"Dead serious."

5

There was a problem with the fraternity date rape case: the victim was the daughter of none other than the Cook County District Attorney, John Speers. Which meant the Office of the District Attorney had an ethical conflict of interest with the girl's assailants.

A search for an independent prosecutor began. Lists of criminal defense attorneys were downloaded and feverishly reviewed, as the more time that went by, the more time the assailants would have to get their stories squared with each other.

After a full day of intensive searches of names, and career highlights, the DA's staff had come up with two names. One of the names was awaiting appointment to the first criminal assistant's desk at the U.S. Attorney's Office. She would have been their first choice as she was not only qualified, she was political as well, and there would definitely be political angles to the case.

The second of the two names was someone equally qualified but without the proven political smarts. Her name was Christine Susmann. It was decided the staffers would send out investigators and learn all they could about the young attorney.

Three days went by. Then the investigators from the DA's office began filing workups.

District Attorney Johns Speers, First Assistant Woody Smitts, and Sexual Assault and Domestic Violence group leader Iona S. Palin liked what they saw. Christine Susmann was in her early thirties, a graduate of Chicago Law, a family woman, and had experience in the legal system with sex crime cases. Of course she had been defending those, but that could be forgiven. Knowledge of the elements of sexual assault and investigative techniques--she had those down. Criminalistics, rape kits and emergency room exams--she had those down, as well. These were the ingredients that went into making for success as a sex crimes prosecutor and she scored high marks.

There was one problem area, however, and that was money. Not whether she would want too much; rather, she was loaded. The money they could offer would be meaningless to a multi-millionaire. So they decided they would appeal to her sense of justice and her parenthood. Two kids, both of whom would be destined for college, would play at her heartstrings and motivate her to accept the offer they were going to make.

"It's a very difficult moment for me," said DA John Speers to the two assistants aiding him in the recruitment. "This is my daughter. I cannot afford any screw-ups. If the independent counsel makes a crappy deal or screws up the evidence, my kid loses her one chance to see justice done."

"Plus you want her to have the advantage of a conviction in her pocket when she files her civil case against the perps," said Iona S. Palin, of Sex Crimes. "A Not Guilty verdict would stop her cold."

"Agree," said Speers. He leaned back from his marble desk and looked past the floor-standing American flag. Beyond the high glass, seagulls coasted on the thermals and eyed the city streets for food debris the citizens discarded on the sidewalks by the ton each day.

Speers clinched his eyes shut. "Anybody. Speak to me."

"She was my second choice all along," said Woody Smitts. Smitts was a Naval Academy/Stanford Law grad who lived his life by the book. "She's personable, from what I've seen. But she's also very plodding, a thinker, a woman who isn't afraid to think and act creatively but still she'll hit the books when necessary. I'm a 'Yes.' Especially after she just kicked my ass on the witch case."

"Lord," muttered Speers. "Iona? What say you?"

"I wanted a female, but only because I think females make the best sex crimes prosecutors. They're on fire because the victim is most often one of their own. Plus juries relate to them in sex prosecutions."

"More than men?" asked Speers.

"I can't say that," said Iona Palin. "I wouldn't go that far. But I've seen her work. Unlike Woody, Christine Susmann is my first choice, not my second."

"That makes for two yeses. I'm too close to the situation, so I'll go with what the two of you think. I have to rely on you and your distance from the facts."

"Yes."

"Smart. I agree, Jack."

"All right, then. Let's bring her in and make an offer."

"She's outside?"

"She kindly agreed to come by this morning. Doesn't even know why."

"Let's do it, then."

DA Speers punched his intercom and told his secretary to bring in Christine Susmann.

"Let's move over here to my conference table," said Speers to his two staffers. "Take away the power chair behind the desk."

They were just settling in when the door opened and his secretary guided the young lawyer into the room. John Speers stood up on the far side of the table and waved Christine over. "Please," he said, extending his hand. He indicated Christine should take the head of the table, which she did.

"Am I in big trouble?" said Christine, only half-kidding. She didn't know why she would be in any kind of trouble in any case, but one could never be too careful when it came to detectives and prosecutors. She had been around the block enough times that she was wary, although her demeanor indicated she was half-joking.

"Nothing, not at all," said Speers. "I've asked you here because I need your help on a case."

"What kind of case?"

"Sexual assault."

"Is this the case I'm thinking? It was in the *Tribune* and it involved a certain family member?"

Speers grimaced. "That is the case. My daughter."

"I was very sorry to hear what happened. I have two kids. I've already told them to stay away from fraternity parties when they head out."

"We don't want to take up too much of your time," said Speers. "So let me be blunt. Would you accept appointment by the chief judge as special prosecutor to bring the assailants to justice?"

Christine carefully examined the faces of each prosecutor. "Seriously? You're asking a defense lawyer?"

"I am. We are."

"Why? There must be a thousand ex-prosecutors in Cook County right now. Why me?"

"You have a record we admire. A record in big cases. And this will be a big case. It will be very political."

"I'm definitely not political."

"You're not?" said Speers. "After you sued the president of Russia and won a few hundred million or so?"

"Well, there's that, I guess."

"Yes," said Iona Palin, "there's that. But one thing I really like about you is the fact that you have two kids. Campus rape must be an anachronism by the time your girl leaves home for school. Don't you agree?"

"I do. You definitely have my attention on that one. Now let me ask you one thing."

"Okay."

"If I do this--I'm not saying I will, not without talking to my husband first--but if I do it, will I also be allowed to speak up for the civil case?"

"You want to sue these boys for my daughter?"

"The boys, the fraternity, the university, the national fraternity. Even the boys' parents. I would like to make everyone responsible in any way come into court and defend."

It would ultimately be John Speers' call, deciding who would bring any civil litigation, as it was his daughter who had the claim. He stood and thoughtfully paced behind the row of chairs on his side of the table. Then he turned.

"You know what? I say yes to that. I would love to have you take on Bussie's case."

"Then let me talk to my husband. Can I have until noon tomorrow?"

"Certainly. But we need you to dig in at twelve-oh-one if you're on board. There's a lot to be done from the gate."

"Got it. I can do that. I have really unlimited resources."

"We know you do," said First Assistant Smitts. "Believe me, I carefully considered your access to bodies when I was considering you for the job."

Christine nodded slowly. "I've been lucky enough to score some wins that mean money is no longer an issue. Anymore I work because it's there. For cases like this one, maybe."

"Then give us a call. You would work out of your own office, incidentally, and we'll assign a full-time investigator to you. She'll need an office and setup."

"She?"

"Winona S. Lindsey. Heard of her?"

"Who hasn't?" said Christine. "She's in the news on some front page sex crime or white collar at least once a week."

"She's all yours. For the duration."

"You really are going all-in."

John Speers looked hard at Christine. "I only have the one daughter. Please remember that when you talk to your husband."

Christine took the elevator to the lobby of the County Building.

She was standing at 69 W. Washington; the Executive Office of the Cook County DA was upstairs in suite 3200. Outside she flagged over the first cab moving in her direction. She gave the cabbie directions.

"One Hundred South, please."

"Missus, that's the high rent area. You must be doing all right."

"Is that a question?"

"No, ma'am. Just a thought. Sit back. Enjoy the traffic jam. I got this."

6

Within a week the court had appointed Christine to the office of special prosecutor. Which meant she was going to be very busy with just the one case.

She began reviewing staff needs and decided she had an immediate need for a second attorney in her practice. She posted notices of a job opening in all the right Chicago law newspapers and the *Bar Journal* and waited. The resumes began pouring in, which wasn't a surprise given the tanked economy and the fact that law schools were producing 125% of the nation's need for lawyers. She and paralegal Billy Tattinger worked their way through the pile and compiled a short list. Then calls were made and appointments set up. One, the final one, awaited Christine in the reception area.

Christine studied Edward Mitchell's resume and slowly nodded. Out of fifty-five replies to the classified ad in the *Chicago Daily Lawyer*, Edward Mitchell was on the top of the pile. He was young--twenty-eight--and ready for a career. He was unmarried, so family life wouldn't interfere with the long hours she had planned for him. He was older than most law grads by five years because he had done a JAG stint right out of law school. The Army had posted him to Iraq and Germany, where he had defended American soldiers brought up on courts martial. Christine, ex-Army herself, liked him even more for serving and it gave him great validation with her. His undergrad major was criminal justice, definitely a plus. In law school he'd done heavy concentration in criminal law, a practice area where Christine needed help. She needed civil experience too, someone who had been around and had gotten beat up once or twice and had learned to give it back in spades. That's what had happened to her and she knew how sometimes hard lessons produced granite survivors.

He looked good, on paper. So she had her old contacts at XFBI take an in-depth look. Then she invited him in to talk.

While he waited in reception, Christine studied a file stamped CONFIDENTIAL: XFBI STUDY. In the upper left corner, in small gold letters on a black rectangle, was his name, Edward Mitchell. The study was a good inch thick, including photographs of the applicant at a juice bar in his health club. A second photograph showed him filling his hybrid vehicle at the pump. The third photograph was problematic: it pictured him standing in the community indoor pool at his condo, talking to a much younger woman. Problematic because it caused a mild jealous reaction in Christine, which she admitted though she hated to. How, she wondered, had jealousy stepped in? She stopped the file review and wondered if she was doing the right thing, interviewing a young man to whom she had immediately felt attracted? She shook it off and plunged forward, flipping pages. How could anyone develop feelings for a photograph? She shrugged it off as ridiculous.

She didn't ask how, but XFBI had learned that he was twenty-eight, single, a lifelong resident of Chicago except for the military years, a loyal Bears fan who had obtained autographs from the entire defense when Urlacher was around, and that he had two job offers: one from the district attorney's office and one from a family law practice. The latter he had zero interest in, while the former had offered the first interview and then a comeback interview to meet the others in the Violent Crimes Unit. He was definitely interested and had as much as told them so in two emails from earlier in the week. His alma mater was Northwestern and thanks to its unfriendly tuition

structure he still owed over $100,000 in student loans, which some-
times he was late in paying. He had even been turned over to collec-
tions two months ago. Christine nodded. She could forgive him that,
especially since she planned to double whatever the DA was offering.
He listed as his last employer the United States Army. He had been
home all of twenty-five days.

Christine handed the file over to Billy, who began flipping pages.
She wanted Billy in on this because he was a great judge of character,
number one, and because he would be answering directly to Ed
Mitchell if Mitchell indeed came on board.

"This guy's my new boss?" Billy asked as he skimmed the file.

"Here's hoping," she said. "He's pretty hot to trot with the DA's
office right now."

"Hell, Chris, just wave Benjamins under his nose. He's been
fighting it, being in the Army. No bucks and credit's shot to hell. He'll
see the wisdom of your offer."

Christine sighed. "I want him to want to be here for more reasons
than money."

"Well, the hours are long and the food downstairs is lousy. You'd
better come up with something else."

She sat forward and spread her hands. Excitement rose in her
eyes. "I want him to *love* his job. That starts with feeling like you're
making a difference. With feeling like you're actually helping people.
That's the secret."

"Like I said, there's nothing wrong with being able to pay all your
bills too."

"You'll get no argument there. My question is, will he perceive me
as someone with leadership qualities, someone he'll follow? Don't
forget, Billy, I was a sergeant in the Army, an NCO. This guy's
discharge rank was captain. He outranks me. There will always be
that, no matter what."

"Is that a showstopper?"

"Only if he lets it be."

"Once he sees what you're made of, he'll jump right in and
follow. There's also the matter of the Silver Star you won in

Afghanistan. Does this Mitchell guy have one of those on his chest?"

"Misnomer. The Silver Star is actually a gold star hanging on the end of a red, white, and blue ribbon. It's very impressive to anyone in the military. It might cancel out the rank thing."

"Can you wear it to the office?"

"No. Besides, Edward Mitchell is going to have to see other traits in me that cause him to follow. I don't want competition in the firm. I want cooperation, a team of team players."

"You've got that as far as me and Melinda out front are concerned."

"I know that. You guys save my life on a daily basis."

"Look here, did you see this? Four bad checks his senior year?"

"Saw and noted. He was a poor boy. Or else his folks had disowned him. Whatever. It was once very common for new law grads to file bankruptcy the day they graduated. That was back when you could get rid of student loans in bankruptcy. They closed that loophole. It's still common for the married ones to file divorce papers on the day they walk across the stage. Not very kind to the spouse who supported them for three years. Those are the kinds of things I would shy away from. Bad checks happen, like speeding tickets happen. They aren't about moral wrongs. More about supply and demand."

"Agree. I know. I was in one of those places."

"I remember. Thaddeus got you out, got you cleaned up, and gave you your first paralegal job."

"God bless Thaddeus Murfee. Even my own mama in Alabama prays for that man."

"He probably needs it. Lots of it. So look, let's bring the guy in. We've made him wait the mandatory ten minutes past the appointment hour."

"I'll go get him. Be right back."

Christine watched Billy walk back through the L-shaped office and disappear around the corner.

He returned minutes later with a tall, dark man carrying a black notebook. He came toward Christine, extending his hand to shake, and she peered into light blue eyes with smile lines at the corners. His hair was black and long on top, short on the sides, and his extended hand was angular in the way of mannish hands, with strong fingers and carefully trimmed nails. "Ms. Susmann, hello. I'm Ed Mitchell."

Christine took his hand in hers, shook it, and tried not to stare too long into those light blue eyes. Feeling slightly flustered, she sat back down and held up his resume.

"I've read this," she said, as if announcing she had found a vein of gold. She wondered at her voice; it sounded as if it were floating in very cold air, threatening to break and fall to the floor. Was she being too reserved because she was attracted? She tried a warmer tone. "Very impressive resume. Very impressive."

"Thank you," he said, and took the nearest visitors' chair when she indicated he should sit.

Then he surprised her.

He leaned forward in his chair and spoke in the friendliest possible way. "I know the usual M.O. for these meetings is you ask, I answer. But would you mind if I asked a few questions first?"

Christine smiled. "That would be cool. Go for it."

Now he sat back and crossed his right ankle over his knee. He pulled at the trouser leg and settled in.

"Well, I've done some background on you. I know about what happened in Russia. You were arrested and jailed. My question is, were you on a CIA mission at that time? The articles I've found seem to think so. At least it's what President Irunyaev was claiming, that you were a CIA spy come to murder him."

Christine said thoughtfully, "Well, even if it were a CIA mission, it wouldn't have been a mission to Russia. Remember, we were skyjacked. We were supposed to land in Zurich and I was making connections there."

"So what was your destination?"

She was pierced with a strong desire to tell him he was way out of bounds now, but she let it slide for one more answer.

"Can't say. Truth be told, I don't even know. I wasn't to find out until Zurich. Which, like I said, we never reached."

"Next question. Is there a future for me here? Or am I filling some sort of long-term need that might peter out?"

"There is a huge future for the lawyer I hire. The sky's the limit when it comes to salary. I'm already thinking two hundred thousand to start, plus a piece of any jury awards."

She could almost hear the air go out of him. He blinked once, twice, and was truly speechless. Slowly, he recovered.

"Excuse me? Did you just say you're paying your new hire two hundred K plus a percent of recoveries?"

"You heard right. Listen, Mr. Mitchell, I never intended for my law practice to turn a profit. Truth be told, I don't need it to turn a profit. As you also read about me, I'm literally fixed for life after suing the Russian president and hacking off four hundred and fifty million of his U.S. assets. But then a funny thing happened. The practice has been self-supporting and has turned a profit from the sixth month and thereafter. Go figure."

"And what's the thrust of the practice?"

"Right now it's public policy work. But in fact I've just been appointed special prosecutor on a case out of the Cook County DA's office. If it looks fun and interesting, I'm in."

"Would I have a say in what cases we accept if I come here?"

"No, except yes to those you bring in. I have to retain my own autonomy when it comes to clients."

"Of course. Hell, it's your law practice. No argument there."

"What about you? Are you looking for long term?"

"I'm looking for a career position. Right now I have an offer pending from the DA. It's fair and looks promising. You're my last interview before I tell them my decision."

"Well, what's your decision?"

"Well, tell me about my autonomy."

"Totally autonomous, one hundred percent. I need you to step in and take over probably fifty heavy-duty cases and run with them.

This thing with the DA's office is going to eat into my day big time. Can you do that?"

"Sure. So long as you're around for questions when I need you."

"Of course. Also, there's a firm car in it for you."

A smile spread across his face. "Did you just make that up?"

"Yes."

"Why?"

She returned the smile. "Because I want you onboard. Biggest reason? You're ex-Army and so am I."

"I know you are. Silver Star. I bow down to that."

"Really? How about the fact that you're a captain in the reserves and my rank was sergeant?"

"It's like a combat mission. We answer to whoever the CO says. In this case, you're the CO. We have no issue there."

"Good. I had to ask."

He played with the cuff of his pants for a moment, then uncrossed his legs and learned forward again.

"What kind of car?" he asked almost sheepishly.

"Your choice. Up to a hundred grand."

"When would I start?"

"You just started. What do you say?"

He extended his hand and leaned forward. His pale blue eyes fastened on her own and held her gaze.

"I say yes. I just enlisted."

They shook on it.

"Welcome aboard. We'll get you provisioned and set up tomorrow morning. Does eight to five work for you?"

"Christine, after my insane hours in the Army, eight to five is a blessing."

"All right."

Now she stood.

"Welcome, Ed Mitchell. I'm glad we have a deal."

7

J amie Susmann was thirteen, the son of Christine and Sonny Susmann, and was often surrounded by a family room full of friends. He had been diagnosed with cerebral palsy at three months and hadn't learned to walk until he was four years old. Now he walked with the aid of forearm crutches and ingested anticonvulsants to control his seizures. Still, Jamie was a happy guy. "My kid with the sunny disposition," Christine called him. "Look at this kid. His smile would light up a tomb."

When Christine arrived home the night of the DA's selection of her as special prosecutor, Jamie was in his bedroom, working on a programming problem in the C# programming language.

"What does all that stuff mean?" she asked, trying to rest her hand on the young man's neck as she came up behind him at his desk. He moved away from her hand--as all thirteen-year-old boys do--and pointed at the screen.

"I'm building software that will recognize facial and body expressions in video and indicate whether the person is lying."

"You what?"

"Sure. There are telltale facial twitches and expressions that are dead giveaways. My software analyzes faces and tells me in what percentile of truth-telling the face falls. It's pretty cool, Mom. Watch. See this feed along the bottom of the screen? It's analyzing videos of my face frame by frame and reporting back truth percentages."

Christine folded her arms and looked at the screenful of code.

"Can you demo it live for me? I'd like to see it work."

"Not yet. Right now I'm working up the recognition algorithms. I'm a few hours away from a demo. But I'll get there before bedtime."

"Yes, you always do. Tell you what, come down and help me fix dinner."

"Do I have to?" His voice went up a notch. Not whiny, but playing around the edges of whiny.

"No, you don't have to. But I'd like you to."

"Not right now, okay?"

"Okay. I'll have to make my plans to go interview some college guys without you. Too bad, because their veracity is very important to my case. I was thinking maybe I'd try your new software on them. The first guy lives in Alaska. That's where I'm headed tonight."

Jamie spun in his chair, inserted his arms in his crutches, and pulled himself upright.

"No way! You're not going without me!"

"That's what I thought. But you're so busy here, I thought maybe you didn't want to be disturbed."

"I'm not *that* busy, Mom. Come on, already."

By the time they got downstairs, Sonny was walking in the back door.

"Hey, everyone," he said. "Dad's home."

He swept up Christine and kissed her hard on the mouth. "How's my favorite barrister?"

She squirmed away. "I'm fine. I'll be even better when you shower then try that again."

"Please," said Jamie. "Get a room, you two."

"Hey," said Sonny to Jamie. "I've never been able to restrain myself when it comes to your mother."

"Sure. I'll bet."

Sonny and Christine took seats at the long table in the

kitchen/family room. Jamie pulled out a chair and sat down at the head of the table. The room was large but made cozy by bright patterns in the furniture and pastel landscapes hung on the walls. The furniture was high-end collectibles mixed with Eames lounge and wireframe chairs.

"So, Mom's going to interview a guy in Alaska and needs me to help out," said Jamie. "Is that okay with you, Dad, if I go to Alaska?"

Sonny was a fit, athletic thirty-five-year-old who ran his own construction company. His days were spent moving men and materials to assignments. Nights were spent moving numbers around on spreadsheets. Sonny and Christine had married when she was in her early twenties and back from a tour with the Army in Afghanistan. He had been twenty-six, almost twenty-seven, and driving dump trucks for a living. Shortly thereafter they had adopted Jamie, who was beset with overwhelming medical problems. She had reluctantly returned to the Army in order to take advantage of the medical benefits her family would receive if she were serving. She had returned to active duty after a year in the reserves and spent a year with the military police in Kabul. During her final year in the service she had trained and worked as a paralegal for a team of JAG officers in Germany. Following that, she had come home and taken over with Jamie as a working mom. Naturally, as a reservist, she still received Tricare medical and dental for her family.

"She needs my help, Dad. Can I go?" asked Jamie again.

Sonny broke into an embracing smile. "Of course you can go. Mom says she needs you, you go."

"Thanks, Dad. Mom, what time are we leaving?"

"In one hour."

"What?"

Christine rested her hand on Jamie's shoulder. This time he didn't pull away.

"We'll be leaving in one hour for O'Hare."

"Can I fly shotgun?"

"You know the rules. FAA says two pilots in a jet. Don't bother asking."

"I know, but I'm working on my private pilot's license and could use the time."

Christine laughed. "You, getting logbook time in a jet, when you're flying little Cessnas for your license? Somehow that doesn't compute with me."

Jamie looked away. "Doesn't hurt to ask."

She squeezed her son's shoulder. "Always ask. You never know. It's like trolling out of a boat. You never know what you might hook."

His face lit up. "Hey, what should I bring?"

"Levi's, sweater, jacket. Weather is volatile in our forty-ninth state. And how about your laptop and video camera? We'll take it out for a spin."

"I'll work on my software on the way up. You need it tomorrow. I'm on it."

"All right, Jamie, now go. I want to talk to your dad."

"Cool."

Once Jamie had headed upstairs, Christine reached across the table and took Sonny's hand. "Busy day?"

He leaned back. "Let me grab a beer. Want anything?"

"I'm good."

"I need alcohol. It was one of those days."

"Tell me."

He bent and studied the interior of the refrigerator. "Coors--ah, here we are." He popped the top and took his place back at the table. There he took a long drink, swallowed, then gave a satisfied belch. "Plumbing's all bent to hell at the apartments. Everything's bass-ackwards."

"So you had another day of undoing LeMarch Plumbing's screw-ups?"

"Pretty much. It adds probably two days to the contract. Maybe just one. Depending on how many guys they send to re-do it. Now, what are you up to? Why Alaska?"

"It seems the DA's office wants me to take on one of their cases. First potential witness is in Alaska. College kid."

"Alaska? Where's the school?"

"Right here, Chicago U. He dropped out this semester and I want to find out why."

"Is he in trouble?"

"Might be. Date rape case."

"This kid raped his date? How's that work?"

"I didn't say that. I'm saying I need to talk to him. I want to let Jamie try out his new software, too. See whether it works."

Sonny took another swallow and narrowed his eyes at his wife.

"Still, why would you be willing to fly all the way to Alaska on a rape case? Isn't there enough work in Chicago?"

She poured a cup of coffee. "This has the potential to be bigger than just a criminal case. This could involve a civil case as well."

"I don't follow."

"Well, if the girl was raped--and we have no reason to doubt her story and the medical workups--maybe the national fraternity should be sued along with the boys. Throw the school in too and the pot sweetens considerably."

"Okay, now I'm getting it. I'm slow tonight."

"No, you're not slow. You're just not a lawyer. You and I think differently."

"Understatement of the century."

"Well..."

"Billy going with?"

"Of course. I can't exist without Billy."

"Good. You need some muscle, he's your man."

"Agreed, but I won't be needing muscle. This sounds like a case with whodunnit overtones. That's all it is."

He nodded and took a guzzle of beer. He wiped his mouth with the back of his hand.

"So tell me about the incident. Was it a fraternity party?"

"I don't know, Sonny. There's lots more. I don't know it all. But I'm a very willing student." She laughed. "You've got to give me that."

"Done. You got that. I can't think of anyone more willing to learn than you. One of the things that makes me wild about you."

She sat back from the table and blinked hard. "That's always nice to hear."

"But you'd like to hear it more from me."

"Hold on. I didn't say that."

"But you've said it before. And you're right. I don't tell you enough how impressed I am with you. Go to Russia, survive a Russian prison, sue the president of Russian, win millions of dollars, pay your way through law school. Lady, I'm duly impressed."

She smiled and looked away. "Don't embarrass me. Anyone would take advantage of the opportunities I've been handed. That's all it is."

"Yes, maybe they would. But you actually did it and I'm proud of you."

She held up her right hand, missing her forefinger and ring finger. "All it cost me was these."

He shook his head. A sad expression came into his eyes. "That's right. That and--"

"And it cost me a hysterectomy. Other than all that, I came out smelling like a rose."

"Hey, you were hurt bad. I'll be the last one to ever forget. Or forgive them. So you go ahead and do what you need to do up in Alaska. I'll stay here and take care of our youngest and do my spreadsheets."

"What do you have planned with Janny?"

"Chuck E. Cheese is all she cares about."

"That's a winner. Okay, we've got her weekend figured out."

"I'll take her someplace neat. Maybe the Shedd Aquarium. Maybe the zoo."

"You're a great dad."

"Deal. Now, do we have time to race upstairs and address my sex-o-rama before you fly off?"

"Not with Jamie lurking around. Don't even go there."

She was being funny, but still she felt a thrill in her body that was very receptive to his suggestion. She loved her guy, loved his arms and back, loved touching them while he was atop her and making his own special kind of love. And she would miss that. *Well*, she thought, *there's always Sunday night. Note to self: be home early enough on Sunday to spend an hour alone with Sonny.*

Now why would she have even the smallest hint of a feeling toward Ed Mitchell when she had Sonny Susmann at home?

Ridiculous, she thought, and pushed it out of her mind.

8

H er customary seat on her Gulfstream was the starboard bulkhead couch. She loved to lie there, cutting through the air at 550 knots, reading and dozing. On the way to Anchorage she was educating herself with an article about Illinois sexual assault cases.

Jamie was sitting at the rear of the cabin, propped up against the shelf of pillows he usually arranged on the port side of the aircraft. He was oblivious to the world as he worked on his laptop. The keyboard was challenging, due to his diminished small motor function, a result of the cerebral palsy. But he had compensated, never being cowed by the disease but always facing it head-on. He even made fun of his jerky movements, telling everyone he suffered from "whips and jangles."

Behind Christine sat Billy Tattinger. She turned around to ask him something about legal experience he might have had. He was wearing sunglasses, and iPod buds sprouted from his ears. "Dream state," Christine whispered to herself, and turned forward. "One foot in this world, one foot in a parallel universe."

Across the aisle sat Winona S. Lindsey, the sworn officer on loan from the DA's office. Winona--Win, as she preferred--was busy putting together a list of all fraternity brothers on the premises on the night of the investigation. She was also pulling together all police and laboratory records for Christine's use. She was a compelling forty-year-old with bleached hair, a bent toward dangly turquoise earrings, and heavy gold bracelets on both wrists. She was extremely studious and a details person, as Christine had learned upon interviewing her at the airport when they first met. And that was exactly what she needed, a details person. Christine could see they were going to get along very well.

There was a four-wheel-drive Bronco waiting at the airport, and they continued the trip at eight in the morning after catching a light sleep on the parked Gulfstream.

CHRISTINE, Winona, Billy, and Jamie drove to downtown Anchorage.

The Exxon Building's twenty-fifth floor was office suites that could be rented by the hour or by the day. Christine had booked one for the day. They took the designated turn-in and parked in the basement, climbed out and headed for the elevator. Christine was wearing jeans, sweatshirt, Patagonia shell, and hiking boots. Winona was wearing navy slacks, navy turtleneck, and a woolly sport coat with overcoat. She carried a gun in a shoulder holster as she was a sworn peace officer. Billy was wearing jeans, Chicago Bulls red hoodie, Northface jacket and hiking boots. Jamie was wearing jeans, red sweatshirt that said "Get Some!", fleece-lined denim jacket and hiking boots. Jamie leaned forward on his crutches as they waited for the elevator and said to Billy, "This is cool up here. You been before?"

"Me? I haven't much been outta Nevada and Chicago. I'm not known for traveling."

"Me neither. I mean, Mom has the plane and all, and we go with her sometimes, but mostly she flies alone."

"I've gone with her a few times before. Once we went to New York, but I didn't leave the airport. We took the deposition right there on the plane."

"That's cool. We could install CCTV on the plane and feed depositions to my software. I think I know how."

"Go for it, kid," Billy said with a smile. "You never stop amazing me."

"Not much to it. It's just some C-sharp and algorithms."

"Right."

"I'm very interested in seeing this software of yours," said Winona. "If it works, you're on to something that could bring you into the national spotlight, young man."

Jamie looked perplexed. "Of course it works. No 'ifs' about it. Why would I make something that didn't work? What's the point?"

Winona smiled at Jamie and nodded.

Billy punched the lobby button. "I'll find a Starbucks and grab some coffee. Jamie, you want anything?"

"Venti cap."

"Cappuccino? You sure, dog?"

"Certain. I could use a jolt about now."

"Whatever."

"It's okay, Billy," said Christine. "It's a special occasion."

Billy got off, and the others headed for the twenty-fifth floor.

Upstairs, the receptionist told them the Tongass Room was open and waiting for them.

Christine led the way. The room was quite large, with an oak conference room table surrounded by twenty-two heavily padded leather chairs. The mandatory pitchers of water and glasses occupied the center of the table. Some kind soul had also seen to it that the guests would have Danish and crullers and all manner of donuts in a long basket next to the water pitchers.

"How will you arrange everyone, Mom?"

"Why don't we put the witness on the far side of the table and you can set up on the opposite side? Right behind the second chair. That will leave me room to sit in the second chair and ask questions across the table while you video behind me. Does that work?"

"Sure," said Winona. "I'll take the chair on your far side."

"Uh-huh," muttered Jamie, who was extending the legs on the tripod and finding its optimal placement.

A few minutes passed and the court reporter walked in with her machine. She set up quietly on Christine's left.

Billy returned with three Venti cups and made the distribution.

Thirty minutes later, the receptionist brought the witness to them.

Noah Adams was the president of Theta Kappa Alpha and had been in the room with Bussie the night of the assault. A basketball star in high school, he was six-six and lithe, with huge hands and muscular arms, and proud, erect bearing. His eyes were cold and dark and his hair was bleached blond in long strips. His natural color was mahogany. He immediately tried to light a cigarette, which Billy prevented, telling him the building was non-smoking. Christine watched this exchange, knowing a little bit about the student, knowing he had been an athlete, which made smoking seem non-congruent. She would have to ask about that, she noted.

Christine indicated where Noah would sit and he calmly pulled out the chair and sat down. He was given the oath by the court reporter--almost inaudibly saying "I do" when he was asked whether he swore to tell the whole truth--then all eyes shifted to Christine, prompting her to begin the questions. She first checked with Jamie that he was up and rolling, then she launched in.

"For the record, please state your name."

"Noah Adams."

"Your age, Mr. Adams?"

"Twenty. Twenty-one in a month."

"Where do you live?"

He gave his address in Anchorage and again withdrew his cigarette pack, only to quickly replace it in a shirt pocket.

"What is your business, occupation, or profession?"

"Unemployed. I'm normally a student."

"Are you a student right now?"

"I'm not enrolled this semester."

"Why not?"

"My student loan didn't renew. Along with all the other members of our fraternity."

"None of you is enrolled this semester?"

"I didn't say that. I said I didn't enroll because of my student loan getting shut off. I don't know about my brothers."

"When you say 'brothers,' how many brothers do you have?"

"Birth family, zero. Fraternity brothers, sixty-five, give or take. Pledges, thirty."

"What fraternity is that--for the record?"

"Theta Kappa Alpha."

"Is that a national fraternity?"

"It is. A social fraternity."

"What is a social fraternity?"

"It's a Greek organization that brings guys together who have similar backgrounds and similar interests. We always look for brothers who have that extra something: athletics or grades or special talents. That kind of stuff."

"What is your something extra?"

"It was athletics."

"Was?"

"Until I had my knee scoped for the second time. It's an anterior ligament tear. The doctor won't release me go back to playing."

"He's afraid you'll re-injure it?"

"Uh-huh."

"Yes or no, please."

"Sorry. Yes."

"Now, directing your attention to last semester, November twentieth. Do you remember that date?"

"I do. It was Thanksgiving weekend. We had a party after the football game that Saturday."

"Tell me about the party."

"Not much to tell. It was a toga party. Four kegs of beer, lots of noise, reggae band."

"Did you serve in any capacity at that time?"

"I was the local president."

"Congratulations. That's quite an achievement."

Noah grimaced and sat back. "I don't know. Truth is, no one else would do it. So they cajoled me into it."

"Noah, what is your major in school?" Christine was purposely jumping around, preventing the witness from thinking ahead and preparing answers.

"Athletic Management. It's a combined degree from the business school and athletic department. Lots of guys doing it these days."

"It prepares you to what--coach?"

"Yes, basketball."

"Who was invited to the party?"

"Everyone could bring a date or one other person. Some guys brought a date. Other guys brought a friend or whatever. There were probably a good hundred and fifty people there."

"Were they all students?"

"What difference does that make?"

"I'm asking the questions. Please answer."

"Hell, I don't even know why I'm here."

"You're here because I'm investigating an incident that happened at your fraternity the night of the party. You are being given the opportunity to make your statement without having to appear before a grand jury. I'm playing softball with you--put it that way."

"I didn't know that. Grand jury? What's that about?"

"A formal criminal inquiry. I've been asked by the Cook County DA's office to do a workup and bring charges against parties who may have committed a crime the night of your party, right there in your fraternity house. Whether you get charged with a crime or not will depend on what you tell me here today and will depend on whether you cooperate with me or not."

"Do I need a lawyer?"

"Your choice entirely. I made that clear when I spoke to your dad by phone."

"So no lawyer. Figures. My dad is very cheap."

"Not if he's sending you to CU, he's not. He's probably very strapped because of the high cost of supporting a student in Chicago. So let's give him a break, okay?"

"Okay. Sorry I said that. Can you take it out?" he said to the court reporter, who ignored him.

"We can't take it out. Just be sure of what you're saying and be sure it's the truth. Perjury is a very serious crime and you don't need that."

"Okay. Well, everything I've told you is the truth."

"Were you present in a room at the house that night when a member or members of your fraternity had sexual intercourse with Bussie Speers?"

"Who's Bussie Speers?"

"You still don't know?"

The young man looked down at his hands. They had started fluttering in his lap when she reminded him about perjury and now refused to calm down.

"I mean, I've found out since then who she is. I know now. But I didn't know that night."

"Fine. Now back to my question about your presence when an alleged sexual assault was made on Bussie Speers. Were you present?"

"No. I wasn't there, no. I don't know what happened except what other guys say."

"What do other guys say?"

"I don't know. That some freshman girl got raped, I guess."

"Who says that?"

"I don't know. Lots of guys. You hear it here and there. Everyone was talking about it after."

"Were you talking about it?"

"Well, the CU police came around and talked to a bunch of guys. Told them what the girl was claiming. That's what got everyone talking. Truth be told, I think she's making it up."

"Making what up?"

"The rape. I don't think she was raped. I think she had sex and got herself knocked up or something and tried to blame someone for it. I think she's the one at fault."

"Did you have sex with Bussie Speers that night?"

"No, I had a date. We're in a committed relationship so we don't sleep around."

"Do you know the names of any boys who had sex with Bussie?"

"No."

"Or who were there?"

"No."

"Remember about perjury, please."

"Still no."

"This woman to my right is Winona S. Lindsey. She's a Chicago police officer. Would you give her a set of fingerprints, palm prints, and hair sample?"

"Sure. Glad to."

"All right. Now, Ms. Lindsey and I are going to step out into the hallway and talk. We'll be back in just a couple of minutes. Please don't move."

In the hallway, Winona fixed Christine with steely gray eyes.

"Son of a bitch is lying through his teeth," said the police officer.

"My take too," Christine affirmed. "But he makes it appear so nonchalant, you almost want to believe him."

"He's a natural liar. He was there. I have no doubt."

"What do you have on him as far as investigation?"

"We found a palm print on the head of the bed where Bussie was stripped and assaulted. If we get a match other than the boy who lived in that room, then we're on to something. That's why I asked for palm prints from all these yahoos."

"He said he'd give you one. Hope it turns something up. So, do you have more questions you want me to ask?"

Winona thought about that. She flipped through her file on Noah Adams. She then flipped through other pages, taking five minutes or more while she derived her answer about more questions. Finally she said, "You know what, I think we're done with him. We can always hit him with a grand jury subpoena and do it all over again, so let's ramp it down for now."

"Will do."

"By the way, I like Jamie. Lots. I'll be very interested to see what his software has to tell us."

Christine smiled. "You and me both. He's my doll baby. But don't tell him I said that."

"Hey, it's all confidential when we speak."

Both women laughed and did a high-five and a bond was formed. Christine knew they were going to feed off each other and make this investigation work. Her confidence in the case had just doubled.

THREE HOURS LATER, they were back in the air and Alaska was a green topography below the silver wings of the Gulfstream.

Christine was back in her bulkhead seat and this time she had her MacBook in her lap. The plane's Wi-Fi provided the necessary connection. She read up on environmental law until sleep overcame her. She folded the laptop and set it aside, yielding, at last, to the several hours of sleep she could get on the return flight.

She was extremely tired, she thought as she drifted off. Sonny would just have to wait for his sex-o-rama--as he called it--for another night.

9

The lawyer and the detective were all eyes, closely focused on Jamie's laptop screen as he explained his truth-telling software. They were in Christine's family room, gathered around the long dinner table where Jamie had temporarily set up camp for the demo.

"A little background," he said. "Computer scientists refer to facial and body language as microexpressions. At first, microexpressions were very difficult to recognize through automated facial analysis because of their short duration. An eyebrow raises and lowers in a twinkling. Follow me?"

"Yes," said Christine.

"I do, indeed," said Winona. "Please proceed, Jamie."

"All right. Look. Standard video is shot at twenty-five frames per second. Twenty-five FPS is too fast for our purposes. So I've used a system I call temporal interpolation to achieve a higher number of frames and Multiple Kernel Learning to improve classification."

"When in the world did you do all this?" said Christine.

"Usually late at night after you and Dad were asleep. I got back up and coded. Silent keystrokes. Anywho. What I came up with is what's known as Spontaneous Micro-expression Corpus, or SMEC. SMEC consists of seventy-seven microexpressions that I've taken from twenty-two subjects. As of now I've emailed government agencies and four universities. I'm trying to land some testing against certified human facial analysts."

"Any luck?" said Winona.

"Not yet. But everything just went out Friday."

"Do we need to copyright this?" asked Christine.

"Done. It was a simple process and I paid for it myself."

"So you own this lock, stock and barrel?" said Christine.

Jamie smiled broadly. "I do."

"So how can this help us?" asked Winona. "I mean, I know how I hope it can help us, but what do you have in mind?"

"Using my camera integrated with my software, I recorded Noah Adams in Anchorage."

"Results?"

"Seventy-five percent accurate he was lying twenty-two percent of the time in response to Mom's questions."

"Where do those percentages come from?" asked the police woman.

"From algorithms based on facial expressions. I'm using standard frame sets for facial analysis. In other words, my software is relying on the same testing performed by human facial analysts. I just do more of it, faster, with immediate results."

"Holy smoke!" exclaimed Winona. "This is incredible!"

"I know," Jamie agreed. "I think I'm on to something that can really help you, Mom. In this case and others, probably."

Jamie stood and supported himself with the forearm crutches. He raised the right one and wiped his long hair out of his eyes.

"So, what can you show us?" Christine asked. "Can you demo what you have?"

"I can do better than demo. I can play back the entire deposition with a crawl across the bottom of the screen that gives you the truth percent and the facial expression that triggered the software to return with a hit."

"A hit?"

"A hit is a microexpression that accompanies a falsehood."

"How many hits did Mr. Adams have?"

"Two hundred and two. Give or take a margin of error of plus or minus three."

"He lied two hundred and two times?"

"No, he presented facial expressions that confirmed a lie. Sometimes one lie produced two, three or even four hits. In other words, a lie can be one microexpression or it can be several microexpressions rolled into one lie."

"How can we use this, Chris?" asked Winona.

"Will it be admissible in court, you mean? Most likely it won't, though you never know. I mean, all scientific methods had a first time to be used in court and each time it was an uphill battle. I think the first DNA evidence allowed in U.S. courts was as recent as twenty, twenty-five years ago. Now it's used thousands of times a day in courts all over the world. But like I said, everything has a first time."

"Cool," said Winona. "I'm not above recommending we use this in court."

"I'm with you there, Win," said Christine. "I fully plan to present it. We'll need Jamie's testimony, too, and we'll need to present him as someone qualified to create this kind of methodology. But in the end, no one ever said an expert witness has to have umpteen college degrees and two thousand hours in court. That's not the rule."

"Great," said Jamie. "I bill my time at one hundred dollars per hour and expect a two thousand dollar advance."

The family room fell silent. Christine's eyes widened as she stared at her son.

"Hey," he came back. "All expert witnesses get paid. I've done my research about this. Also, most of them charge five hundred or a grand an hour. I'm letting you off cheap."

"I guess you have to," said Christine with a smile. "After all, your methodology involves untested software and unproven methods and interpretation by a machine that hasn't been vetted. One hundred per hour seems pretty nervy to me."

"That's my bottom line," said Jamie. He began closing up his laptop.

"Open that right back up," Christine said. "We want to see the video workup you've done."

"Actually, I didn't do it. The software did it."

"What do you call your software?"

"I call it FACCE. Stands for Facial Analysis Criminal/Civil Evidence. You pronounce it 'face'."

"Face," said the lawyer and the detective together.

"I like that," said Christine. "You're sure this copyright is solid?"

"Sure I'm sure."

"Would you mind if I had an intellectual property lawyer look it over?"

"Don't mind at all, Mom. Thanks for that."

Christine hit a button and a video screen lowered at the far end of the table. Jamie connected his laptop to the video system and the playback began.

"Now, let's hold it right there," said Jamie, and he paused the video action. "Right here is where the software is normalizing his face. We're doing this through the use of an accretion of frames where the innocent questions were being asked, such as name, residence, job, and so forth. The software is creating a database of the guy's normal expressions. We have to know normal before we can differentiate. Follow me?"

"Yes."

"Yes."

"All right. Now listen to the next couple of questions and answers."

QUESTION: Were you present in a room at the house that night when a member or members of your fraternity had sexual intercourse with Bussie Speers?

ANSWER: Who's Bussie Speers?

QUESTION: You still don't know?

"Now look at the feedback in the crawl. The FACE says he's lying right now, and it's 87 percent sure of that."

"Shit," said Winona.

"I know," Christine said. "Go on, Jamie."

"Well, watch the next three seconds. He looks down at his hands. His hands are moving all around in his lap. See the microexpressions on the face? The eyes breaking away, the grim mouth. Now, the other part of FACE is something I haven't told you about yet. It's the surprise."

"Which is?"

"FACE also analyzes voice. A lie is said in a moment of stress. When there's stress in the diaphragm, the air supply is compromised and the voice involuntarily lowers. That's what the second line of crawl is on the screen, the graph. You can see the graph head down where he says he doesn't know Bussie."

"Which corresponds to the eighty-seven percent certainty of lie in the next lie above it. Amazing!"

"Jamie, you're a genius," said Christine. "I am *so* proud of you."

"Okay, keeping on--"

QUESTION: Now back to my question about your presence when a sexual assault was made on Bussie Speers. Were you present?

ANSWER: No. I wasn't there, no. I don't know what happened except what other guys say.

"Read it and weep, kid," Jamie said to an imaginary Noah Adams. "Eighty-eight, and look at the voice analysis nosedive. Straight into the back forty. Ladies, this guy was in the room the night the girl got hurt. Trust me on this."

"Sick," said Winona. "I hate these bastards. Excuse my French, Jamie."

"That's all right," said Jamie. "It's nothing like middle school between classes out in the hallways. Nothing."

"Jamie," said Christine. "You understand this isn't just about a girl being hurt?"

"Yes."

"You understand it's about rape? Probably the worst thing you can do to a woman besides taking her children away?"

"Yes."

"Okay. We're going to call it sexual assault when we talk about her situation, okay? That just works better than to say she was hurt. She was hurt, yes, but what those boys did is an extremely serious crime. They'll spend many years behind bars after we track them down and sort it all out."

"I hope you put them away for a long time. But I get what you're saying."

"Okay. Now go ahead with your presentation, please."

"Okay, here we go."

QUESTION: Were you talking about it?

ANSWER: Well, the CU police came around and talked to a bunch of guys. Told them what the girl was claiming. That's what got everyone talking. Truth be told, I think she's making it up.

QUESTION: Making what up?

ANSWER: The rape. I don't think she was raped. I think she had sex and got herself knocked up or something and tried to blame someone for it. I think she's the one at fault.

"Right here he's at ninety-three percent. Lying through his teeth. And voice analysis has him a minus thirty-five. It's the lowest the chart has swung."

"All right," said Winona. "We have one of them."

"Agree," said Christine. "Let's go forward, Jamie."

QUESTION: Did you have sex with Bussie Speers that night?

ANSWER: No, I had a date. We're in a committed relationship so we don't sleep around.

QUESTION: Do you know the names of any boys who had sex with Bussie?

ANSWER: No.

QUESTION: Or who were there?

ANSWER: No.

Jamie flipped on the lights. "That's about all. But the last part is beyond not only a reasonable doubt but beyond any doubt. You have one of Bussie's rapists in Noah Adams. I make you that promise."

"Okay," said Christine. "So what do we do next?"

Winona fielded it. "You go out and talk to the girl. Suggest going to her place rather than making her leave her home, just for right now. She's injured and laying low, poor kid."

"Okay, I'll give her a call and set it up. What are you going to do?"

Winona smiled. "I was saving the best part for last. You know the palm print we got off the bed where she was assaulted?"

"Yes."

"Guess whose print matches it? Noah Adams!"

"Bingo! Defendant number one, please stand and identify yourself to the studio audience."

Jamie spoke up. "You're doing *What's My Line*, Mom. That's a TV show out of the Jurassic era."

"It's not that old, buddy boy."

"Mom, can I ask you one other thing?"

"Sure. What's up?"

"Remember I said I needed two thousand for a retainer?"

"Yes."

"Mom, where's my check?"

10

"You said you wouldn't be comfortable coming downtown, and I can appreciate that," said Christine. She was standing just outside Bussie's front door, waiting to be asked inside. "So I agreed to come here and talk to you woman-to-woman. May I come inside?"

"Come in, please. Dad said you would be coming and I did get your phone message. Forgive my getup. It's just too hard anymore to worry about how I look."

Bussie was dressed in sweats, wool socks and running shoes, and a nondescript red top that was several sizes too large. Christine knew it was the typical type of non-revealing clothing often chosen by female victims of sexual assault in an effort to hide their body contours.

Christine had reviewed file notes from the girl's father. Bussie Speers was eighteen years old, had scored in the ninetieth percentile on the SAT test, was modest and tasteful by nature, and had always been challenged by social functions where the serial meeting of people was expected.

Her father had noted that it was beyond comprehension that she had been a willing attendee at the type of party described in the initial police reports. Which had led Christine to consider that the girl had either been duped into attending or she had a more adventuresome streak than her father gave her credit for. Either way, it had been her first time at a function where the goal was to drink to intoxication, vomit, and drink some more.

"According to the registrar's records, you had a 3.8 GPA at midterms. It must be terribly hard to give that up."

"It wasn't by choice. Would you like something to drink? We have coffee, water, and I can make tea."

"Nothing right now. I want to just get to know you, Bussie. Kind of get a feel for who you are and how this ordeal has impacted you. I'd also like to know about the night of the party."

"It was just a dumb party, Ms. Susmann. I didn't know I was going until my roomie's best friend came down sick. I was a fill-in. So we ripped the sheet off my bed and made me a toga. My sheets hadn't been washed since September, beginning of school."

"I remember being eighteen."

Christine did remember. She knew it would be devastating at that age--or any age--to have your nude pictures posted worldwide. She shuddered and plunged ahead.

"Why don't you tell me a little about the party."

"Cindy--that's my roommate--talked me into going. But I was curious anyway. It wasn't that I was a goody-goody, I was just slow to grow into someone who would go to a drunk-o-rama. That just wasn't in me. Until that night, when I sort of got teased into it. So we walked to the TKA house and the front door was wide open. There was a sign on the wall with a giant arrow pointing downstairs. It said 'Enter if ye dare.'"

"What did that mean to you?"

"I guess it meant what it said. But I didn't figure that out until it was too late. Anyway, we go downstairs and it's so noisy we can't even talk to each other. There's a band playing reggae and everybody's either dancing or making out or screaming at each other to be heard. *Girls Gone Wild* kind of scene."

"Have you ever seen a *Girls Gone Wild* video?"

"No, I just know about them. Three boys immediately ask me to dance. So I figure what the heck and I go dance with all three of them at once. They're doing sexually explicit things while they're dancing."

"Such as?"

"Oh, pretending to be masturbating or humping. Stuff like that."

"Sounds romantic."

"I should have left right then. Truth was, the place was so crowded it was almost impossible to get back to the stairs. Besides, I didn't want to leave Cindy there alone."

"Where was Cindy while you were dancing?"

"A boy had come up to her and spilled some beer on her white shirt. She had gone back upstairs to use someone's blow dryer. It was stupid."

"As college parties can be. I'm no prude, Bussie. I've been to these shindigs myself."

"Anyway, I should have left but I didn't. Then this boy named Jackson something--he handed me a red plastic cup filled to the top with beer. They wanted me to chug with them and I did."

"Why?"

"It just seemed like the thing to do. I knew I wouldn't get drunk on one cup of beer and I would leave after. Peer pressure, I guess."

"I totally understand. So what happened next?"

"I drank maybe half and that's the last thing I remember."

"What happened next?"

"It was just before sun-up and somebody had taken me into the living room and put me on a couch. I woke up and immediately was hurting. I ran into the bathroom and looked, but I wasn't bleeding. But lots of stuff was coming out. I figured I must have met someone and gone to bed with them."

"Had you done that before?"

Bussie looked away. "Is this confidential?"

"Yes. Totally."

"My dad won't see your notes--ever?"

"I promise."

"Well, I did do it one time with my second cousin. I was fourteen and he was nineteen. I never did it again because it didn't feel all that great."

"Would you say you passed out that night?"

"Definitely."

"Why would you say that?"

"Because I remember nothing. The whole night is gone from my memory. It was never in my memory."

"Do you have any idea who the boys were who took your picture while you were nude?"

Tears flooded the young woman's eyes. "No. If I did, I would take my dad's gun out of his desk and go shoot them."

"Please don't. I know you don't really mean that, Bussie."

Tears began rolling down the girl's cheeks. She wiped her eyes with the back of her hand.

"No, I do mean it. I would shoot them so they could never hurt someone that bad again. You can't even begin to know what it feels like to know there are boys around the world leering at you and getting off on you."

"No, I can't. But please, no shooting. Leave the payback to me, okay?"

"I'll try."

"That's more like it. I can promise you, Bussie, that I will find these guys and I will make them pay. That's a solemn promise and you can count on it."

"I believe you, Ms. Susmann. Dad says you're the best prosecutor he's ever seen."

"Well, that's nice of your father."

"He wouldn't say that if he didn't mean it."

"Okay, good. Now, according to my notes, you found out about the pictures the next morning?"

"Yes. Janessa--one of my best friends--texted them to me. She knew I had to see them and she wanted them to be from someone who cared."

"What did you do?"

"I went into shock. I couldn't even talk."

"What happened?"

"Cindy took me back to the dorm. I finally got up the nerve to call my dad and he came and got me. We drove home. Then Winona had a doctor examine me at University Hospital. He had a nurse and they did swabs and stuff. Then Winona Lindsey questioned me. She's a detective in my dad's office."

"She's working with me on your case."

"Oh, great!" exclaimed Bussie. "I like her. She was the first woman besides Cindy that I told about this. And she was so gentle with me."

"Have you talked to your mom about it?"

"My mom was in France, studying watercolors. It was her first chance to do something for herself, now that I was away at school. There was a course there she was taking for eight weeks this past fall. She came right back, though, and we told her what had happened."

"What did she do?"

"We cried and hugged. She held me and let me cry until I went to sleep the night she got home. It was the first night I was actually able to sleep."

"Good for Mom."

"She's my truest best friend."

"How about your dad?"

"He is, too. Best man friend."

Christine sat back in her chair. "You know, I would like that coffee now. Does that work for you? I'm just not quite done and I know you must need a break."

"Be right back."

Bussie bounced up and excused herself as she headed for the kitchen.

Christine looked around the living room. It was very formal, and she guessed that Bussie's father probably saw business associates-- police and detectives--here during off hours.

Floral designs on the couch under the front window. Wingbacks on either side of the couch, done in a light shade of pink with a pattern of yellow fleur-de-lis. A giant glass coffee table ran the length of the couch and was supplied with automotive magazines and daily newspapers, presumably for guests to while away time with while they waited to meet with the DA. Various chairs and a love seat with throw pillows completed the furnishings. The walls were festooned with Impressionist prints, mostly Degas, as the owners seemed to prefer the raw earthiness of the dancers and cabaret depicted. Which told Christine something about the occupants, though she wasn't sure exactly what.

Bussie returned with the coffee and an eggshell-colored tray. Cream and sugar and two silver spoons were provided, so Christine helped herself and then took a sip.

"Thank you. Now, Bussie, we need brighter days ahead for you. What are you thinking might come next?"

"Two choices. One, I think Cindy was right the very first time we talked. Dye my hair, cut it short, colored contact lenses, name change, California or New York. A whole new life."

"And what's two?"

"Two is becoming a nun."

"Seriously? You would do that?"

"My parents are very Catholic. I guess I am too. We even talked about it one time when I was about fourteen. I'd just had sex with my cousin--second cousin--and I was feeling guilty, so I guess I brought it up. At that age, the last thing I wanted was another boy in my life and I figured the nuns were a way to avoid them."

"What about now?"

"We're very religious. I'm seriously considering it. Maybe working in a third-world country."

"But you wanted to be a doctor, your father said."

"Wanted. Past tense. That was before."

"You don't think you could do that now?"

"Truthfully? I haven't given it much thought. Mostly I just sit around and look out the window. It's almost winter, you know. We've already had two light snows. I love winter. I love that insular feeling of being inside in front of the fireplace in the den, all snuggled up with a comforter."

"What do you think about when you do that?"

"I don't think. I cry."

"Does anything make it better?"

"No. I used to read a lot. Now I don't so much anymore. It's like I can't concentrate like before."

"So you're suffering emotionally and mentally both."

"I guess so."

"Snuggling up by the fire: do nuns get to do that?"

"No, and I get what you're saying. But I love it."

"That sounds like just the place for you to spend your winter. Well, I think we're done here."

"That wasn't so bad. You made it easy, Ms. Susmann. Thank you for doing that."

"Hey, this case is the most important case in my office. We're going to see justice done."

"Can you get the pictures off the Internet?"

"No, unfortunately not."

"Then justice won't really be done, will it, Ms. Susmann?"

11

Bussie's father was averse to carrying the gun concealed, but there were times in his duty as district attorney that he was forced to. Usually when particularly violent men or mafia drones were being brought to justice.

After thirty minutes of searching his bedroom, she finally found the gun downstairs in his office, in his top right-hand desk drawer. It was old, a Model 59 S&W in a brown IWB holster. The hammer was secured by a holster strap that looped it.

She had learned to shoot with this gun. She knew that to fire it, she needed to work the slide, push the safety forward, and a 9mm projectile would exit the barrel at a speed of 1250 fps.

The shells were JHP defense loads, constructed of material designed to enter and then piece apart, shooting up, down, and sideways inside the body or limb. In short, the rounds were meant to stop an oncoming bad guy, to kill him. Her father had told her that when one of the loads entered the cranial vault, it spun and spun until the brain was soup.

Bussie removed the weapon from the drawer and shed its holster. She then turned and made her way upstairs, holding the gun down at her side as she'd been taught. Into her bedroom she went, straight to her bed, where she sat on the unmade sheets and lifted the gun to a horizontal plane. There she gazed at it, considering what she knew about it and considering what her life had become since she was twelve years old and learning to shoot the piece. In just six years she had had her life turned into an unlivable catastrophe. She might as well have had an inoperable brain cancer, the way she was feeling. She was just as doomed. Death seemed the inevitable end result of the collision between her life and that of the man who had taken the pictures. She was at an impossible impasse, lacking the will either to go forward or sideways.

She easily worked the slide, and the gun's mechanics allowed a 9mm round to come off the top of the magazine and be loaded into the breech. Now the gun would fire one round and thirteen after it. Her father was well armed with this weapon and she felt good when he carried it, knowing how efficient it was.

But now she felt the gun was her best defense too: her defense against the world at large and its pictures of her nude body and drugged face. The gun would defend against that, if used properly. Meaning if she put the gun to her temple and pulled the trigger.

So she lifted the gun and placed the muzzle against her right temple. She said two Hail Marys and asked for forgiveness.

Suddenly an image of herself riding a tricycle entered into her thoughts. It was a photograph she had seen in the family album, taken on the sidewalk in front of the tiny two-bedroom house her parents had rented after her father had graduated law school. She was wearing a pink dress, puffy-sleeved with arm openings that were tight against chubby baby fat. Her front teeth were missing (she thought, but wasn't sure), and her dimpled hands clutched the handlebars as she leaned back and laughed into the camera. She had been a beautiful little girl, she had to admit. She marveled that that child's life was so soon over.

Other images came to mind as she sat, the gun at her head, eyes closed, remembering then and comparing it to now.

12

After leaving Bussie's house, Christine pulled into Barrington's only Starbucks. She waited in line, drumming her fingers on the headrest of the passenger seat. Her turn came and she ordered her favorite: skinny latte mocha on ice. Odd, but memorable, as far as she was concerned.

She pulled up to the window, held out her phone for the Starbucks scan, and received her drink. Then she pulled away, turned left, followed by another two lefts, until she was again on the highway out to the freeway.

"Poor girl," she said to herself. "Her life is virtually over. At least as she knew it before."

She couldn't begin to imagine what Bussie must be going through. The girl had just turned eighteen in July before school started and had known nothing about the world out there that was waiting to gobble up young girls like her. Going to a fraternity party and accepting a drink you didn't see come out of the keg? No one in their right mind would do that. Certainly no worldwise female ever would. But this child had; she had blithely trusted strangers that night. She had trusted them because she thought their world was pure, like hers. She hadn't ever encountered evil before. But now she had. Now it was Christine's job to seize it and choke it off.

Her cell phone chirped. Winona.

"Hey, Win," said Christine. "I just finished up with her."

"How was the girl when you left?"

"I would have to say she was resigned to her situation. Guess what? She's thinking of becoming a nun."

"A nun? I've known Bussie for ten years. She's always wanted to be a doctor. Or a veterinarian. When did the nun business start?"

"When a team of assholes took nude pictures of her and posted them on the Internet for the whole world to inspect. That would turn many of us toward the nunnery, and a life in some third-world country caring for the sick."

"I hear that. Well, what's our plan?"

"I'm thinking I'm going back to see Noah again. This time with Jamie's video and its FACCE markup."

"And doing what? Confronting him?"

"Yes. You have his palm print, I have the video. Wouldn't you think he'd be ready to take a deal to help us nab the others?"

"Yeah, but I don't like the idea of dealing him out. He's the king of the assholes, far as I'm concerned."

"Hey, you'll get no argument there. If I had my druthers he'd receive the longest sentence of them all for straight-out lying to me."

"What would be an alternative course? I've already interviewed the guys from TKA who attended the party. Nobody knows anything. Bullshit, but there you are."

"Yes, it is a load. That's why I think Noah's our man. Say, what about offering him a deal that requires a year in shock?"

"Shock incarceration? They do have that in Illinois."

"They do. IDOC has a system called Boot Camp and consists of physical labor, education, counseling, and a point system. It lasts six months. I say six months of shock and tack on six months of regular prison. It would be an experience he'd never forget."

"Of course it doesn't come close to matching the impact on the victim's life. That's what I'd like, a *quid pro quo*."

"I hear you. Me, too. But as the prosecutor on the case, I think I need this kid enough to offer him a one-time deal."

"Does he have a lawyer yet?"

"Unknown. He said something about his father being tight-fisted. Maybe this is the time to hit him up again, before he lawyers up. Look, let's do this. I'm in my car, so if you would, call him and make an appointment for me to go back up there and talk. This time I've got the offer in my pocket, the video, the palm print."

"Sounds reasonable. I'll call him, then get right back to you."

"Thanks."

They signed off and Christine drove several miles, eating up the next fifteen minutes in deep thought. Five miles west of Chicago, on the Kennedy, the traffic began its normal stop-and-go tangle.

The cell phone chirped again. Winona.

"Hey, girl, what you got?"

"You're going to meet him at ten tomorrow. Same place. I made the arrangements."

"That just leaves time for me to run home, grab some clothes, kiss everyone hello and goodbye and head for O'Hare. I'm on my way. Thanks, Win."

"You got it. Just do me one favor when you see this guy, okay?"

"Sure. What's that?"

"Kick him in the sack. Nobody will ever know."

"You don't know me. I could do much more damage than that and easily live with it," Christine said. "I don't need encouragement."

"All right. Well, forget I said anything."

"I won't forget. I just might go for it."

"Please call me when you're done. I'm itching to know about the deal."

"Will do. Later."

"Later, Chris."

She was just turning off the freeway onto Washington Street when the cellphone ended her reverie. Winona again.

"Yes?"

"They just found Bussie."

"Who found her? Doing what?"

"Her mom came home from her volunteer work. Evidently Bussie was on her bed, her dad's loaded gun in her hand, fast asleep. Her dad's on his way home. He let me know."

"My God. I'm so sorry for her. Anything we can do?"

"Drill that son of a bitch tomorrow. If there's the slightest hesitation, come home, convene the grand jury, and get him under oath. We get a perjury count that way, when he lies and says he wasn't there. That and the rape will put him behind bars for twenty years without possibility of parole."

"I'm just sick. I hope they don't think it was something I said."

"Not for a second. They know she's been drifting into deeper depression every day. Your visit is in no way in question."

"Okay, good."

"I've got your back down here. You go to Anchorage."

"I'm all but in the air. I will be in about three hours. I've already called my pilot and he called his partner and they're having the plane gassed this minute. I'm off."

"Call me when you know."

"Will do. Hey, I thought of something else I'd like you to do."

"What's that?"

"Call about ten of the boys on your list. Tell them we're offering a one-time deal to anyone who will come forward and cooperate."

"I like that. Like cold-calling prospective buyers."

"We do have something to sell. We're offering a low down payment on freedom."

"I'll start right now."

"If I'm guessing right, one or two of them will immediately turn around and call Noah and tell him about the deal. That should scare the living hell out of him. Then I'll tell him first come, first served."

"Smart lady. I'll get them all called before I leave."

"Thanks, Winona."

"S'long."

Christine hung up and then dialed Ed Mitchell. His private desk phone was picked up on the second ring.

"Ed Mitchell here."

"Ed, Chris. I need you to take a ride with me tonight. We're going to work on the lawsuit I started you on."

"Evan Rushdie?"

"Yes, Evan Rushdie versus the witch girl's father."

"I can do that. I have no plans tonight. When are we coming back?"

"We'll be back by closing time tomorrow or thereabouts. Wear something warm and bring a coat. It's still cold up there."

"Where?"

"Alaska."

"Jeans okay?"

"Better than okay. That's my usual getup for the outback."

"Where do I meet you?"

"Come to the General Aviation Terminal at O'Hare. Just go to the lobby and wait for me there."

"I'm on my way. Are you headed there now?"

"Got to go home, kiss the hubby and kids, change my clothes, then I'm there."

"Okay. Well, see you there, boss."

"Thanks. And bring the Rushdie file."

"One step ahead. It's already on our server. Everything's PDF or images now."

"Good work. So just bring your laptop. *Adios.*"

"Goodbye, Christine."

She hung up and found she was feeling excitement deep down in her gut. Or lower. *Now what the hell*, she thought. Then she fought off the thought. *Just keep it all business and everything will be all right. You can't be frolicking with the help.*

Besides, you've got Sonny. No woman could want more than Sonny.

At least not me.

13

"Is there ever a time where deadly force such as what the girl's dad used on Evan is legally justified?"

They were on the Gulfstream, discussing the witch case while en route to Alaska. Outside it was dark and the strobe lights were winking in the frigid air.

"Yes, there is," said Ed to Christine. "My research has turned up plenty of cases where deadly force is used in defense of another."

They were sitting at the port conference table built mid-fuselage on the Gulfstream jet. Christine was wearing jeans and a white button-down with a gray sweater draped over her shoulders and tied in front. Ed was dressed similarly, in jeans and a pale blue broadcloth button-down, sans sweater. The cabin attendant had outfitted both passengers with new moccasins, intended to protect the soft leather seats from rub-off shoe polish. Christine was ever-so-picky about her fifty million dollar aircraft, and no one blamed her.

She sipped her coffee.

"Well, I know guns are used to defend others. That's a no-brainer. But what about kicking a kid in the head several times? And protection from what?"

"I've got the answer to that. Here's what I think the defense might try." He stopped and gathered his thoughts. "Evan was actually engaged in the commission of a felony when he had sex with the girl."

"Statutory rape?"

"Yes, exactly. She was underage. It doesn't matter that he was underage too. He can still be guilty of stat rape."

"Go on."

"So I'm thinking the defense will argue that when the father came into the room and found them having intercourse, the father was within his rights by stopping the commission of a crime from proceeding."

"Brilliant. A jury might not like it so much, but you're thinking they might get a summary judgment so the case never sees the light of day."

"You read my mind."

"Interesting. So how do we work around this?"

"By breaking apart what happened. We can argue that the father might have been within his rights by separating them. But then, when he got Evan down on the floor and began kicking him--that was force that wasn't necessary to stop the commission of the crime of stat rape."

"Agree. I like your thinking."

"Thanks. Anyway, I've found a boatload of case law that supports this."

"One question. What if the parents come back and counterclaim against Evan for the rape? What if they get damages from him? Even punitive damages?"

"Hmm. Hadn't got that far, to tell the truth. But I'll look into it. You're right, it might be a big hole in our case."

She sat back from the table and toyed with her cup and saucer.

"Of course, there's always the fact Evan is penniless. So they sue him, so what?"

"No, he won't always be penniless. And they can revive any judgment they get and keep it around forever."

"And bankruptcy on the judgment wouldn't work--"

"Wouldn't work because you can't get rid of civil awards based on criminal acts. So bankruptcy won't save our boy."

"You know, I really can't see the jury hitting him with any kind of award. Kids are kids."

"Probably. But let me work through it and get back to you."

"Sure. Take your time, in between all the other work I pushed off on you."

He ran his hand back through his long black hair. He blinked heavily, and she could see--through those beautiful eyelashes--that he was suddenly quite sleepy.

"How about we grab a couple hours of sleep?" she said.

He yawned. "You'll get no fight out of me, Chris."

She stood and began making her way to her bulkhead seat, where she had several pillows and blankets waiting. She lay down, not bothering to remove her warm moccasins. She thought about Ed and she thought about Sonny. An air phone was installed on the cabin interior next to her. She picked it up and called home.

Sonny answered on the first ring.

"Thought you might call," he said without asking who it was. "We haven't seen you much around here this week."

"I know, and I'm sorry. I just called to say I love you and wish you could be with me."

"That's good to hear. I love you too. The kids are doing their homework. At least one of them is. The other one is camped in front of his computer, working on his software."

"That's our boy."

"Yes, thank God. He is our boy."

"We're very lucky. We're blessed."

"Yes."

"Let's never do anything to mess up what we have."

"Like what?" he said. "What could we possibly do wrong?"

"I mean let's just take care of our family and give it all the love we can."

"I think we're doing that. We're both working, supporting the kids and ourselves. You would never have to turn another tap, truth be told. Not with the few hundred million you've got squirreled away."

"*We* have squirreled away. You're on those accounts as much as I am, Sonny."

"I know. It's just something that never enters my mind, all that money. It's great to have, but I want a normal life. I want a job, a not-too-big house, a mortgage, two cars and good food. That's about it."

"We have a good thing going, that's all I'm saying. And we're keeping what's ours."

"I'm all in, Christine, you know that."

"I do."

Suddenly she was too tired to fight off the cross-current of the two men in her mind. Sonny and Christine said their goodbyes and she reached back and replaced the phone. She closed her eyes and gave in to the night and sleep.

THE FLIGHT PLAN called for a six hour flight, Chicago to Anchorage. With a strong headwind, however, the flight took a half hour longer. They touched down at two o'clock in the morning, Anchorage time.

Christine opened her eyes long enough to hear Ed snoring on his side of the cabin. She had already prearranged with the pilots that they would disembark and leave the two lawyers to sleep on the plane, rather than going through the rigmarole of finding a hotel in the middle of the night, checking in, getting three hours of sleep, checking out, and all the rest. So she closed her eyes and immediately fell asleep again.

Four hours later, she awoke rested, if a bit cramped in her legs. She'd had her couch built long enough to fully stretch out on, but somehow she always woke up feeling out of sorts. Today was no different.

A catered breakfast was brought onboard at eight a.m. The meeting was set for ten o'clock, so Ed and Christine rejoined each other at the dining table and had a very luxurious, very filling breakfast of Canadian bacon, ham, sausage links, scrambled eggs, toast, coffee, orange juice, and a basket of fresh fruit from California.

They talked very little while they ate, and Christine was careful to avoid eye contact with her employee. *There*, she thought. *That's better. He is, after all, my employee. I owe him respect and courteous distance. And he shall have it.*

She took the forward bathroom and he took the aft to freshen up and get ready for the day. Once, they met briefly in the aisle and there was a moment of embarrassment while they squeezed by each other. She wondered what aftershave he was wearing and in the same thought realized Sonny didn't wear aftershave. And so what? Why would that even come to mind? It was time to buckle down and start thinking about the upcoming deposition.

It was decided that Ed would remain behind on the plane and continue working on Evan's case while Christine went off to meet Noah Adams. They said terse goodbyes and she walked down the stairway. He followed moments later and caught up to her. He said he was going to stretch his legs with a walk around the airport. She didn't reply, only nodded and leaned into the strong Anchorage wind sweeping down off the mountains.

Yellow cabs sat nose-to-tail out front. She climbed into one and was off.

As the car pulled away, she craned around to look out the back window.

He was nowhere to be seen.

∼

THE RECEPTIONIST GREETED Christine and said the Tongass Room was open and waiting.

Christine knew the way. Once again there were Danish and crullers in a long basket next to the water pitchers. She helped herself to a Danish and chomped down. It was flavorless but sweet and she immediately wished she hadn't eaten it. *Mental note: extra thirty minutes on the treadmill tomorrow.*

The receptionist brought Noah Adams to the room. He came in wearing chinos, a plaid wool shirt, Patagonia shell, and roper boots. Christine saw he wasn't smiling and he didn't smile when they shook hands. He was, in fact, grim and looking white around the mouth.

"Have a seat there," she said, placing him across the table from her.

"Thanks."

"Noah, I want to be straight with you. I'm prosecuting this case, but the girl who was raped is the district attorney's daughter and he had a conflict of interest. I don't have a conflict of interest because I don't work for the DA. I have my own private practice. Now, there are some things you should know about me. One, I don't suffer fools gladly. This means that I don't put up with bullshit. You following me so far?"

"Yes."

"Second, I have a very mean streak in me. If it were up to me, I'd probably send a hit man after whoever did this to my daughter. You might say that I'm that hit man, masquerading as a lawyer. I say that because the damage I'm prepared to inflict on you will make you wish you were dead, if I get you into the right prison and get you mixed up with all the wrong people. Those people would love a taste of your sweet ass."

"Shit."

"You should shit. Now you know a little about me. Let's review what we know about you. You were the president of TKA on the night of the rape. We also know you were present in the room that night."

"But I wasn't--"

"And I call bullshit! I call bullshit because CSI found your palm print on the headboard of the bed. I also have a video of your last meeting with me. It's been processed by software that tells me exactly where you were lying to me and tells me why we know this. I'm going to play that for you now."

She opened the laptop, called up the video, and swung the screen around for him to watch. He leaned forward on the table and held his head between his hands as he watched. He wasn't a bad-looking kid, she decided, but he was one evil son of a bitch and she planned to make him pay. The video ran for fifteen minutes. When it was done, he looked even whiter around the lips. His hands perceptibly shook when he released them from his head and sat upright in his chair.

"Now you know where my head's at, Noah. And it's not good for you."

"So what happens now? Do I just go to prison? Or is there a trial? What's next?"

"There will be a trial. You will be found guilty of rape and perjury, and the judge will put you in a miserable Illinois prison for twenty years with no possibility of parole. The inmates will pass you around like a girl and do whatever they want with you. You'll probably die in prison of AIDS. You'll die in a sunless, bare room, no family, no wife, no kids, with prison nurses ignoring you. Nobody likes a rapist in prison. You're the lowest of the low. So that's your future. Unless."

His hands were placed on the table and his fingers scratched and jittered at the hardwood. Sweat was beaded across his forehead. He was breathing in irregular gasps and now his entire face was white.

"Unless what, Ms. Susmann?"

"Unless you cut a deal with me. Right here, right now, no bullshitting around."

She slid the plea agreement across the table. "Read it," she commanded.

He read it. All the while, his movements and complexion remained under the cool observation of the special prosecutor. She was taking her job seriously and she had told him in no uncertain terms what she had in mind for him. *It's his day to shit or get off the pot,* she thought.

"This says I go to prison for a year."

"You go into Boot Camp, also known as shock incarceration. It won't be pleasant. I'm told it's worse than Army boot camp. I've been to Army boot camp in today's new army, and I can tell·you that you won't like it a damn bit. Then six months in regular prison."

"But I don't wanna go to jail. I've never done anything wrong in my life. Doesn't that count for something?"

She reached across the table and jerked away the plea offer.

"Fine. No deal, then. Your call."

She stood and began unplugging and closing down her laptop.

"Wait. Please. I didn't say I didn't want to do it. I do. Please let me sign it."

"Are you sure?"

"Yes."

"The third page down is a waiver of counsel. Do you waive your right to have a lawyer represent you?"

He was hesitant, but then remembered her admonition. "Yes, I give up my right to have a lawyer. I just wanna sign and get it over with."

"And the plea agreement says you will give up the names of the other boys present and testify against them at any and all times as I may request. Do you agree to that term?"

"I didn't know--I mean, can we negotiate around that?"

"No. That's a stone-cold requirement."

"God, they're gonna kill me."

"Who could blame them?"

She removed the pages from her folder for a second time. She slid them across the table and dropped her gold ballpoint on top of them.

"Then sign. I'm getting really bored and I don't like being around you any more than absolutely necessary. Sign, before I change my mind."

He scribbled his name and handed back the documents and the pen.

"Omigod," he breathed. "I'm going to prison."

"You're damn right, ducky. Right where you belong. Now, I want the names of the other boys who were in that room when Bussie was raped. By the way, have a fricking Danish. You earned it."

He proceeded to give her the names of all the boys present with him that night._

They ended the meeting. She caught a cab back to the airport; he went downstairs to the street and climbed inside his pickup.

He was sure of one thing: it was time to call his brothers.

14

N oah flew to Chicago later that day. He arrived just after midnight and took the L train into the city, caught a cab, and went straight to the fraternity house.

The next day the others straggled in. By three o'clock they were all there.

Steve Emel, the junior from Piscataway majoring in computer science, arrived first. He had administered the cherry meth and worried sick. The call from Noah hadn't been at all reassuring.

Then came Hanley Miscont III, the coolest of all the brothers, driving his own Rolls Royce.

Jordan Weeks came in nervous and talking nonstop.

Parks N. Swansong, the sophomore pledge from Virginia, walked in just at three. He knew he was TV handsome and this knowledge made him more sure of himself than the others.

Noah Adams himself was waiting as they arrived.

They met in the cafeteria. The room was deserted. Behind the articulating service door the food staff was busy preparing supper, but they wouldn't interfere with the boys' meeting.

Noah went first. "Men, I've asked you all to come here because we've got problems."

"Boo!" cried Hanley Miscont III. "We're too cool for problems!"

"Shut the hell up, Han Solo," said Steve, the computer engineer. "Let's hear what the president has to say."

"All right, gents, thanks for your vote of confidence. Anyway, I've been visited twice by a district attorney named Christine Susmann. She wants me to turn over your names in return for me getting a light sentence for rape. I know the school has already interviewed all of you. Evidently everyone played along and kept their mouths shut, which is good. But this lady says she has my palm print off the headboard of Franklin's bed."

"So is Franklin being blamed?"

"Unknown. I mean, he wasn't there, so I don't think he's in any kind of trouble."

"We won't rat him out," said Jordan Weeks.

"So what's the haps, bro?" said Hanley. "Are you giving us up to this bitch?"

"No way!" cried Noah. "I said I would, just to buy some time. But I really won't go through with it," he lied, keeping from them the fact that he had already turned them in yesterday when he met with Christine.

"All right, Mr. President," said Steve Emel. "Good on you."

"So what happens next?"

Noah waved them closer. They leaned in and were all but whispering.

"We need to make this bitch go away," said Noah.

"Agree," said Hanley. "We hire someone to take her out."

"But won't they just send someone else in her place?" said the wannabe TV anchor. "It only seems logical they would kick it upstairs to someone else."

"Maybe, maybe not. That's what we're here to talk about. Something needs to happen. And soon."

Hanley looked around at the faces of his fraternity brothers.

"Can you guys give me a minute alone with Noah?"

The others grumbled but stood and walked out into the hallway.

"Look, bro," said Hanley. "I know some people who will do certain things."

"Such as?"

"Off this bitch."

"You serious?"

"For a price."

"How do we pay?"

"You don't. I do. I'm planning on attending Princeton next year. I've already been accepted post-grad and I'm not letting some bitch waste my future. I'm on it."

"You've got the green light, dude."

"I'm on it, like I said. Let's not speak of it again."

"I'm good with that," said the president.

"One last thing. Stand up and raise your shirt. Just gotta make sure there's only one target I'm after."

Hanley's words were cold and suddenly chilled Noah. He stood and peeled his shirt up to his nipple line.

"I'm not wired, if that's what you're worried about," he said.

"Just being cautious. My dad always says, caution today, live again tomorrow."

"Should I get the others back in here?"

Hanley shook his head. "Naw. Just tell them we're done here. Under no circumstances are they to discuss what happened that night with anyone."

"They already know that."

"Tell them again."

"Sure, Hanley. I'll make sure they know. Same routine, different day."

"Now tell me where this bitch is. Everything you got on her."

15

J ackie Barre was an Akron torpedo for the gang that controlled the unions in Ohio. You needed someone hit, you called Jackie Barre. He bore a remarkable facial likeness to Abraham Lincoln, including the beard, but he was short in stature. He stood only five-two, barely tall enough to see over the steering wheel of his Escalade.

Barre was embarrassed to be seen in direct light, as he was heavily pockmarked from an unrelenting case of wildfire acne that had pursued him even into his twenties. The beard was a spotty cover-up.

He was in his forties now, unmarried, no children, and spent his days in the back room of Spatz's Deli in Akron. He gathered there with lesser and greater lights of the union mobs, where deals were cut, poker was played, and insults were hurled from dawn to dawn.

Barre's nights were spent clubbing and killing. Usually no more than one hit a month, but some months got busier, especially during those times when hand-picked union officers were up for re-election and were facing competition. Which was not all that common, as word had spread that running for a union office in Ohio could result in having your brains splattered on your pillow as you slept.

Hanley Miscont III steered his Rolls into the open spot in front of

Spatz's and got out. He was wearing the getup required by his father whenever he was going to present himself at the tire plant: three-piece pinstripe, reflective dress shoes, white shirt and regimental tie. His long hair was neatly combed. Hanley's smile had been constructed by thirty thousand dollars worth of orthodontia and twenty thousand dollars worth of refrigerator crowns. He was proud of his smile and was quick to flash it. Rich boys, he figured, could afford success, so smile, smile, smile. Even when you're worried about prison.

He strode inside the deli, shooting his French cuffs. Up to the counter he came, where he observed the bored looking woman cutting paper-thin ham slices.

"Can I help you?"

"I'm looking for Jackie Barre."

"No one here by that name."

"I'm Hanley Miscont. My family makes tires and I was told I could find Jackie Barre in your back room."

She jerked upright from her work. She smiled and pointed.

"Of course, Mr. Miscont. Go on back where the sign says NO ADMITTANCE on that far door."

Without another word, Hanley marched to the door and let himself inside.

All talking heads inside the room swiveled to size him up.

"Gents, I'm looking for Jackie Barre. I've got a job."

All heads swiveled the other direction. Jackie Barre was playing Pinochle with three other men. He was ahead and didn't appreciate the business-looking guy tracking him down. Immediately, Barre worried the guy was IRS--he looked it and smelled it.

"I'm Hanley Miscont. My family makes tires. I've got work for you."

Barre looked relieved and stood up from the table. "Follow me."

Barre led Hanley through the alley door. Outside they stood in the cold wintry air.

"Shit, the hawk flies today," muttered Barre. "Make it quick, kid."

"Like I said, my family makes tires."

"I know about your family. What can I do for you."

Hanley reached into his pocket and pulled out a bulging manila envelope.

"Take this and kill someone."

Barre seized the manila envelope and spread it open.

"How much?"

"Twenty grand now. Twenty grand on completion."

"Shit, kid, you just bought yourself a contract. Who's the lucky guy?"

"No guy, a woman. A bitch."

"Who is this bitch?"

"A lawyer in Chicago."

"Is she working for the cops?"

"You could say that. She's prosecuting a case where I have exposure."

"When we talking?"

"Yesterday. Do it yesterday."

"Gimme some details. Got a picture?"

"An address and a name. The rest is up to you."

"How do I know you're good for another twenty?"

"Mr. Barre, I don't ever want you looking for me."

They shook hands and Barre went back inside, tucking the envelope into his pants.

Hanley trudged along the icy alley, turned the corner, and headed for his Rolls.

That was almost too easy. He hadn't really appreciated the full power of his family's money where desperate measures were required.

He was liking his name more and more.

16

J ackie Barre opened a dossier on Christine, something he did on all his jobs. There were pages for photographs, addresses, travel diaries, and known family members.

He hopped a Greyhound in Akron and slept on the ride up to Cleveland. From there he boarded the ten o'clock Capitol Limited Amtrak to Chicago. Using a phony name and driver's license, paying in cash, he was a hundred percent certain no one knew where he was. The hit wouldn't know he was coming and no one in Akron had any interest in this little problem one way or another. No one except Hanley Miscont III, and he was one of the good guys. At least he was in Jackie Barre's world.

After various station stops and interludes while he catnapped in his chair, Barre arrived in Chicago just after dawn on a blustery, snow-spitting morning in January. He climbed down off the train and was immediately pierced by the cold of Chicago's innards as he made his way up along the tracks to Union Station. Once inside, he went into the Amtrak lounge, bought a cup of machine coffee, and waited for a half hour to locate surveillance.

After seeing there were none, he made his way up the escalator and stepped outside. It was lightly snowing, mixed with sleet, and the sidewalks were slippery. He hated snow and ice and cursed himself for the ten thousandth time for not moving to Vegas where there was sunshine year around. *What the hell is the matter with me?* he wondered. With the forty thousand he was about to knock down he could move anywhere in the world.

A cab ride behind an urban turban took him to Christine's building across from the Union Title and Trust Building. He found her on the downstairs signage and boldly rode the elevator up to her floor.

Then he was there, standing just beyond her glass door, out of sight of the receptionist, feeling the weight of the forty caliber Sig Sauer P229 in its shoulder holster. The worst thing possible would be to barge in and shoot her where she sat. Too much opportunity to be captured by nearby cops who just might be sitting out front. That would be just his luck, so the thought of a quick mass execution of everyone in the office was quickly discarded.

He left and did his homework, locating her law school and buying her student records, along with a three-year-old student ID bearing her picture. She was a beautiful woman, a top student, and was at that time married with a daughter. Another child had passed away, according to her admissions essay, and she was returning to school filled with grief and desiring a prodigious change in her life.

He returned to her building, where he made notes and drew a hasty sketch of the office and hallway. Everything would have to be known before a trigger was pulled. Then he decided to find a location where he could wait for her and follow her home when she left work. It would be impossible--or at least very fortuitous--to score a parking slot out in front of the building, plus she probably parked underground and wouldn't be coming that way anyway. So he caught a cab over to the downtown Hertz office, rented a Taurus, and made his way back to her building, where he located the parking for the building's thousand denizens and double-parked where he had a clear view of the elevator lobby. Now to wait.

Sure enough, around four p.m. he recognized her face. He watched her climb into a new Sierra 3500HD. He reasoned that it must be her husband's truck and that, for some reason--maintenance, maybe--she hadn't arrived at work in her customary Mercedes. When she bumped up and out of the exit ramp, Barre was right on her tail.

Back to the freeway they went, then turned westbound on the Kennedy. While they traveled the freeway, he kept one lane over to her right, so she couldn't suddenly take an off-ramp and catch him in the middle lane. Most of the trip he was two or three car lengths back and she clearly hadn't noticed him in the nondescript Taurus.

Finally they took the Barrington turnoff and began winding along a two-lane surface road.

Fifteen minutes later, she turned down a lane leading toward a modest home that sat on several acres of land. There were two horses and a swing set in the front yard. Barre saw no other inhabitants or visitors around and he drove right past after his prey had turned in. He drove north another two miles until he arrived at the next red light, where he pulled over and considered his next move.

CHRISTINE WENT inside her house and trotted upstairs. She peered out the bedroom blinds and scanned the roadway in both directions. Her line of sight gave her about a hundred yards either way from her front property line.

Then she went to her closet and opened the gun safe cemented in her floor. She withdrew her Glock 17, shoulder holster, and two spare clips.

"Son of a bitch followed me from the parking garage all the way home," she muttered. She had been watching for that very thing, knowing that the other boys had been notified by Noah Adams that she was on their trail. Billy Tattinger had turned up the name of a kid who had way too much money, a kid by the name of Hanley Miscont III. In situations like this, she knew the rich never took things lying down and she guessed this kid wouldn't either.

The hit man was expected; in fact, he was damn near trite, as far as she was concerned.

What to do? Definitely not the police. They'd never catch him and would only make her more vulnerable with their stumbling and bumbling around. No, she wanted to ambush this guy and beat some names out of him. If he refused to talk, she would decide then and there what next step was indicated.

She shut the blinds and went to the phone at her bedside. She dialed and waited two rings.

"David Graham, please."

Lines clicked, and after a momentary wait, he came on.

"Christine? Our system says it's you. This is Dave."

"Hey, Dave. Yes, it's Chris. We've got a live one."

"Male or female?"

"Male."

"How many?"

"One. So far."

"Who is he interested in?"

"Me. Which I'm not all that concerned about. But my family-- that's the worry."

"Sure, I can appreciate that. What kind of setup do you want? We recommend rotating shifts twenty-four/seven on each family member. Probably two in shifts on you. You're very mobile and we'll need the usual seats on your aircraft, that sort of thing."

"Whatever you think. Just tell everyone to bring a big gun."

"If we lay hands on this guy, what do you want done?"

"I want to talk to him. Alone. Preferably away from everyone."

"We've got a safe house where you can do that."

"That would be perfect."

"Chris, give me two minutes."

She waited on hold.

Then he returned. "I've dispatched a team to your house. I would also recommend two snipers overnight."

"Whatever you think, Dave. Just do it, please. And tell your guys that no-view by the family would be optimal."

"Sure. We're not there to frighten anyone."

"Excellent. I'll tell Sonny, but the kids I'll leave in the dark."

"Sounds good. Now, are you packing?"

"I am."

"All right--the worst exposure times for you are going to and coming from court. You can't take a gun into the courthouse, so you're unarmed then. If this guy's worth a damn, I'm sure he knows that. In fact, I'm guessing he's probably counting on that."

"My feeling too."

"We'll have cover in the next thirty minutes. In the meantime, please remain inside."

"Of course."

"Okay. Talk soon."

"Thanks, Dave."

She hung up and crept down the hallway. Jamie's door was shut. She stood at the door and listened. No sound. She knocked.

"Come in, Mom!" he shouted.

She went inside and found her son at the computer, as she'd expected.

"Mom, I've got this wired now. Everything's working. I'm ready for another video session."

"Hey, hello to you too, my son."

"Hi, Mom. What do you think? You got a suspect or something for me?"

"One? I've got four of them. We'll probably be into them by this time next week."

"Are they bad guys?"

"Very bad."

"What did they do?"

She stood at her son's unmade bed and swept aside sweats and a school jacket, making a place to sit.

"They raped a girl."

"Is this the same case as the Alaska guy?"

"Yes, Jamie. Same case. And listen, I don't want you discussing any of this with your sister, okay?"

"Janny doesn't know squat. I never tell her stuff. I wouldn't do that to you, Mom."

She smiled. "I know that."

She nodded and turned away.

"Mom, you seem very quiet tonight. Is anything wrong?"

"Not really. I just wanted to ask you to stay inside the house this evening. Please don't go outside."

Jamie lurched to his feet and planted his crutches so he could swing over to his windows.

"Sweet," he said, peering through the curtains. There's someone out there and they're after us, right? You can't keep stuff from me, Mom. Let's hear it."

"Because of the case I'm working on, there's a bad man after me."

"What's he want?"

"Honestly? He wants to kill me."

"Mom, no way!"

"Yes, way. But you're not to worry about that. I have my gun and there are men coming to protect us. So, if you see men following you or notice the same faces around you over the next few days, just chill. They're my guys."

"This guy who's after you. What does he look like?"

"Truthfully, I don't really know."

"That's bad."

"Been there, done that. I can handle myself. It's you and Janny and Dad I'm concerned with. You guys are civilians. So help is coming and you'll be safe."

"Okay, Mom."

"Okay, then. Now, get back to your software. Dinner's around six. Come down before so we can all see you're still with us, okay?"

"Okay, Mom."

"Thanks."

She watched her son swing across to his chair and resume work.

Which left Sonny to tell. He wasn't going to be as easy.

F inding the Mercedes in the parking garage was simple: he had already bought her license plate online. The black Mercedes 65 AMG coupe was parked where the GMC 3500H had stood the previous day. With his lock picks he opened the trunk, climbed inside, and pulled the lid closed. Now to wait.

He had with him a KA-BAR knife and a silenced gun.

Just after five he heard footsteps. The driver's door opened, and he felt the weight shift as the driver sat down behind the wheel. Then the door slammed shut and the engine purred to life. Moments later the muted blast of the sound system roared to life.

Lying on his side, he felt the car climb the exit ramp and cross the sidewalk into the roadway. She squealed her tires getting into the flow of traffic and from then on it was stop-and-go out to the freeway, where the on-ramp speed accelerated in a rush. The way he had it planned, he would be driving this very car later. He admired her taste in vehicles.

Thirty-five minutes of stop-and-creep movement on the freeway. But it was a Mercedes and the trunk was secure from exhaust fumes and the freezing cold winter, so he was relatively comfortable.

Then he felt deceleration coming down the off-ramp and a stop for a stop sign. The car turned right and began a series of long S-curves as Christine neared home.

At the garage she slowed almost to a stop and he heard the garage door rising.

Then they were inside the garage and the car rocked to a stop. She opened and closed the door and went inside.

Jackie Barre didn't move. It wasn't time yet.

CHRISTINE WENT to the family room and found Janny at her Playskool desk, busily coloring.

"Hello, my baby," said Christine as she lifted the little girl from behind and kissed her on the neck.

"Mommy! Look at my colors!"

Christine released her daughter back into her seat and knelt on the floor beside her.

"Show me everything," she said.

"This one is Oscar. He's all blue."

"Okay. I like that blue."

"This one is Bert and this one is Ernie."

"Oh, excellent use of colors. Maybe you're an artist, Janny. You ever think of that?"

"I love colors. But I'm hungry right now. Do we have cookies? Nana wouldn't give me any."

Nana came up from behind. She was a sixty-year-old retiree who had taught in the Chicago public school system.

"Nonsense," said Nana. "I let you have two cookies. Now you get fruit or carrot sticks."

"But that was *hours* ago," Janny complained to her mother. "And I hate carrot sticks."

"Fine, then you can have pear slices," said Nana. "C'mon now and let's let Mommy change her clothes."

"All right."

Christine kissed her daughter again and gave her a playful swat on the seat of her jeans as she followed Nana into the kitchen. Then she climbed the stairs and was immediately bowled over by the rap music thumping in Jamie's bedroom.

"Hey!" she cried over the noise. "Who are we listening to?"

"What?" came Jamie's reply.

"Who's that rapper?"

"Snoop Dog. I love this guy!"

"What happened to the computer? Why aren't you coding?"

"It's finished! It's a wrap! Now I'm breaking out with my main man."

She waved him off and continued to her bedroom, where she went straight to the bed and lay down. It had been a hectic day of too many phone calls and not enough real work getting done. And it had seemed that each time she turned around she was staring into the soft eyes of Ed Mitchell. *Now there's a face that would stop a clock*, she thought. *In a good way.*

Thirty minutes later she blinked awake. The sensation of--no, it was no sensation; someone actually had his hand up under her skirt and was fondling her buttocks. She dreamily swatted it away.

"'Lo, Sons. What time did you get home?"

"Just now."

"Well, why don't you mount me and show me what you've got?"

Sonny pushed up from the bed. "Can't. Nana just left. Little Bit will be hammering on our door any second now."

Sure enough, two minutes later, as Christine was coming fully awake, a clamor arose outside the bedroom door.

"Let me in!" shouted the little girl. "Dammit, right now, Sonny!"

"Wonder where she got that?" Sonny said.

"Certainly not from her mother," Christine replied. Busted. She'd have to watch that kind of talk about Janny.

Sonny unlocked and pulled open the door.

"Hey, Janny, you've got to lay off the cuss words."

"Okay, Daddy."

"Yes, little girls don't talk like that."

"Mommy does."

"But she's Mommy. She's very old. You're young and you don't need to talk like that."

"Very old? Very old? Very funny, ha-ha."

"Well, you know. In her eyes we're probably ancient."

"It will only get worse, the older she gets. I remember thinking my parents were relics of an earlier civilization."

"How about some coffee?"

"Let's do it. I'm going to throw on some jeans and a sweatshirt. Be right down."

After they were gone, she stood up and removed her suit jacket. It was hip length and purposely cut very full. Next came the shoulder holster and Glock, the reason for the full jacket. Unbuttoning her dress shirt, she shivered even though the house temperature was warm enough. Where, she wondered, was the guy? She had taken two off-on ramps coming home and no one had followed, leaving her perplexed. And more: she was downright alarmed at the fact that the XFBI didn't have eyes on him.

It was a trying time. Two XFBI cars were parked out front in the circular driveway. The agents had nodded at her when she drove in. It was a good feeling to know they were there. Sonny was excellent with a pistol, but he wouldn't carry one. He said it would scare the hell out of his crews if he showed up with a gun. They might even walk off the job, and he couldn't chance it.

She shed her dress and slip and pulled a sweatshirt from a shelf in the walk-in closet. Jeans followed, with wool socks and moccasins to keep her feet warm against the chill outside. She replaced the holster and gun in the gun safe, spun the combination lock, and went downstairs.

～

HIS ROLEX FACE lit up the dark trunk. 12:22 a.m. Time to move? He decided to give it another hour, just in case someone was working late. He closed his eyes.

He came awake with a start, and tried sitting up. His head

smacked against the trunk lid and he realized where he was. 2:10 a.m. Time to move.

He turned his back to the rear bumper and began kicking the back seat. Three hard jolts and it gave way, moving forward enough that he could see around it, even as dark as it was in the garage. With his hands he then pushed the seat forward and, on his hands and knees, crawled into the interior. It was then a simple matter to unlock the door and exit. He closed it carefully so as not to make a sound.

Up the three steps, then the lock picks found the purchase they needed and he heard the lock release. Quickly he stepped inside the house and found himself in a very dark mud room. He held his breath, listening. Then, there it was, urgent beeping just through the door. In the kitchen, glowing green on the wall, he found the security system key pad. Now came the most dangerous moment for him. Using the blade of the KA-BAR knife, he peeled the keypad from the wall and quickly cut the attached wires. The beeping immediately ceased.

And he was inside.

One more item before going up. He needed her keys. He planned to get away in her car, using its high-speed capabilities to disengage all pursuit. He would leave them in the dust in that Mercedes. He knew that in most families keys were hung up or placed in some kind of bowl or recess for others to use. His instincts told him the pantry. He opened the sliding doors, after he had tried several others, and ran his hand down the inside of the wall. "Got you," he whispered. The small LCD on the key fob lit up. Sure enough, Mercedes key. He pocketed the key and turned. Now to find the stairs. He moved soundlessly from room to room until he had located the stairway.

Ever so slowly, feet spread wide so as to avoid creaking steps, he began climbing. He would take a step, stop, listen for ten seconds, and then step up again. Two minutes later, he had scaled the stairway and stood at the end of the long hallway. Two doors led off to the left and one led off to the right. That would be the bigger room behind that door, he knew--the master bedroom. So he crept to just outside that door and listened. Was that snoring? If so, it was very subdued.

He stopped and considered. If either or both of them slept with a gun at their bedside, they would be looking for a silhouette coming through the doorway. Most likely they would hesitate in order to confirm it wasn't one of their children coming in. What if he turned the doorknob and found the door locked? Would the sound of the doorknob turning awaken them? Alert them? Alternatively, the door might not even be locked. Probably not, given that there were kids sleeping up here, kids they would want to have access to them.

He decided to wager the door was unlocked. So what to do? Go crashing in, aim and fire, or go in by stealth? It made no sense to storm the door because that would startle them awake and they'd probably be reaching for their guns. No, he would try stealth.

He reached out and put his fingers on the knob. He encircled his thumb just below, and began twisting. The knob went all the way to the right and didn't feel locked, so he tried opening the door an inch. There, it opened. Now he could hear no breathing, nothing. Had they discovered him and were waiting?

He pushed the door open a little more. There was a door leading off the bedroom to the left, which Barre guessed was the bathroom. Probably through a walk-in closet. At the far side of the room was a portico leading into what looked like another room. He guessed that would be the sitting room or a small reading area, some such thing.

Moonlight filtered through the bank of windows along the far wall. As his eyes adjusted to the silvery light, he began to make out two figures sleeping in the bed. He could not separate man from woman just by looking, so he decided to shoot them both.

Outside in the circular drive, in the lead Chevy Suburban, sat two XFBI agents, Reith Pollard and Sevel Mahoney. They were both in their fifties, retired from long and honorable careers in the FBI, and both were carrying semi-automatic pistols. Atop the roof of the house a sniper sat with his back against the chimney that emptied the fireplace out of the master bedroom. Across his knees lay an M4 automatic rifle, the same weapon issued to American GIs in Afghanistan. Occasionally he would put the scope of the rifle to his eye and scan the front and back areas as well as the side yards around the house.

At night he used infrared, with the capability of locating dark targets well before an optical scope would have.

As Pollard and Mahoney sat lost in a deep conversation about retirement medical benefits, their ear-comms suddenly crackled and recorded sirens played. Someone inside the house had hit a panic button. At the same time they heard the alerts and were piling out of the car, they heard four quick gunshots come from the upstairs, followed by a fifth and sixth gunshot and then, five seconds later, a seventh. Both men knew they were hearing different calibers. A gunfight had just occurred.

As Jackie Barre entered the bedroom and drew down on the closest sleeping figure, he hadn't counted on anyone being awake.

But she was.

Unsure whether it was one of the children turning the doorknob, Christine had waited until she saw an unfamiliar silhouette enter the bedroom. At that point, seeing that it was neither child--no crutches, no small girl--she rolled out of bed onto the floor, seizing her gun from the bedside table as she went. Lying prone on the floor, she shuddered when four quick shots rang out. Then it was still momentarily and she sighted beneath the bed at the legs of the intruder. She snapped off two quick shots and the intruder cried out sharply and dropped to his knees and rolled to his side.

Both of her shots had found their targets. Incredibly enough, Jackie Barr lay shot in both legs. Christine was quickly on her feet and around the bed. She found the man lying on his side, his arm upraised as if to shoot whoever appeared. Before he could react, she had fired a third shot, this one catching him just behind the ear. It was a mortal wound and the man died where he lay.

In seconds she was peeling the bedclothes from Sonny. Then Janny was there, switching on the overhead lights. "Mommy?" she said. "It was loud."

"Go in my bathroom," commanded Christine. "Now!"

Before she could assist Sonny, Christine jumped into the hallway with her gun, assuring herself that there wasn't a second target lurking nearby.

"Mom?" she head Jamie say. "Mom?"

"Stay in your room, Jamie!" she ordered. "Don't come out! Do you hear me?"

"I'm staying here, Mom. But I wish I could help!"

"It's all right."

By now agents Pollard and Mahoney were charging up the stairs.

"Who got hit?" cried Pollard.

"Sonny--I think he's hurt bad."

They ran past her and into the bedroom. She followed right after.

Pollard had jumped onto the bed and was turning Sonny face-up. He began administering chest compressions. Mahoney forced open Sonny's mouth and reached to clear his airway, which was when he felt the wound.

"We've got a wound here, soft palate," said Mahoney to his partner.

Pollard stopped and listened for breath sounds. He felt for a carotid pulse.

Then he turned to Christine and shook his head. It was apparent that one of the bullets had entered obliquely through Sonny's neck, made its way upward through his soft pallet, where it entered the brain and destroyed the cerebral cortex, ending Sonny's life.

"Oh my God!" cried Christine. "Sonny, no!"

Agent Reith Pollard immediately crossed to the intruder's body and felt for a pulse. "Good shooting, Christine. You caught him right in the head."

"I should have," she cried. "I was standing right over him!"

"We won't repeat that."

She crawled up on the bed and took her husband in her arms, pulling him to her.

Tears came and she wept for several minutes. Janny reappeared from the bathroom. Then Jamie could be heard swinging on his crutches as he clumped down the hallway.

Now, both children were standing at the foot of the bed and Jamie dropped his arm over Janny and pulled her tight against his hip. "Sssh," he told her. "They're doing everything they can."

"Daddy's hurt real bad."

Christine turned her head toward the little girl. "Sevel, you guys please take the kids downstairs."

"Police and an ambulance are headed this way," said Pollard.

Christine nodded. She moved away from Sonny's body and slid backwards off the bed until she was standing. Now she was alone in the room with her husband of twelve years. Shock and horror were flowing through her body and making her dizzy, as if she were about to faint. But then it came, her old ally, the anger. It filled her chest slowly at first, then spread into her arms and legs and inflamed her thoughts. She would find whoever had caused this bastard to be here. She would find them and finish them herself. No need to discuss it with anyone or get anyone's consent; she had her mind made up.

And she knew just where to begin.

18

In his will he had requested cremation, and that his ashes be spread over Lake Ganymede, and she followed his wishes. First, however, there was a memorial service on Monday, allowing all of Sonny's family, friends, employees, and acquaintances to pay their last respects. The chapel was a small, non-denominational chapel, funded by the donations of area residents. Memorial services were routine here; a retired Methodist minister, who graciously accommodated everyone on short notice, oversaw the place. Thaddeus Murfee flew in from his Flagstaff office, along with Albert Hightower, his law partner, and their wives. The District Attorney John Speers, was there with his wife and Bussie. Accompanying him was First Assistant to the DA, Woody Smitts. Billy Tattinger was there from the office, along with Ed Mitchell and Melinda, the receptionist. Two other paralegals staffed the office that morning in the absence of Billy, Ed, Melinda, and Christine. One answered the phone while the other cleared Christine's calendar for the next four weeks.

Sonny had been religious, so the minister read passages from the Old and New Testaments. A flute solo navigated a classical piece. One by one, friends and family took to the podium and said their words in remembrance. Christine, sitting with the two children in the front row, never did stand and speak. She knew she would be weepy and grasping at words--because words weren't enough to recount Sonny's life--and she especially didn't want to upset Janny any more than the little girl was already.

Then it was over. The parking lot quickly cleared out. Christine was left with a ceramic urn bearing Sonny's ashes, and the two children. She started up the Mercedes and they headed for Lake Ganymede, followed by Thaddeus and Katy Murfee, Albert Hightower, and Sonny's parents.

The lake was essentially frozen over, but Christine slipped and slid down the embankment to the water's edge while the others watched from above. She lowered her head and said goodbyes to her husband, whom she had treasured ever since freshman year in high school. Then she unscrewed the urn and pitched its contents out across the ice, as Sonny had requested. She knew that one sunny day the ice would melt and Sonny would become one with the water. Then she watched as the wind picked up and scattered the gray ash further along the lake's frozen cover.

Thaddeus came down the embankment and helped her back up to the top; then, from above, Albert helped Thaddeus back up. There were hugs and blessings and wracking tears from family and friends as they all stood at the top of the embankment and took one last, lingering look.

"I want to talk to you about all this," Thaddeus told Christine. He had taken her by her gloved hand and pulled her aside. "I know you too well not to say what needs to be said."

"I know what's coming, but say it anyway."

"Let the police handle this, Chris. Turn your anger loose on the boys you're prosecuting. Cut no deals, put them all away. This is one of those times where a mallet is better than a scalpel. Get them all behind bars and you've avenged Sonny."

"You've obviously discussed the case with John Speers?"

"Huh-uh, Winona Lindsey. She called me. She knew I was your best friend and she knew some of your history and she was worried you'd make a wrong turn."

"Well, I'm glad you spoke up, but you needn't worry. I've put my guns away. I'm a lawyer now. That other stuff, that was a long time ago."

"Chris, seriously? Reith Pollard let it out that you virtually executed this Barre guy after you had wounded him in both legs."

"But that was self-defense. I was only worried he'd keep firing. In fact, he raised his gun at me."

"I understand. I really do. But let's put those guns away now, today. Will you promise this for me?"

"Thaddeus, my mind is so foggy right now. I don't know what I do and don't promise. Please don't try to force me."

"I'm only thinking of you and the children. You're all they have now. They don't need you out having gunfights."

"Point well taken, Thad. Thanks for that."

"No problem."

"I've got to get back to Janny. I can hear her crying for me."

"Okay. Just remember, please."

"I will, Thad."

"Remember, no guns."

"Tell that to the bad guys too, would you?"

"Chris--"

"Okay. No guns."

"Okay."

XFBI continued their patrols and tailings. Detectives came out from the sheriff's office and took statements. The identification of the dead intruder was made and inquiries made into just who Jackie Barre had been. NCIC was searched and eleven hits came back, for everything from armed robbery to grand theft auto. The offenses dated clear back into the man's early teens and had resulted in incarceration three times, including juvie, for a total of fourteen years behind bars. He was last known to be living in Akron, Ohio.

From there it was an easy matchup for Christine. She obtained the five boys' records from the university and reviewed them for home addresses. Then, there it was, in black and yellow: Hanley Miscont III, City and State: Akron, Ohio.

Now she had her husband's real killer. And she knew it had really been meant for her to die.

Sonny was collateral damage, as the Army would have called it. But in truth, he had been her life. Now that was over and she knew where she would go next.

Their freedom was about to be lost.

19

Following Sonny's memorial, Christine gathered up Janny and Jamie and loaded them on the Gulfstream. It was time to get far, far away from Chicago. The kids were totally traumatized and grasping. As was she. She wanted them to have time to slowly come back to life and to feel safe for the first time since that night.

They flew out to San Diego, where Christine's sister Rosalind met them at the airport. Rosalind helped with bags and got the threesome loaded into her Buick. She then headed south. They crossed the border at Tijuana and kept going.

Rosalind and her husband were ex-pats living in Rosarito. Roberto Sanchez was a Mexican-American and he managed a string of resorts for a consortium out of L.A. Rosarito was the company's Mexican headquarters location.

Rosalind kept the conversation light and easy on the thirty minute drive south, never bringing up the shooting--not in front of the kids--and instead just shared information about her life, her inability to have children, and Roberto's job. During the day, Rosalind volunteered at a mission to feed the hungry. She did some of the cooking and always worked the serving line. Nights, she and Roberto would usually eat out, trying out the establishments in and around their bustling tourist town.

It turned out Rosalind and Roberto wanted Christine and the kids to have some privacy and time for being alone and grieving, so Robert had set them up in one of his company's condos. It was ocean-front property with a beach just outside the back door.

"All right, guys," said Christine to the children. "Let's change and go down to the water."

"I don't know, Mom," said Jamie. "Crutches in sand?"

"You'll manage. You're a tough guy," said Christine. "Time to man up."

"Good grief. The woman's mad."

"Enough, junior. I really think you can do this."

And sure enough, he did. It was a struggle, but doable. Jamie was very proud, stretched out on his own beach blanket. The iPod was nearby, sunscreen was administered, and he was king of the beach. Janny likewise got slathered in SPF 50 before she ran for the ocean and started trying out the waves. By the end of their visit a month later she would be riding a boogie board and having the time of her life. Jamie stared wistfully at his sister's fun, but there were limits and staying out of the ocean was one of them. His use of his legs was limited; swimming was all but impossible.

Christine accompanied the kids to the beach every morning, early. Sometimes she would go into the water and sometimes not. Her mood was very dark and she did her best not to be sullen--at least not while the kids were watching. She missed Sonny terribly and cried herself to sleep at night. She was bound and determined to minimize the horror of what had happened in the bedroom, as far as the kids were concerned. But she'd had her life ripped away from her by Jackie Barre and she would never forget that. Nor would she forget who had hired Jackie Barre. she had a special place reserved in the hell of prison life for one Hanley Miscont III.

"That dirty son of a bitch," she told her sister through her rage.

"They'll prosecute him for Sonny's death?"

"Absolutely. The wheels are already turning. He'll be prosecuted for conspiracy, murder, and a dozen other crimes after I'm done with him."

"Will you handle the case?"

"Negative. That one's back in the DA's office."

"Got it. So, where does my little sister go from here?"

"Honestly, I just want to take care of the kids at this point. They've been to hell and I'm trying to bring them back. Janny cries in her sleep and Jamie's gone almost catatonic at times. He's a great kid and tries to comfort me, but then he lapses back into his own grief."

"My God."

"Yes, as you might imagine. We're all just numb."

"I know, I know. Please let me know how to help."

"Sis, I honestly don't know. Just allow us to be with you and Roberto these next few weeks, I guess. We'll just take it one day at a time."

"What about Thaddeus? Has he been around?"

"Thad drops by and spends time with us. Which isn't easy for him, as much as he's on the go."

"Love that guy."

"Yes, Thad and Katy are my two favorite people in the world, after you and Roberto."

"He's meant so much to you."

"He has. But he's doing great and business is out of control for him. For both of us, I guess."

"Why didn't you go into practice with Thad?"

"Really? One law practice can't have two commanding officers, that's why. We couldn't both be in charge and we're strong-willed enough that both of us need to be in charge."

"So you guys discussed going in together?"

"Oh, sure. But it just hasn't been the time or place. And now I'm trying to move more into public policy kinds of cases and he's not. So it just wasn't a good fit."

"I see. I'm glad it wasn't something else."

"Never. Thaddeus Murfee and I are joined at the hip. Always will be."

"Good to hear."

~

TWO WEEKS INTO THE GETAWAY, Winona flew out to meet Christine in San Diego. There was an important development in the date rape case and she needed Christine's input. Christine agreed to meet in San Diego because she was actually going to venture out on a shopping spree up there, "Just for the hell of it," she told Rosalind.

Actually Christine had all but cried herself out. Never around the children, always at night, always into the pillow, which would still be damp with her tears by morning. She grieved and told God how angry she was and she pounded the pillow and wept some more. Then, one day, that part suddenly felt better. Christine had always told other women that they were the stronger half of the human species, but only in one curious respect. *Women,* she would say, *don't bottle up their emotions. They get them out and when it's over, it's over. Men can leave their wives for a younger woman and at first the wife will cry and cry and cry. But soon,* she liked to say, *you don't need to bother calling the marriage counselor, because the tears are done with and you no longer want to reconnect with the guy.* That was how Christine perceived it. At least, that's how she was. So she agreed to meet Winona and at least for part of one day try to stick a toe into the tepid water of work.

They met at the airport, shook hands, and found a nearby restaurant.

"So what do you have for me, Win? What brings you west?"

Winona pushed aside her coffee cup. "I was approached by Steven Emel's attorney."

"What's the name?"

"Her name is Charlene Abboud and she's out of Denver."

"Denver? Why Denver?"

"That's where Emel's from. She probably knows his dad. Anyway, Emel wants to make a deal."

"What kind of deal?"

"Avoid prison in return for testimony."

"Nope, won't do that."

"That's what I told them. So they've agreed to cooperate in return for your recommendation to the court of ten years in prison. A cap on time served."

"That just might work."

"I thought so. And as the chief law enforcement officer on the case, I would recommend we take them up on it. We need the testimony, now that Noah's screwed the pooch."

"You mean the murder conspiracy? Well, what can this Emel kid tell us?"

"I've been told by his counsel that he will name names and describe the whole incident."

"Was he sober?"

"Turns out he was. Normally he's the hardest partier of all of them, but that night he was going to turn in early because his parents were in town for homecoming. His mom was an alum and the family was getting together for breakfast. They had a suite where he was supposed to spend the night with them. They had him coming in no later than midnight."

"He didn't make it, I don't believe."

"Evidently not. But the point is, he had stopped drinking at ten. So when the rape went down he was sober as a judge."

"So he was there and he was lucid. I'm liking it so far. What else?"

"He can also tie Noah Adams in with Hanley Miscont on the day of a certain meeting where the murder of your husband was first planned. Seems the other boys were dismissed from that meeting, but later Noah Adams told Steven what had happened. He knew they were going to kill Sonny."

"He knew but he didn't tell anyone."

"Right. But there's no legal requirement that someone go to the cops when they have knowledge a crime is about to be committed."

"No, there's not. This sounds like what we need. But wait until I get back and let me finalize the deal. There are certain stipulations I want. For one thing, I want his full confession, on video, before we sign anything."

"You want Jamie's software to review the confession?"

"Exactly. I need to know the truth is being told. I need to know this isn't some bullshit deal to help him avoid ten years."

"I don't blame you for that. I figured that might be what you'd want to do. I told them I had to talk to you."

"Is that about it?"

"I think so."

"Thanks, Win. This is a score for our team."

"I agree. We're seeing our case come together."

"Okay. I'm out of here. I've got the credit card itch and it needs scratching. I'm off to the shops."

"Well, you're sounding better. It's great to hear."

"I'm doing better. Tell everyone in Chicago that Christine is down but not out. I'm coming back ready to go to war."

"Will do."

"And tell that son of a bitch Emel if he's lying I am personally going to see to it that he goes to prison and winds up in a cell with the craziest bastard in Illinois. Tell him that."

"Done."

"Okay. Later, lady."

"Later."

20

T O: NOAH ADAMS

FROM: CHRISTINE SUSMANN, SPECIAL PROSECUTING ATTORNEY

Dear Mr. Adams,

It has come to my attention that you with several others combined and conspired to effect my murder. Accordingly, the plea deal you entered into with my office is declared null and void. This is predicated on the small print in paragraph 4, where you stipulated to abide with all laws and engage in no further criminal activity.

/s/ Christine Susmann, SPA

She sent the letter to the Anchorage PD with a request they serve it on Adams.

All bets were off. She had no doubt that word had been passed from Adams to Miscont that she was after the five of them. Adams and Miscont had then plotted to murder her. Instead, Sonny was murdered. She and John Speers were now free to go after all five of them not only on the underlying rape charges--Christine's role--but also the murder and conspiracy to commit murder charges--John Speers' role.

Christine took the case before the grand jury. Her only witness was Winona Lindsey. With the grand jurors rapt and attentive, Winona reviewed her workup and what Noah Adams had said during his interview. She also recounted how the boys had had Jackie Barre come after Christine to murder her, and that Barre had murdered her husband instead. An indictment was voted on the first vote. And it was unanimous.

The indictment was filed with the Court Clerk and arrest warrants were issued for the five young men. They would be arrested and brought to jail from wherever they were.

As it turned out, they were all located in the City of Chicago, still in school, some for their final semester before graduation. One by one they were snatched out of their lives and put behind bars.

The defendants were set for initial appearance on February 15. The location was 2654 South California Street in Chicago, the criminal courts building, commonly known as the "California Court."

Christine arrived, parked in prosecutors' parking, and headed for the building entrance south of the courthouse itself. Coming up the sidewalk, she admired the eight Doric columns across the front of the building. She opted for a closer entrance as the temperature was well below freezing and it was beginning to sleet. Through a glass atrium she made her way and was immediately greeted by the equivalent of Homeland Security. There were two lines: a long one on the left for men and a much shorter one on the right for women.

She still had a half hour before the initial appearance. Christine took the stairs to level two, the cafeteria floor. She went through the line and opted for the deli, where she located a fruit cup with a plastic spoon attached. Eating at a nearby table, she was once again reminded of the horror chamber the California Court cafeteria really was. The placed reeked of industrial floor cleaner, yet the floors were spattered with grease and littered with culinary castoffs that had come from God only knew where. She tried to ignore the ambience as she slowly chewed and swallowed.

She had to admit she was nervous. She had never been a prosecuting attorney before and the importance of the assignment she had undertaken was not lost on her. Following the fruit cup, she went back through the line and purchased a coffee to go. The half-and-half didn't curdle when administered to the drink, a relief.

Then she rode the elevator up to her courtroom.

A recess was underway.

The place was filled with the usual courtroom denizens: clerks, bailiffs, security, and prosecutors scanning massive carts of colored file folders. As the assistant DA's shuffled files they searched for notes that gave some clue what the cases were about. Criminal defense attorneys strutted their stuff inside the bar, the quality of their suits depending on the luck they had encountered in their practices. Some sported razor-cut hair, others had let their hair grow long and some had fashioned their locks into ponytails meant to indicate they were flaming liberals and woe to the police officer who might have made an arrest or stopped to investigate without the kind of probable cause that could readily be found in the casebooks. Everything was up for argument at $250 per hour. Nothing was settled, not even the date and time.

And then there was Christine, an interloper, neither resident among the prosecutorial staff nor blending in with the defense bar. She was rootless, without assistants to scurry here and there and do her bidding, but she felt strong, alive, and ready to fight for what she knew was right. Then she eyed Winona Lindsey sitting in the jury box with a dozen uniformed cops who were waiting for their cases to be called. The cops were snarky and exchanging outrageous comments about the defense bar, but always in low tones that couldn't be overheard. Still, the smirks and guffaws were an ugly patina over this assemblage of self-proclaimed good guys. The only exception was Winona, who sat quietly apart. She saw Christine enter. Their eyes met and Winona nodded toward the hallway. Christine nodded back.

They hooked up just outside in the hall.

"You see our boys?" asked Christine. She was referring to the orange jumpsuit crowd, cuffed and shackled and spread along two benches at the far edge of the courtroom. These were defendants who had been arrested when indictments were served. "I think I saw Noah Adams, but I couldn't tell for sure. If it was him he's looking very chastened this morning."

"I saw two of the boys I interviewed," said Winona. "One drives a Rolls, and the handsome one is bucking for a TV job. They were sitting next to each other and whispering. They even smirked while I was watching."

"That's because they can't imagine what kind of case I have, given that I don't have any confessions except the plea agreement signed by Adams."

"Oh. I just thought they were dumber than dog shit. Anyway, I hope Her Honor drills them on bail. Seven-fifty or higher and we've probably got their asses locked up. All except Miscont, who can afford to pay any amount."

"Yes, it worries me that the judge will set their bail inordinately low because they look like good old college buddies."

"Not Judge Agatha Duchamps. She's death on sexual assault cases. She and I go way back."

"Is that good or bad?"

"Are you kidding? I just hope she gets the trial assignment too. That rarely happens, but I'm hoping anyway."

"How much bail do the Assistant DAs usually ask for in these cases?"

"One million is common. You'll probably see it set at around one hundred fifty thousand. Ten percent of that is something most of their families can do. A million requires a hundred grand. Most of them can't hack that. The judge knows that, so be ready for bail on the low side."

"Too bad. I was hoping we'd keep them locked up. It's easier to break them down that way."

"I know. But it likely won't happen."

"Okay, I've got ten straight up. Let's go inside," said Christine, ending the pow-wow. She tossed her paper coffee cup in a receptacle and followed Winona through the doors.

This time, Christine took a seat at the far end of counsel table reserved for prosecutors. "Special prosecutor," she whispered. Heads nodded and looks confirmed: here was the woman chosen to torture those responsible for the rape of DA James Speers' daughter, Bussie.

Judge Agatha Duchamps appeared and teetered to the bench. She was an unsteady seventy-something who was highly regarded among the prosecutors with whom Christine had spoken during three visits to the DA's office. She was small, delicately built, with pale blue eyes and wispy hair dyed a shade somewhere between flaming orange and stop sign red. There was a mischievous look around her eyes and mouth. Christine had to admit the woman exuded the kind of robust dedication that bespeaks people who love what they do. She also came with a massive stage voice, which she demonstrated to the participants and spectators when she switched on her mike and said, "All right, everyone, places. Let's get this shindig on the road!"

For the next forty-five minutes the same drill was repeated over and over as defendants circulated before Her Honor like fish nipping surface delicacies: Name, Address, You Are Charged With (Fill-in Name of Crime Here), Do You Understand The Charges, Conditions of Release, Be a Good Boy (or Girl) Lest You Violate Bail and Go Straight to Jail. Not exactly in keeping with the rules of criminal procedure, but no one was arguing with the judge. It was her court and clearly she was going to do things her way, as she had for thirty-some years.

Christine alerted when her case was called.

"State of Illinois versus Noah B. Adams, Hanley Miscont III, Steven J. Emel, Jordan P. Weeks, and Parks N. Swansong, Defendants."

The five defendants were unlocked from the chain that slithered among all the defendants. The quintet made their way to the podium, hands shackled in front to waist chains and feet shackled to prevent a sudden dash for freedom.

At just that moment, the rear doors of the courtroom opened. All heads swiveled.

Bussie, accompanied by District Attorney John Speers, strode confidently down the aisle and together they took saved seats on the front row. A large blue tick shoulder bag rested in Bussie's lap. She toyed with it, shifting its weight around. John Speers looked the boys over and a sneer curled his lip. For her part, it was all Bussie could do to even be there. She avoided eye contact, but when the boys turned back to face Judge Duchamps she glared at the backs of their heads. Christine, watching this entrance, knew Bussie would kill all of them on the spot, given a chance. She wondered whether the girl had been searched for weapons, given that, with who her father was, she had probably used a back entrance to the courthouse that required no security procedures.

"State your name for the record," the judge said to Christine.

"Christine Susmann, Your Honor. Representing the People of the State of Illinois as Special Prosecutor."

"Very well. Welcome, Ms. Susmann."

"Thank you, Your Honor."

"Defendants, please state your names for the record."

"Hanley Miscont the Third."

"Parks Swanson."

"Steven Emel."

"Jordan Weeks."

"Noah B. Adams."

"For the record, in Illinois criminal courts, upon a defendant's arrest or voluntary appearance in answer to a charge, he must be taken before a judge without unnecessary delay. You five were arrested yesterday, so that has now happened. The judge--me--informs you of the charges against you and provides you with a copy of those charges. The sheriff has already served the indictments on you. I must advise you of your right to be represented by counsel. If you are indigent, a lawyer will be appointed to represent you here today. I will then fix bail in a reasonable amount necessary to ensure your further appearance as required. Are you all with me so far?"

Each defendant indicated by verbal response that he was with her.

"So let's do some housekeeping. No lawyers have come forth with you, so let me ask each of you, do you plan on retaining private counsel or are you requesting that I appoint the public defender's office to represent you? Starting with my far right, Mr. Adams?"

"My dad can't afford a lawyer for me," said Noah Adams in a hushed tone.

"Very well. The public defender is appointed. Next, Mr. Swansong?"

"My mother said she would have a lawyer for me, but nobody has contacted me yet."

"Is Park Swansong's attorney present in court?" boomed the judge to the entire room.

There was no answer after several seconds of everyone looking at each other.

"The public defender is appointed to represent Mr. Swansong. Mr. Emel?"

"I have a lawyer being hired today, Judge. She's on her way to Chicago. She would have been here, but the ice storm in Denver delayed her flight."

"Very well. Hanley Miscont?"

"That's Hanley Miscont the Third, Your Honor," said Miscont with a smile, which was all but lost on the judge. "My lawyer is downstairs in another court but he said to tell you he'll be joining us."

"How thoughtful of him. We'll pass on you for the moment. Jordan Weeks?"

The youngest man blanched. He was all but speechless momentarily, then managed to say, "I need someone, too. I don't have money and my folks said it's my problem."

"All right, gentlemen. Now, the public defender is appointed to represent you all with the exception of Mr. Miscont and Mr. Emel, who have retained private counsel."

To the public defender's enclave at the left-hand table, the judge continued, "Ladies and gentlemen of the PD's office. Please take the next fifteen minutes to meet with your clients. If there are conflicts, please file your reasons with the court and outside defense counsel will be appoint--"

At that moment four gunshots rang out in the courtroom. Heads ducked and spectators ran for the back doors. The defendants stood frozen in place, except for two whose luck had run out. Parks Swansong fell straight to the floor, mortally wounded in the back of his head. Jordan Weeks likewise fell and then tried crawling off before succumbing to two wounds in his back that had pierced both lungs.

Standing just behind the bar, Bussie worked the action on the pistol she held. Evidently the gun was jammed. Two burly deputies rushed her and threw her to the floor, spread-eagled her, and pulled her wrists together from behind.

Christine had been standing at the far right end of the row of defendants and was unscathed. A battlefield veteran, she fell to her knees to attempt lifesaving measures with Jordan Weeks, clearing his airway and beginning chest compressions.

"Ladies and gentlemen--" The judge's voice broke off and she stood up from her high-backed chair. "Is anyone else hurt?" she cried, surveying the courtroom.

Pandemonium had everyone fleeing for the doors. The chained defendants had watched, awestruck, as the victim of the sexual assault voted with her gun. Now they sat subdued, awaiting instructions from their jailers. Not one dared move.

One of the public defenders was an EMT and she rushed to the aid of Park Swansong. She probed the head wound with her fingers and then sadly looked up at the judge and shook her head. She mouthed the words, "He's gone," and the judge nodded.

Bussie's father had turned to stone with the first shot and did not move. Some would later say that he was letting his daughter have her way, but those who knew him and knew what a staunch prosecutor he was, knew better. Truth was, there had been no indication from Bussie that anything like this was going to happen. In fact, she had at first resisted her father's request that she accompany him to court. She should attend all the court sessions involving her attackers, he had told her. What neither he nor anyone else would know was that her father's strong suggestion that she attend all court sessions had been the final straw for Bussie. She had simply come undone. The notion of sitting through months of hell in court separated by weeks and months of excruciating waiting periods was more than she could fathom. So she had done what she had thought was best--she had attacked back.

No one knew, that morning, that the bullet that was a hang-fire in the semi-automatic pistol was in fact one she had intended for herself. She had meant to shoot and kill as many of the young men as she could and then take her own life.

"Her shooting was damn good," Winona later told Christine, as they left the courthouse together. "She had shot up targets for years. Those boys were no challenge."

Following the shooting, the judge declared the court in recess and continued all of that day's hearings and appearances into the next day. The maintenance crews, standing by as detectives and CSI swarmed the room, would have the place ready by then.

One astute courtroom bailiff, once the shooting had stopped, lunged for the courtroom doors and locked them from the outside so no more could leave. He knew the police would want names and tele-phone numbers for later contact. That included Christine, who was, as coolly as possible, already weighing in her mind what would happen if she bowed out as prosecutor and instead took Bussie on as a client in the criminal case that would ensue. She was torn; the girl needed her now more than ever. She would have to speak to John Speers about this. On the way back to her office, she called Speers' office and made an appointment to see him the next day.

As it turned out, she didn't have to wait that long. He called her at her office just after four o'clock.

"Hello, Christine. John Speers."

"What happened? You brought her in the back way?"

"Exactly. I have my ID and private entrance. There's never security where I enter."

"Why's that?"

"Oh, my staff and I. We're in and out dozens of times a day. The chief judge set it up."

"John, this should never have happened."

"Agreed."

"You gave her the opportunity to smuggle a gun and damned if she didn't do it."

"I know. I'm likely to be prosecuted myself for being an accomplice. It wouldn't surprise me."

"If I were you I'd circle the wagons. There's going to be a shitstorm and you're smack in the middle."

"Christine, ease up, please. I feel horrible. And Bussie, if her life wasn't over before, it is now."

"I can't ease up. You killed two of the assholes I was going to send to prison for twenty years. Now they won't suffer like they should have."

"Christine, I've just left Bussie."

"Can she even speak?"

"She was able to ask to use the restroom, but not much more. I wasn't even sure it was my own daughter I was talking to."

"She's segregated."

"Uh-huh. Psychiatric evaluation is pending. Jim Bruner will see her tonight. He's a police psychiatrist we've used forever. In case she needs medication, Jim'll see to it she gets that tonight."

"Then what?"

"Well, that's something I wanted to talk to you about."

"Go on."

"Bussie really liked you. She trusts you."

"I can't defend her, John. I have a conflict."

"Oh, I know. But I think she might at least talk to you. If you could go see her."

"That I can do. And I will."

"And impress on her that her mom and I love her deeply and we're supporting her."

"I'll go by tonight."

"Bless you, Chris. Thanks so much."

"And what about you, John? What steps will you take to defend yourself?"

"I've already made some calls, looking to get yet another special prosecutor set up."

"To prosecute Bussie."

"I have to stay out of that decision. It's not mine to make."

"Agreed. You appoint a special prosecutor and then back the hell out, John."

"I plan on doing just that. It's such a mess. I'm sick about it."

"Get over it. You're going to be on the defensive. The special prosecutor might see a better case against you than against Bussie."

"I know. I never saw this coming."

"Lawyer up, John."

"I will."

"Okay. I'll drop in on her later"

"Thank you."

"I was thinking of trying anyway, before you called."

"Thanks, Christine."

"You got it. Goodbye."

They hung up and Christine swiveled in her chair to gaze out her window. Snowing again. The seagulls were swooping through the freezing air, still on the prowl for sidewalk scraps and open dumpsters.

She closed her eyes and let her mind begin telling her what would come next.

21

E d Mitchell was no longer desirable to look at. No man was. Christine was still in love with her husband and she was beginning to realize her love for Sonny would never end. She had no idea how to move on from there and really didn't want to anyway.

He came into her office the first day she was back, ready to update her on his case assignments. They were meeting at nine o'clock on the sixty-fourth floor of the Warner Building, in Christine's L-shaped office that looked out across Lake Michigan to the east and toward Evanston to the north.

"Welcome back, Christine," he said, and held out his hand to shake.

She reached across her desk and took his hand.

"Thanks, good to be back," she replied, and released his hand. "Grab a seat. Let's talk."

He was wearing gray slacks and a dark brown sport coat flecked with gold. His gray and gold striped tie brought the outfit together, over the white shirt. As usual his hair was longish and slightly wind-blown, but who in Chicago had hair that wasn't always windblown?

He was prepared to go down a long list on his legal pad.

"One second," she said, and went to the wet bar for coffee. The Keurig kicked out a quick cup and she returned. She was wearing a navy suit with red shirt and a flourish of a tie. She had no need for blush as she had soaked up the warm Mexican sunshine and was looking fit and tan. She was still wearing her wedding ring and she doubted she would ever remove it, even if she remarried--which was an event that had never crossed her mind.

She nodded for him to begin.

"All right, first up, there's a couple from Indianapolis here to see you. Their case came in over the Internet and I thought it sounded interesting enough for you to at least talk to them."

"Tell me about it."

"I can do better than that. They're in the waiting room, hoping you can see them today."

"Let's not make them wait. Bring them on in, please."

Two men. Everyone shook hands and names were traded and then Christine was given background and details.

Frank was an architect and Francis worked for the City of Indianapolis Department of Sanitation in Human Resources. Frank specialized in HVAC systems for a chain of supermarkets constructing new stores across the country; Francis worked with men and women who chose to participate in the City's confidential counseling services for people with addiction issues. He was a primary counselor there, holding a Master's in Family Counseling and bringing twenty years' experience. They had been ejected from an Indianapolis eatery because they were gay.

Five minutes with the men indicated nothing about their sexual preferences or the fact they cared deeply for each other. Which left Christine trying to understand how the owner of Riversouth would have imagined his guests being troubled by Frank and Francis eating there. As Christine talked about current law, there was a moment when Frank patted Francis on the knee. It happened when the smaller man described his horror at being ejected from the restaurant even after they had been seated, had ordered, and were working on their Manhattans. But that pat was quick, wasn't sexually aggressive or overt, and had it happened in public, in a busy restaurant, it would most likely have gone unnoticed by even the diners seated at the next table.

Fifteen minutes into their meeting, Christine was struck by how ordinary and how minimal were their displays of affection for each other even there, in her office, where they were safe.

But still she was bothered. And what bothered her, she soon realized, was this: Even if Frank and Francis had been overtly "gay" and loving and even kissing each other, how would that be different from the man and woman seated one table over who were on their honeymoon or maybe celebrating an anniversary, who openly held hands, openly cuddled, and even kissed without remonstrance? How was it different? And even if it were different, did the law allow that "difference" to be used as a legal roadblock to food service?

Soon her thoughts were racing. She decided that sometimes reality outpaced social norms. Gay displays of affection were further down the road than what society—outside of progressive San Francisco—might accept. In short, gays and lesbians shocked straights when they were affectionate. And that was the gist of what the laws of Indiana meant to legislate against. It was all cloaked, of course, behind religiosity that reserved the right of vendors who claimed some religious persuasion to refuse service.

So she explained these perceptions and impressions to her visitors. None of what she talked about surprised them. But they needed to be heard, so she opened the discussion and said she was ready to quit talking and to listen instead.

Frank went first. The son of an architect-engineer who had built electric plants in the Middle East and traveled the world with his family, Frank was the tall one, the cool one, the analytical, probably plodding, half of the couple. He would be the one who kept the checkbook and changed the oil in the cars. But he was also a deeply feeling human being.

His blue eyes flashed and he ran his fingers through his razor-cut hair.

"To be honest, I really don't know how this idiot knew we were even a couple. There was no hand-holding--not because we were avoiding it, but because we had had a tiff earlier and were keeping our distance from each other."

"*That* was fun," said Francis, the smaller man whose hair was cut very short and who wore tortoise-shell glasses that glinted in the early morning sunlight. "Tell Christine what *that* was about, please. I don't want her to get any wrong impressions here."

Frank sank in his chair. "My son. He's graduating from college after the first summer session. His fraternity is hosting a graduation dinner and I wanted Francis to accompany me. Now, Francis is like Rudy's second father. He's always been there for my boy and sometimes I think they're even closer than I am with my son. So Francis, always putting Rudy's feelings first, declined the invitation, saying if Rudy showed up at his fraternity with two fathers it would be a huge embarrassment. I said that was bullroar, that it was tough darts. I said young people are much more liberal and accepting. But Francis refused. So we fought and I threw a glass--not at Francis--at a picture of the two of us. So we weren't even speaking when we got to the restaurant. It wasn't like we weren't being ourselves and holding hands or whatever. It was just that we were both very pissed, hardly speaking, but Riversouth is a month in advance for reservations so we both knew we wanted to go, regardless of the tiff."

"That wasn't all of it," said Francis. "Tell the part about Marge."

"My ex--Marjory Ilene--she wanted me to leave Francis home and she wanted to go to the graduation and dinner with me as if we were still a couple. In order to spare Rudy's feelings, or some such crap. I had refused and told her off and now she was threatening not to go at all, and Francis was angry because that was directly hurting Rudy and somehow that was my fault too. I was damned if I did and damned if I didn't."

Christine nodded and made a few notes.

"Whew," she said. "There's nothing quite like being in a relationship. We all need lots more of that joy in our lives."

Her humor relaxed the men and just briefly they joined hands.

"So," she said, "how did you get my name? May I ask?"

"Google. I searched 'gay rights' and your name came up," said Francis.

"You have got to be kidding me," she said. "I wonder how my name got connected to gay rights?"

Frank shrugged. "Is this something you'd rather not handle?"

"Not at all. This is exactly the type of case I want to handle. I'm just surprised, that's all. Pleasantly surprised."

"Well, if you take us on, your name will be out there for every other same-sex couple in the world to call. So get ready."

"You'll need a few more incoming lines," said Francis.

"So here's what I'd like to do," said Christine. "I'd like to staff up this file, get the latest case law and statutory law on Indiana and the feds, then talk to you again, probably next time by Skype so you don't have to make a trip back over. Can we Skype next Saturday, same time?"

Frank said, "You bet we can. You can know something by then?"

Christine looked at Ed, who nodded. "Like I said, I'll put a couple of people on this today. We'll be writing a legal memo by Thursday, which I'll email to you by Friday night so you're up to speed on what we've found out. Sound good?"

"Excellent," they said.

"Good. Now about my charges, my fee."

"Okay," said Frank, the checkbook partner.

"Off the top of my head, I'm thinking lawsuit against Riversouth. But there's more to it than that. Probably a lawsuit would be dismissed in the pleading stages, based on Indiana's new discrimination law. In other words, the restaurant would succeed in having our lawsuit thrown out. Which would give us quick entrée to the federal courts, where we could strike fast and get this crazy law overturned before it does more damage. I would ask that you pay me hourly for my trial court time, but I would be willing to do all appellate work *pro bono*. Which means I do it on my own nickel."

"Why would you do that?" asked Francis.

"Because I can."

"Good grief, how could we refuse?" Frank said.

"Well, trust me, this works for me. And it's more than fair to you."

"Agreed."

Handshakes followed, and hugs followed handshakes.

After the men were gone, Christine and Ed reviewed cases for another hour. There were new emails, new inquiries, and new pleadings on cases to be sorted through.

Then came the witch case and their client Evan Rushdie.

"We have effected service on the father and the daughter. I emailed you a copy of the complaint while you were away and you signed off, so we're good there. Now we're just waiting for the defendants to answer, then we're off and running."

"Good, good. How is Evan doing, after the scare of his life being on trial?"

"He's doing fine. But I also talked to his mom. There's a question of cognitive deficit."

"His brain might have been affected by the kicking?"

"We're having him do some testing with a psychologist. Unless there are gross anatomical changes, cognitive deficits can only be ruled in or out by pen applied to paper in the form of tests. Those tests can even tell you what part of the brain isn't functioning normally."

"Well, you've done a hell of a job while I've been away. Thanks so much, Ed."

"And I wanted to remind you, I have to leave at noon on Friday. I have Army reserves this weekend."

"Yes, I remember. How's the Army treating you?"

"This is just more training. The UCMJ has been amended and we're up for more classroom time. No big deal."

"So we're not on the verge of war and you're just not telling me?"

They both laughed. She saw again the appeal he'd initially had for her, and why.

But her initial feelings had vanished.

She was dead inside and wondered if she might always be.

22

Three months sped by. The kids were back in school, Christine was back to full speed in the law practice, and things were only getting better in her spirit. She was beginning to love the mornings again and the kids were back to piano lessons (Janny) and serious computer time (Jamie). Christine bought them two pound puppies, a Shih-Tzu for Janny and an abandoned male Doberman for Jamie. Total cost at the pound: $660, including neutering for Furball, Janny's new friend.

Bussie's rape case was set for trial in May. A flurry of activity ensued the month before. Then, the night before, Christine and Winona and Ed met to review case law and witness examinations.

"So you put Steve Emel on first? Or me?" asked Winona.

"I put you on first, Win. We always want to start with a police officer who has a twenty thousand foot view of the case. You'll be able to tell the jury about the investigation start to finish, including medical workups on Bussie, the DNA stuff, and the fact we have Steven Emel's statement. We can also review your interviews of the boys."

"What do we do about my interview notes with Emel before he

came over to our side? He denied the whole thing at that time. Now he's admitted it to you."

"We let the jury know the facts. They'll have to decide whether he was telling the truth when he first talked to you or when he later talked to me."

"And what do we do with the fact that someone was outside the door pounding on it while the rape was going on? Franklin, maybe?"

"I'm going to put Franklin on the stand. At least he can ID the boys who were in the room when he stuck his head in."

"Good enough," said Ed. "But how does he remember their names? He only looked in for a split second."

"We have to take him at his word. I agree, there's room for some difficult cross-examination there, but we'll cross that bridge when we come to it. For now, he and Emel are our case in chief."

"What can you do with Noah Adams' signed plea agreement?"

"I guess I didn't tell you. We just got the ruling yesterday and the court has ruled the agreement isn't admissible."

"That's a crock!" cried Winona. "The little bastard admitted he did it when he signed that plea!"

"We know that. But it turns out that negotiations and statements during attempts to settle a case aren't admissible. We can't use it."

"That's a crock!" Winona repeated.

"And of course he won't testify," said Ed. "The defense will never call any of the three to the stand."

"No. But I get to call Emel. He's our ace."

"Did you check his video confession with Jamie's software?" Winona asked.

"I did. It appears he's pretty much telling the truth."

"Pretty much?"

"Jamie and I could subtract out those places where he tried to minimize his own involvement. He was lying through his teeth at those times."

"Figures," said Winona.

"You won't try to use it in court, will you?" asked Ed.

"You already know the answer to that. Only if he changes his story. Then we can impeach him with it."

"I figured that would be it," said Ed. "I did that piece of research and wanted to make sure we were on the same page."

"What kind of deal did we make with Emel?" asked Winona. "How did you leave it?"

Christine answered, "Basically he gets a cap of ten years on any sentence. But he still has go to trial."

"So he could still be found not guilty?"

"Not after he tells the jury what I've got him saying on video."

"What else do we have?" Winona asked.

Christine traded a look with Ed.

He said, "That's about it, Win, unless you've got some other ideas."

"The palm print from Noah Adams. The rest of it sounds weak to me."

"Agree," said Christine.

Win continued. "Have we done any testing on Bussie?"

"Such as?" asked Christine.

"We could call a psychologist to testify her problems are consistent with what rape victims ordinarily present."

"Nobody's denying she was raped. They're only denying it was them. So I don't see how that helps."

"We use it in child victim cases. A lot."

"Understood. But I don't think we need it."

"Okay."

"Well, that's about it, ladies and gentlemen."

"Okay. 'Conviction' on three. One, two--"

They joined hands in the center of their small group, then, "Three! Conviction!" they all cried in unison.

"Now it's my turn," said Christine. "These sons of bitches are going to regret being born. I promised Bussie that and I'm going to deliver."

"Will she be there?"

"Just for opening statements. Just let the jury see her. After the new special prosecutor hit her with the two murder counts she was released to her parents' custody. Low bail; I think Mr. Speers posted a property bond. But she'll be there. She's promised me."

"One other thing," said Winona. "We've also got the CSI workup. We'll need to introduce it through the technician."

"Palm print," said Ed.

"The smoking gun," said Christine. "Bang. Welcome to the Department of Corrections."

BACK AT THE OFFICE, Billy was waiting with a handful of messages. One of them was a possible new case.

"Who've we got?" she asked Billy.

"More whiners. And that new guy again. The one about the house in the river."

"Let me call the complainers first. They're too easy to put off."

"No, call the Alaska guy first."

Fifteen minutes later she hung up from the call to Alaska. She buzzed Billy back into her office.

"We're going to Alaska," she told him.

His eyes lit up. "I'm in! When?"

"Tonight. We'll leave at eight. See you at O'Hare."

"Be there. How cold is it up there?"

"Find out online. I'm clueless."

"See you at eight. Dress warm, I'm guessing."

"Thanks, Billy."

23

Ketwautnee, Alaska

The house was nothing to write home about: two bedrooms, one bath, narrow kitchen, faded wallpaper that pre-dated the Second World War, and plumbing that moaned like an old man passing urine. However, the house had the one key feature everyone wanted: a paid-off mortgage.

It was owned by Jesse Osako, a fourth generation fisherman who lived in the small house with his toothless wife, Milee. Joining them were two Weimaraners with watery blue eyes and seven fat cats. (There's always an abundance of fish when your owner's a fisherman.) The thing was, the place was priceless to Jesse and Milee, for the house was warmly insulated against the Alaskan winters, there was no rot in its bones and a new roof kept it dry even in Alaska's snow monsoon. Move outside and you would be stepping into Alaska's coastal rainforest--like walking into a cathedral. Two-hundred-foot spruce and cedar trees soared overhead while sunlight filtered gently through the canopy to the forest floor like dreams of calm. Amid the lush shrubs and ferns and damp, mossy remnants of fallen trees, you might see deer browsing or a grizzly bear ambling its way to the nearby salmon river.

Pristine, yes, but things were changing.

The U.S. Forest Service continued to offer large tracts of the surrounding old-growth forest for intensive logging. Private interests--having already logged their own portion of this ancient forest--constantly lobbied Congress to put more of the Tongass National Forest in private hands. Yet, further clear-cutting would come at the expense of those who relied on the forest to support the region's fishing and tourism industries. Meanwhile, large areas that had been clear-cut were slowly growing back into dense thickets of young trees that were nearly impenetrable to wildlife. Old logging roads sprawled in disrepair, filling salmon rivers with erosion and blocking the way for fish. Rivers overflowing their banks, rivers running amok were the new order.

Jesse's home was situated on the bank of one of those rivers intent on cutting away its banks. Once a friend to Jesse and his wife and a source of much of their diet, the river was now a mounting threat as it eroded and undercut man's best efforts at taming the Alaskan wilderness.

Jesse had put on a new roof two years ago. Padded knees against shingles, pounding tacks on the rooftop, he had watched the salmon spawn in the whitewater of autumn lust--but that had been two seasons ago. Now the fingerprints of industry were everywhere upon the land and last fall there had been no spawn. The fish had moved on--to where, the ancient fisherman had no idea. "They've gone wherever fish go to die," Jesse told Milee over Folgers dark roast. "They won't be back, not in my lifetime."

The spring also brought with it the rising waters of the snowmelt. With each passing day the river grew deeper and wider. Jesse kept a wary eye on the water. But he believed because there had been other passive spring times and snow melts, this melt would flow away to the Pacific Ocean just as passively.

But the erosion knew better. The erosion knew the loggers had removed the trees and grass that held the riverbanks in place. Now the erosion wanted to gobble up Jesse's house.

So it waited until the pre-dawn hours, and in its swirl below the riverbank that supported Jesse's house it washed away the concrete foundation.

The house cracked in the center and slid halfway into the rushing current. The upriver side of the house collapsed and the water cascaded into the bedroom. It then blew apart the downriver wall, leaving a free-flowing river where once there had a been a warm, dry bedroom.

Jesse awoke with a start, astonished to find himself floating. The water was freezing cold. Milee's hand briefly protruded from beneath the waterline. He reached for her, but he was too late. The downriver wall breached, and Milee, like the puff of an extinguished match, was gone. Taken by the river, not to be found until six miles away, a trout-fishing Indian spotted her nude body on the sandbar where he was wading. The rocks and sand had peeled away her skin. When the authorities brought Jesse in to ID her, they showed him only her head, leaving the rest covered with a sheet. But even that was too much, for her nose was missing, sanded away. He wept and had to be helped from the morgue.

Overcome with grief, Jesse returned to his ruined home and spent the next three days retrieving what belongings he could from its carcass. He found he now possessed a dresser drawer, a gun cabinet, a two-drawer file cabinet that had refused to float away and sundry clothes that had once been part of his life but were now water-soaked and mostly useless. His old Sony laptop was still intact and, miraculously, fired right up. He spent his first three days of widowhood on the computer.

His next three days were spent purchasing a new double-wide and moving it onto the lot where his house had stood--but further away from the river by twenty yards. He declined to allow the seller to set it in place permanently--he wanted to be able to hitch up to the double-wide and move it if the erosion kept doing its worst.

On the seventh day he made a phone call. He found the lawyer in an Anchorage newspaper story about a young man named Noah Adams. Jesse studied the woman's picture at great length. She had the look of honesty. Her name was Christine, she worked out of

Chicago and she would fly up to see you if she thought you had a case.

He called her up and introduced himself and told her what had happened.

She said she would touch down in Ketchikan by the next morning and drive all day to reach him. Would he wait? Of course, he said. He wasn't going anywhere. Even if they pushed the whole damn forest into the river, he wasn't leaving.

But he hoped it wouldn't come to that. She thought it wouldn't. She told him she had an idea.

So Jesse slept soundly that night as he waited for Christine to arrive. Three times he felt across the covers for Milee and discovered only a flat, empty place where she had spent sixty years of her life.

He began counting the hours.

Christine Susmann, the lawyer, would be there in eighteen hours.

He was timing her.

~

ON THE WAY TO ANCHORAGE, Christine was educating herself with an article about the Tongass National Forest.

"At nearly 17 million acres, the Tongass National Forest in Southeast Alaska is our country's largest national forest," the article said. "This magnificent landscape of western hemlock, Sitka spruce, western red cedar and yellow cedar is part of the world's largest remaining intact temperate rainforest. The Tongass comprises thousands of mist-covered islands, deep fjords, tidewater glaciers and soggy muskegs that host some of the rarest ecosystems on the planet. It is ideal habitat for a vast array of plant and animal species-- including all five species of North American Pacific salmon, steelhead and resident trout, brown and black bear, Sitka black-tailed deer, bald eagles, and wolves, among many others. The Tongass includes more than 15,700 miles of clean, undammed streams and 4,100 lakes and ponds that provide optimal spawning and rearing conditions for the region's abundant wild salmon and trout."

She read it again. Seventeen million acres? That was bigger than several states in the Lower Forty-Eight. Massive.

Christine, Billy, and Jamie, who had once again accompanied her on the flight, picked up a rental car at the airport and continued their trip. Falling in behind them was a gray minivan with Alaska plates. It was directly behind Christine's rental vehicle as it drove up and into the ferry to Ketchikan.

The driver of the minivan was Arthur Andrews, who was an Iraq War veteran, honorably discharged from his duties as a Marine sniper, and a Risk Management employee of Great Northern Timber and Energy, a conglomerate operating across the dark, cold reaches of the globe. GNTE's home office was Anchorage but they had eyes everywhere, including Ketchikan. All non-local private aircraft were routinely monitored by Great Northern Timber and Energy in its various installations around the globe; the fact that their computers had selected Christine Susmann as a person of interest was not extraordinary, but it meant she would be surveilled while on the ground in Alaska.

Andrews allowed two cars to off-load ahead of him. They turned north on Tongass Highway after unloading from the ferry. Sometimes he had a clear view of the Bronco; sometimes he lost it on a curve. Eventually the in-between vehicles turned off, leaving Andrews a mile to the rear. Which was exactly how he liked it.

Wearing binoculars slung around his neck, Andrews steered the minivan through the forest. Every few miles he would put the glasses to his eyes and zero in on the Bronco transporting the threesome he'd watched arrive on the Gulfstream. The names of the aircraft's occupants had been obtained from the flight manifest and a quick study had turned up the owner of the aircraft as Susmann Law Firm, P.C., a business incorporated under the laws of the State of Illinois. A Subchapter S Election had been made with the IRS and the sole shareholder listed was Christine Susmann. When the driver of the minivan paid more cash for more data, Christine Susmann, it turned out, was a lawyer based out of Chicago who had let it be known she would be concentrating her law practice in public policy law.

When the Bronco stopped for gas, Andrews drove right on past and picked them up again at the next overpass. When they stopped for lunch he lolled outside in the minivan, snacking on Dolly Madison cupcakes and Diet Pepsi, chased with two bags of Corn-Nuts.

~

CHRISTINE, Billy and Jamie took the designated turnoff, followed directions for two miles, and rolled in at half past two that afternoon. Driving the Ford Bronco from the airport had been a breeze, Christine told Jesse.

Jesse looked over his three visitors: Christine wearing jeans, sweatshirt, windbreaker, and hiking boots; Billy wearing jeans, Bears sweatshirt, navy jacket and hiking boots; and Jamie, wearing jeans, navy sweatshirt that said "Wired," fleece-lined denim jacket and hiking boots.

Jamie leaned forward on his crutches and smiled at Jesse. "This is cool up here," he said. "What kind of fish do you catch?"

"We catch all kinds of fish. We net them."

"Net. Is that real fishing?"

Jesse shook his head. "I don't know what that means. Does it support Milee and me? Yes. That's about all I know."

Christine formally introduced her crew and shook Jesse's hand.

"Now," she said, "why don't you show me around?" She held up her camera as she said it.

"What do you want to see first?"

"Show me the flooded house and then we'll look at the forest."

Jesse was eighty-one and walked with a limp, thanks to a fall one stormy night on his fishing boat. A titanium knee now occupied the knee capsule where before there had been flesh, tendon, and bone. His walk looked painful. Still, he got around well enough that his time on the water didn't suffer as he fished for his livelihood.

With Jesse in the lead, they made their way from the double-wide to the bank of the river. Unseen by any in the group, the Andrews minivan crept past and beyond Jesse's property, circled east, and came back up behind them, hidden from view by the trees and underbrush. Andrews climbed to the top of the van, where he sat cross-legged, studying the group through his binoculars and munching Corn Nuts.

Upon viewing the half-submerged house, Christine asked, "Do you have flood insurance?"

"Can't get it. Not this close to a river."

"That's too bad. So what do you do about the wreck?"

"Dunno. Leave it, I guess. I've already gathered up the good stuff and put it in storage."

They walked around the east side of the house and made their way to the river. Jesse was impressed when Christine sat down, removed her hiking boots and socks, and waded knee-deep into the water for a better look. Billy and Jamie and Jesse watched from the riverbank.

"Oh, yeah," she yelled up to them. "You can see where the current undercut your foundation. Big slabs have been washed away."

"Figured."

"Let me get some shots here. We're going to need them."

For next half hour Christine took every imaginable picture of the river, the house, and the gaping hole where once there had been foundation. Then she moved inside, taking pictures of all the rooms, the water damage, and the bed where Jesse and Milee had slept when the water invaded. As she took her pictures, Billy dictated a continuing narrative of the house and damage and his impressions into his phone.

Jamie struggled on the slanted floors of the remaining structure, but he was game. He made it through with the rest of them, just like he always did. Watching her son bringing up the rear, Christine felt a warmth spread through her chest--pure love for the boy. He always persevered, always managed, somehow. *He's just not going to be held back*, she thought, and she was glad he'd come along—at his insistence.

Then she waded into the flooded portions of the house and took close-ups of the walls and of what could be seen of the foundation and floor. Finally she was done and waded out of the house and onto dry ground.

She looked at the back of her Nikon. "I've taken a hundred and four shots. That should get us started."

"Nice. What next?"

"Take me upriver a mile or two. Let me get pictures of upriver changes along the bank. Then we'll work our way downriver and do the same thing. Billy, you and Jamie wait here. Take measurements of the house. Do you have the tape in your pack?"

Billy nodded. He had brought along a backpack laden with tape measures, baggies, Sharpies, crime scene tape, a second camera, legal pads, and other items used in investigations.

Christine and Jesse set off upstream.

Twenty yards into the Tongass Forest, it wasn't easy going in either direction. The scrub trees and bramble bushes hugging the river made it all but impossible to pass. In spots, Christine waded into the water and made her way along, this time with her boots on her feet. Jesse patiently followed.

"No need to worry about wet feet," she told him. "Boots will dry out. What you've lost won't ever come back."

He nodded sadly. His wide brown eyes squinted and tears ran down his cheeks. "She's gone. She's all I had, my wife. She's all I ever wanted."

"I understand."

Christine waded out of the water, climbed up on the bank, and approached the diminutive fisherman. She pulled him close, patting his back as he shed tears for his wife. She told him she respected how great his loss was and that it was okay to express it even with her present. A bond of trust began forming, and Christine knew she could never let Jesse down.

Then they continued upstream until they had gone a mile. Along the way they saw no other houses or people. Christine made her way sometimes in the water, sometimes fighting through the brush with Jesse. It was all running together in her mind, all looking the same, and she began to wonder why she had wanted to walk up this way. But she also knew her own methods: she would literally leave no stone unturned.

She took pictures of cut banks. She followed an abandoned logging road for several hundred yards, taking pictures of how the road had washed away back down to the river. Then she called a halt.

"We've come far enough," she said. "Frankly, we've had a fairly good overview of what logging has done here. But this is far enough."

Jesse came up to her. "Do I have a case?"

"You have a case. What it all means, I'm not sure. But I promise you this: we will find out."

"How?"

"Well, there's much to be done, just like there always is at the beginning of court cases."

"Such as?"

"For one, we need to find other plaintiffs to join you in the lawsuit. I want at least ten names on your side of the 'versus' in the lawsuit. Let's go back and we'll make some plans. Do you have coffee in that double-wide? I need a coffee and a bottle of water."

"Got just what you need," said Jesse. "As long as you like Folgers."

"Folgers, Smolgers. It's all good, Jesse."

Back in the double-wide, the foursome gathered around the dining table. Smells of coffee filled the air and steaming mugs were passed around. Jamie opted out, choosing a Diet Coke instead. Then came bottled water and parched throats were salved.

Christine launched into her background statements.

"There has to be a way for me to be compensated for the time, effort, and money I'm going to put into your case."

Jesse waved at their surroundings. "My money is tied up in this new home. I'm broke. I need to fish."

"Well, there's a way this is done," she told him. "I don't expect you to make payment up front."

"Thank God."

"Second, there will be a need for a great many expert witnesses," she told him.

"What will that be?"

"Well, we're going to need water engineers. Men and women who understand hydraulics. We're going to need forestry experts, men and women who understand what natural resource husbandry is really all about. And we're going to need economists to testify about economic loss. Last but not least, we'll need the medical examiner to testify about cause of death. All of this takes money. Over a hundred thousand dollars to develop and get the case into the courthouse."

"I don't have anywhere near that. I used my only three thousand dollars for a down payment on the trailer."

She reached across the dining table and patted his forearm.

"I know that, Jesse. But I *do* have that kind of money. And I will spend whatever it takes to make this happen. You will repay me out of whatever money we win or settle for."

"What if we don't win?"

"Then you won't owe me anything. This is called a contingent fee. Your payment and my payment are contingent on our winning an award from the jury. Like the yellow page ads say, 'No recovery, no fee.'"

"I see that on TV too."

"Sure. It's what makes American law accessible to the little guy."

"I'm a little guy."

"You are. I was a little guy too, until I had my own lawsuit. Things changed for me after I got an award from a very sympathetic judge."

"Was it for your hand?" he said, referencing her right hand where two fingers were gone.

"That was part of it. We'll go into it at some point. Today's not the time for that. We need to talk about your case."

"All right."

Mugs were refilled. The restroom was used.

Then the talk resumed.

An hour later, they had run out of things to say. Jamie was tapping on his iPad, making notes of the conversation and possible angles described by Christine. Billy had likewise filled seven pages of a legal pad with notes. Still Christine continued, explaining the type of case they would be looking at and how much time it would take and who all would be involved.

As they were leaving, this time there was a hug between Jesse and Christine instead of a handshake. Then the threesome piled back into the Bronco and pulled away. It was getting dark out, so Billy turned on the headlights as they headed for the airport.

The minivan picked them up on Tongass Highway South. All the way back to the airport he followed, while remaining invisible to the travelers ahead.

At one point Christine had the distinct feeling they were being followed. But when she turned to look, there was nothing to be seen.

Andrews was there, but always just out of sight.

24

Trial officially began when Judge Duchamps roared from her seat high in the air, "Court will come to order!"

The courtroom was jammed with members of the venire, commonly called the jury pool. On June 4 it consisted of citizens of Cook County called to serve on a reasonably random basis.

Christine could feel those random eyes on her back and finally, unable to stand it any longer, she turned to have a look. What she saw was a discontented, restless-looking crowd of civilians she was sure would rather be anyplace than in that courtroom on a beautiful late-spring morning. The final release of winter on the soul of Chicago came hard, and these people deserved to enjoy what came after winter. Instead, they had all received a yellow envelope from the Cook County Circuit Clerk bidding them to present themselves forthwith on such and such a date and other dates as might be required. So they had descended on the courthouse rankled by the lousy parking, endured the cardboard food dished up by the underpaid cafeteria staff, and now found themselves in a cold, barren courtroom sentenced to a week or more of endless droning from lawyers and witnesses in a case they couldn't care less about.

That was the hand Christine realized she had been dealt when she turned back around. Winona, on her left, nudged her and smiled. To Winona's left sat Bussie, who was managing to avoid eye contact with any and everyone. At the table to Christine's right sat the three college boys, all wearing suits and ties, their three attorneys, and a fourth attorney for Hanley Miscont III, whose father had supplied him with two lawyers from two different firms to jointly defend the rubber heir.

For the occasion, Judge Agatha Duchamps had applied paint rollers to her wispy hair and now sported an acrylic-looking do that existed somewhere on the far edges of Queen of Hearts red and throbbing pinball orange. Suffice it to say she came all decked out for the trial, at least as decked out as one could be inside a black robe the size of an Army surplus pup tent.

Christine felt her mind racing with the absurdity of the event. She fought hard to pull herself together, realizing in one crystalline moment that the role she had been schooled for, taken the bar exam for, and had, in the end, even earned, was now being thrust upon her. She and she alone was responsible for seeing to it that justice was rendered against the three remaining students who had ruined the life of Bussie Speers. She took a deep breath and forced herself to listen to the judge's first admonition of the morning.

"--names will be called and we'll ask you to come forward and take the top right seat in the jury box. Those who come after you will fill in each succeeding seat until we have finally selected our first panel. Madam Clerk, please read the names as you draw them, beginning with number one."

The clerk then read the names and sixteen jurors filled the jury box. Christine watched them file by: a black man in a chartreuse coat and canary yellow slacks; a matronly white woman with two behind-the-ear hearing aids that looked to have missed the latest decade's worth of electronic upgrades for the hearing disabled; a young black man wearing a two thousand dollar Gucci suit with shiny sleek shoes that fit the look perfectly; and a wellspring of other citizens who, in their dress, shape, color, and manner, were homogeneous, an admixture of common, loyal American citizens. *Good people*, thought Christine, as the last of them was seated.

The judge launched into the stock explanation.

"Now is my opportunity to ask all of you some canned questions. As I ask these questions, please raise your hand if it applies to you and I'll allow each of you to respond. These questions are not designed to embarrass or harass or pry; they are asked to help the attorneys and the court get a sense of who you are and to give those of you with problems being here at all a chance to be heard. And let me forewarn you, because the fact that you don't like being here isn't reason enough for me to excuse you. Having a child at home with no sitter would be. Having medical problems or hearing or vision problems that would affect your ability to judge fairly and impartially would be a reason to be excused. So if I happen to miss what it is that you feel I should know, please keep your hand raised after I am done and I will ask you to come up here beside me and tell me what needs you might have that I haven't addressed."

With that, she launched into the basic inquiries judges always undertake. While the *voir dire* continued and rambled along, Christine drew a visual of the jury box and placed names and brief notes into each square. She would refer to these later when the time came for her to ask questions.

An hour and a half later, that time arrived. Four jurors had been released for various reasons and their seats had been filled by four more of the unwilling but stuck. But Christine noticed the effect lawyers refer to as "jury bonding." It was already happening. The jurors were becoming a community that interacted among themselves. There was a communal smile whenever one of them performed; there was a smattering of conversation when the morning recess of fifteen minutes was taken. By the end of the fifteen minutes, small cliques of jurors had begun to emerge: three older women who had much to share; two shell-bellied gentlemen who seemed to have much in common and talked seriously back and forth; the housewives group; the businessmen who would, at some point further down the line, exchange business cards; and then there were the loners, the unattached, the same people who probably, since high school, had endured the endless torment of never quite fitting in.

Christine walked to the podium when told by the judge it was her turn to ask questions. She placed her yellow pad with its drawing of the jury box, and the notes she'd made, before her.

"Mr. Heilman," she said, beginning top right, "I believe you said you might have heard something about the case?"

"Yes."

"Without telling us what you might have heard, may I ask where you might have heard it?"

"Is this the case about John Speers' daughter? The district attorney?"

"The alleged victim's name is indeed Bussie Speers. Would what you heard in any way bias or affect you so that you wouldn't be able to sit as a fair and impartial juror?"

"No, ma'am. And to tell the truth, I can't even recall what it was I read or heard. I'm as impressionable as new snow right now."

Fine. The first one up couldn't recall the courtroom shooting. She could certainly live with that, so she moved along.

"Got it. Now, Myrtle Evanaugh? I believe you said you live in Arlington Heights?"

"Yes."

"And that you have a nineteen-year-old granddaughter?"

"Why, yes."

"The alleged victim in this case is nineteen years old. Would that present a problem for you or unduly prejudice you?"

The reason for the question was to establish up front that this old woman, whom Christine wanted on the jury, had no prejudices that the defense attorneys would try to establish in order to disqualify her. She would be horrified and shocked by the facts of the case and that was the nature of the juror she wanted on her case.

"No, I won't be prejudiced. Actually my granddaughter doesn't give me the time of day, never comes around, no birthday cards, so I won't have any feelings about kids that age. Except maybe hurt feelings."

Great. The strategy hadn't totally backfired, because she might have stumbled on a reason for her not to have the old woman on the jury. She decided to pass and come back to that. A wise man had once said that when picking a jury, the lawyers are really left with the lesser of all the previous evils that they had managed to get rid of. Point being, no juror was ideal. You just tried to send the really bad ones packing.

For the next ninety minutes Christine worked the jury with her questions. She came as close as possible to extracting promises from various jurors that might help her case, but in truth the line she was walking was sacrosanct and she dared not go so far as to obtain actual promises. Then she passed on the panel and it was the defense's turn to act.

"We'll take the noon break right now," announced Judge Duchamps. Christine checked her watch. 12:17. "Be back at one-thirty, please, and in your chairs."

Resuming at one-thirty sharp, the defense lawyers were next up. They had decided on the order among themselves. Noah Adams' public defender would go last, while the paid lawyers would go first. Which they did.

Over the next four hours the jurors were sweetly examined and occasionally buffeted by the defense bar, trying to locate those who had no gripe with rape, those with distaste for the court system in general, those who had themselves committed crimes--the exact opposite of the jurors Christine was looking for.

At half-past five, the defense lawyers conferred at their table and finally announced that, of what was left of the panel after several replacements and after striking a number they plainly didn't want, they were passing the panel. Meaning, what was left was accepted.

Christine passed too, and the jury was now set.

Tomorrow would begin with opening statements.

On the way back to the office, Christine, Winona and Bussie exchanged notes on what they'd seen that day. District Attorney John Speers hadn't missed a minute of the day's program; clearly, he was going to be there start-to-finish to support his daughter. At his side was Bussie's mother as well.

No one on the jury had remembered the shooting incident. If they did, they had perjured themselves in covering up what they knew. That was one of Christine's key concerns: that Bussie would lose the jury's sympathy if it became known she had shot and killed two of the boys indicted for her assault.

Good fortune had prevailed, Christine told Winona and Bussie as they pulled into the underground garage.

"I think that what's left up there is as fair and impartial as we're ever going to get."

They headed upstairs for the daily debrief with John Speers that the DA had requested. It was a common practice among prosecutors on high profile cases. And it became immediately apparent that no case had ever had a higher profile than this one, as the press and TV converged on all moving bodies.

"Remember this, please," Christine told everyone that night. Tomorrow the press will jam the hallways and the courtroom. They know who you are now. Remember to smile but don't speak. Just walk straight through them and take your seats."

"I know you are talking directly to me," said Bussie.

Christine smiled. "You are now excused from attendance. The jury has seen you, they know you are real, but I don't want them to see you're doing all that well. I want them to hate these sons of bitches."

"I'll stay home then."

"Yes, perfect."

The day was officially adjourned.

25

"We've got an offer on the witch case," Ed told Christine that same night following jury selection.

John and Bussie Speers had left and Christine and Ed were back to the other events of the day. They were in her office across the desk from each other. Ed had shown up with two fresh cups of coffee from the Starbucks in the lobby of their building. He looked very tired but also had a happy lilt in his voice. Christine decided the job must be agreeing with him. And why wouldn't it, at two hundred grand per year? Which she was very happy to pay, because he was working out beyond her best hopes. He arrived earlier than she, got the phones under control, and wrestled with the whiners during the day while producing prodigious amounts of billable hours and work product. Plus, he stayed later than Christine, helping Billy clear her calendar of what was left over from the day. That way, she was able to come in fresh in the morning without unreturned calls from the day before to answer or pleadings left over to write. Worth every penny.

"Who made the offer?" Christine asked.

Ed sipped his coffee.

"Offer was made by Mutual of Missouri. It's the father's home-owner's carrier."

"His insurance carrier. The policy extends to such things as kicking your guest in the head?"

"Lucky for us, it does."

"How much?"

"Three hundred thousand."

"After we take one third, that doesn't leave much for Evan."

"No, it doesn't."

"Do we have that neuro testing done?"

"Yes. Negative. He's very lucky. He was concussive, but there is no cognitive deficit."

"Thank God," she said. "Yes, thank you. He's a nice young man who just happened to be in the wrong place with the wrong person."

"Agree. I mean come on, what senior girl really wants to be a witch?"

"Really. All right, present it to Evan and his folks and see what they say."

"Roger that. Will do tomorrow."

"What else have we got?"

"The usual stuff. Small criminal matters, turned down a divorce, that kind of stuff."

"Excellent. So, Ed, let me ask. How are you getting along here?"

He smiled and straightened his back.

"The people are smart and easy to work with. I have an unobstructed view of the lake. I have a caseload that I handle as I see fit, with very little feedback from you--a big plus. And then there's the money. I'm actually closing on a condo in two weeks. What's not to like?"

She laughed. "I'm so glad. I want you to be very happy here. Truth be told, I'm excited about your work. And the way you keep my calendar up to date is nothing short of miraculous. Thank you for that."

"And you?" he asked. "How are you getting along?"

What was this? she thought. *Was he asking professionally, or personally?* Christine decided to treat it as a professional-level question.

"I like my caseload and love my clients. They're great people, some of whom stood too close to the fire and got burned. But it makes my day to see one of them pulled away from the flames and made whole. You know what I mean? To restore someone to a good place in life, there's no bigger reward for me."

"Agree. And you yourself? Are you feeling any better since Sonny was taken away?"

She decided to answer. It was innocent, the question of someone who genuinely cared about her.

"A little. Some days are up, some days are down. The sadness comes in waves that bury me. But they recede each time, little by little. It's the kids I'm more worried about. They don't talk about what happened that night. They're both seeing counselors and I can only assume they're getting it all unloaded that way. I've tried talking with them about it, but they're still pretty tight-lipped."

"Understandable. But you know, I was thinking. The Bulls basketball season is underway and they're in the second round of the playoffs. Would you mind if I swung by some night and took Jamie to one of their games?"

"Ed, I would love that. It would mean so much to him. And to me. He needs an adult male friend. Thaddeus is trying to help, but he has his own kids and an extremely busy law practice. So, thanks for asking."

"Sure. In fact, Saturday night they're in town. If you don't mind, I'll give him a call."

"Please do. I'll mention it to him, too. I'll encourage him. He can't spend his whole life in front of his computer. That's not healthy."

"You know what, it's not unhealthy, either, considering the other, less acceptable crap kids can get into. I don't think I'd try to micromanage that part of his life right now. But that's just me. What do I know? I haven't got any kids."

"Yes, maybe you're right. I've kind of taken the approach of 'don't rock the boat' so far. They're amazingly resilient, it appears. Much more so than I am."

"Isn't that how it always is? Kids are incredibly strong. And astute, when it comes to judging character."

"Okay, well, yes, please do call him. I'm sure he'd love it."

"I'll get the tickets lined up before I leave here tonight. Then I'll give him a buzz. I'm really anxious to catch one of the playoff games. Hey, you could come too, if you like."

"Oh? Well, I've got Janny. I need to spend some time with her. It'll give us some good girl time together. But after the game, when you bring Jamie home, be sure to come inside. We'll have coffee and hot chocolate and you guys can tell us all about your night."

"Excellent." He stood to leave. "Talk to you later, Christine."

"Later. And thanks again."

"Don't mention it."

26

"What defense counsel and I are about to tell you isn't evidence," Christine admonished the jurors, supplying the stock phrase that is delivered in all jury trials. "What I will be doing right now is called an opening statement. This is the State's opportunity to present to you what we believe the evidence will show.

"First, we will put on the stand Winona Lindsey, the chief law enforcement officer on the case. Winona is a twenty-two-year veteran of the CPD and a detective who heads up the CPD's sex crimes unit. She will present you with a big picture view of our case."

Christine then spent thirty minutes reviewing the witnesses and interpreting what the physical and scientific evidence would prove.

When she was finished, she thanked the jury and took her seat, at which time the defense asked the court for a brief recess. The court granted the recess and defense counsel immediately approached Christine. They wanted to talk.

The five lawyers retreated to the private conference room off the north end of the courtroom. Winona accompanied them as well.

Albert Adelman was one of Miscont's two lawyers and he went first.

"We would like to propose a resolution to the case. All four of us met last night and we think we know how to construct a plea bargain that will satisfy everyone."

"Mr. Adelman, that's fine. But let me tell you," said Christine, "I'm not here to satisfy either you or your clients. I'm here to put as many of their deranged asses behind bars as I possibly can for as long as I can. Do you read me?"

Adelman had been rocked back on his heels, but quickly recovered. "I didn't mean to say we were looking to satisfy our clients. Just that we want to satisfy the justice this case cries out for."

"I don't even understand what the hell that means, sir."

"We want to satisfy you," said the second of Miscont's lawyers, as the first was now visibly flustered. His name was Xavier Delfino and he was an Argentine who had immigrated to America in his early teens. He was handsome, soft-spoken, and a plant meant to lure the ladies into a defense mindset.

"I'll be satisfied when your clients are single-celled with violent men who think date rape is something you do to your cellmate. Nothing would make me happier."

"Of course," said Delfino the smoothie. "Of course you want that."

By now Adelman had reconstituted himself and came roaring back.

"Your case is full of holes," he began. "We want to give you the opportunity to get some of that jail time you're aching for, and to not risk a defense verdict."

"You didn't just seriously tell me you might walk these three morons out of here?"

"I wouldn't call them morons."

"I would. Only morons would spread a young girl's nude pictures across the Internet for the entire world to see. Your clients are morons. And that's being nice."

At which point Winona touched Christine's sleeve. It was time to let them have their say, her look said. Christine decided to back off for a moment and hear what deal these gentlemen had decided to offer.

"We're thinking ten years in prison, with the possibility of good time or two-for, with a plea to aggravated assault."

Christine couldn't help herself; she laughed and shook her head. Laughter tears came, genuine tears. "You're screwing with me, you guys," she managed to get out. "C'mon, Winona, let's get back to our jury."

"Wait, please," said Delfino. "One more item."

"Which is?"

"The three boys would also ask for pleas to lesser offenses than attempted murder when it comes time to be heard on Bussie's murder case. In other words, our boys won't be looking for attempted murder convictions but assault pleas instead."

Christine had to admit, that offer had some merit.

"I can't speak for the prosecutor on the murder case, and I don't know who defense counsel will be. How do you propose we bind two unknown people to such a strange deal?"

"We don't. We're only saying what we would recommend to the court when pleas are being discussed."

"Well, that can't be all bad, so thanks for playing. But frankly, I don't think Bussie is guilty of a damn thing except being driven momentarily insane by these asshole clients you're all stuck with. End of conversation."

"That's it? No counteroffer?"

"No, nada, none. Now I'm headed back to court. Winona?"

"Right behind you, Christine. Let's get some fresh air. The air in here reeks of privilege."

The two women banged out of the room and left the four lawyers to nurse their hurt feelings. *Not even a counter?* they said. *How could that be?*

The remainder of the day was consumed with the defense attorneys explaining why their clients wouldn't testify. They also took a swing at Christine's case, but the jury was ignoring all the lawyers by then, waiting for the testimony and evidence.

Recess for the day was called at four o'clock.

27

T hen trial began.
"State calls Winona Lindsey!" Christine said to the court.

Winona pushed away from the counsel table and crossed to the witness stand. She was the picture of health for a forty-year-old. Her hair had been freshly bleached and her small nose gave her the air of a middle-aged movie actress who had been taking good care of herself. Rather than the usual dangly turquoise earrings, she was wearing small gold studs, and a single gold bracelet adorned her left wrist. She sat down in the witness chair, nodded ever so slightly to the jury with a small smile, then turned her attention to Christine.

"Tell us your name and the city where you live."

"Winona Lindsey. Chicago, Illinois."

"What is your occupation?"

"I'm the chief investigator for sex crimes, District Attorney's Office, Cook County."

"How long in that position?"

"Sworn law enforcement nineteen years."

"You are the lead investigator on the Bussie Speers case?"

"I am."

"What kind of case is that?"

"It stems from a very common occurrence on college campuses which is called, in the press, date rape. I prefer to call it what it really is, which is Aggravated Criminal Sexual Assault."

"Tell us what that means."

"Aggravated Criminal Sexual Assault in Illinois is a Class X felony. Broadly speaking, it requires delivery of a controlled substance to the victim. A first conviction calls for six to thirty years of mandatory incarceration. For a second conviction the mandatory incarceration is for life."

"So date rape in Illinois isn't some laughable little problem that happens at college, but because it happens at college the legislature treated it as less than it really is?"

"Not by a long shot. Unless you call thirty years' mandatory incarceration a laughable little problem."

"Tell us about the administration of a controlled substance in this case."

"Objection!" one of the defense attorneys called out. "Foundation."

"Overruled," the judge replied. "She can tell us what she has learned from any reports. Counsel, I'm assuming you're going to introduce lab reports?"

Christine said, "I am, Your Honor."

"And they will provide foundation for what the witness is about to testify to?"

"They will."

"Then proceed, please."

Christine went on, "The question asked that you tell us about the administration of a controlled substance in this case."

Winona nodded. "Laboratory analysis was done of the victim's blood from samples drawn the next morning."

"Who drew those samples?"

"I did."

"In what capacity?"

"I'm a licensed phlebotomist."

"Why is that?"

"Because the collection of blood samples in my job is so common. It was decided a good dozen years ago that I should be licensed."

"And what did you do with the blood samples you drew?"

"They remained in my custody until I delivered them to the Illinois Crime Lab in Chicago."

"Were they analyzed there?"

"They were."

"Can you tell us generally about the results?"

"Certainly," Winona said. "The victim had ingested gamma hydroxybutyrate, a CNS depressant. It's commonly known on college campuses as Cherry Meth. It has that peculiar sweetening added."

"Did Bussie Speers knowingly ingest Cherry Meth?"

"She did not."

"How do you know that?"

"She told me in our first interview, the morning after. She said she had had part of one beer and then woke up hours later."

"Woke up where?"

"On a couch in a fraternity house. She was nude but someone had covered her with an old blanket."

Christine continued, "Going back to your investigation, tell us what you know about the events surrounding the alleged rape of Bussie Speers."

"It was the night of November eighteenth-nineteenth last year. That was homecoming weekend at Chicago University."

"What occurred that night and the next day?"

"It was a Saturday night. Bussie Speers hadn't planned on going out that night. She had finals less than a month away in several of her science classes and she wanted to spend the time studying. Her roommate had a date that night with one of the defendants, Steven Emel. Her roommate's friend was supposed to tag along but came down sick. So the roommate begged Bussie to go in her place. Bussie said okay."

"So Bussie went out with Steven Emel?"

"And her roommate. They walked across campus to the TKA house."

"Theta Kappa Alpha?"

"Yes."

"What is that?"

"A social fraternity. As near as I have been able to pin down, the sole reason for its existence is to throw parties. There are no community services provided, no good works, no special regard for scholarship or any other worthy expenditure of student time. It is a party-hearty place."

"What happened after they arrived there?" Christine asked.

"Several boys began dancing with Bussie at once. A boy she recalls as Jackson-something or something-Jackson went to get her a cup of beer. He returned with two, one for himself and one for Bussie. He handed her the one in his right hand and raised his own like they were making a toast."

"Toasting what?"

"God only knows. The next thing she knows, she's waking up downstairs on the couch and it's very early morning, before sunrise."

"Does she recall what happened to her during the night?"

"Not at all. She has zero memory, which isn't unusual with gamma hydroxybutyrate. That's why they call it a date rape drug. The date is knocked out and remembers nothing."

"What happened next?"

"After she woke up? Somehow she winds up back at the student union with her roommate. Somebody texts her nude pictures of herself dated the same date, her roommate takes her back to their room, and about nine-thirty she calls her father, in tears and desperate for help."

"Objection! Move to strike 'desperate for help.' Attempts to describe state of mind, no foundation," shouted Charlene Abboud, Emel's attorney.

"Sustained," the judge agreed. "The jury will disregard 'desperate for help.'"

Christine nodded and studied her notes momentarily.

"Did you see Bussie that morning?"

"I did. Her father called me from home. He had her there."

"Who is her father?"

"John Speers, District Attorney of Cook County."

"He's your boss?"

"I guess you could say that. I'm actually pretty much independent of stuff that goes on in the office."

"What did you do?"

"Drew blood and took her for a rape exam."

"Where?"

"University Hospital."

"Was a rape exam done?"

"Yes."

"Swabs of the vaginal area?"

"Yes."

"DNA tests run on those swabs?"

"Yes."

"Saying what, the DNA tests?"

"Objection," said Xavier Delfino. "Calls for hearsay. Your Honor, we've been pretty patient about a continuing string of hearsay problems, but this we must object to. This calls for a scientific background and this witness isn't qualified to be cross-examined on that issue."

"Sustained. Move along, counsel."

"Yes, Your Honor, thank you," Christine said. "I believe at this point I'm finished with this witness except I reserve the right to recall for purposes of impeaching other testimony that may be produced during the trial."

"Very well. Defense may cross-examine."

Albert Adelman, Hanley Miscont's lead counsel number 1, strode confidently up to the podium. He rubbed his hands together and straightened his tortoise-shell glasses. He then removed them, blew across the lenses, and held them up to the light, peering through the glass as he waited for the tension to build.

Then he said, "Ms. Lindsey, my name is Albert Adelman and I'm the attorney for Hanley Miscont the Third. One of his attorneys."

"I know who you are," Winona replied. "We met on break yesterday. You must have forgotten."

"Thank you for reminding me," said Adelman with a winning smile. "Now. Down to business."

"Yes, let's."

"You say the victim has absolutely no recollection of what happened to her that night?"

"None."

"Then how does she know she was raped? Penetrated?"

"Semen was found in her vagina."

"Semen. Do we know whose semen it was?"

"No."

"Was it my client's semen?"

"We don't know."

"Yet you've helped organize a lynching party against my client even though you don't know if he even had sex with the so-called victim?"

"Objection!" Christine called out. "A grand jury is not a lynching party. I can explain why that is true if the court would like."

"The court is well aware, counsel," said Judge Duchamps. She twisted a lock of red-orange hair, thinking. "Please re-ask your question. Please substitute 'grand jury' for 'lynching party.'"

"Very well," Adelman agreed. "My question is asking, even though you didn't know whether my client had had sex with the so-called victim, you still testified before the grand jury that he had?"

"Grand jury testimony is secret, sir."

"It is secret," said Christine. "Object on that basis."

"Sustained."

"Well, let me ask it this way. Is there any scientific or medical proof that my client had sexual relations with Bussie Speers? Yes or no, please."

"No."

Adelman turned from the witness and slowly made eye contact with every juror. "Are you listening?" his gaze asked. Notes were being furiously inscribed in notepads and several jurors nodded at him.

Then he said, "So it's somebody's word you're relying on to prove that my client violated your client. Rather, your victim?"

"Yes, that's correct."

"I take it the so-called victim has no memory of who did what?"

"True," Winona said.

"Was DNA testing performed?"

"Yes, it was."

"How about DNA testing results? Did my client's name swim up?"

He already knew the answer, having been given copies of all the lab reports two months ago. Christine knew he was using it to exonerate his client; she had known this moment was coming, but it still hurt.

"No," Winona admitted.

"Results of DNA testing?"

"Inconclusive."

"Why inconclusive?"

"The samples contained many different DNA types, as I understand it. No one of them could be attributed to any of the defendants we took samples from."

"You took hair samples from all of the defendants?"

"Yes."

"And none of them returned positive for DNA, not even the dead boys?"

"No."

"So you have no proof my client had sexual relations with the so-called victim?"

"Just testimony."

"Well, we'll cross that bridge when we get to it. That's all for now." Adelman paused, then said, "Oh, one more thing. Do you have any proof my client was even there that night?"

Winona hesitated. "No."

"Do you have any proof that Ms. Speers didn't consent to having sex that night? Perhaps she had an alcoholic blackout that is preventing her recall?"

"No proof."

"That is all. Thank you very much, Detective Lindsey."

"Mr. Knoell?" said the judge. "Any questions on behalf of Noah Adams?"

Knoell replied, "Can we stipulate that if I asked the same questions regarding my client the answers would be the same?"

The judge turned and looked at Christine. She saw no reason not to stipulate. It would be one way of avoiding the painful repeat of the process that had just been completed.

"So stipulated, Your Honor," she said, rising briefly to her feet.

"Noted," said the judge. "And Ms. Abboud, any questions on behalf of your client, Steven Emel?"

"Same stipulation, please."

"Ms. Susmann?"

"So stipulated," said Christine. Of course Emel was her whole case--almost--but the stipulation again avoided the same pains.

"Anything further, counsel?"

All the attorneys shook their heads and muttered, "No, thank you."

Winona stepped down from the witness stand.

28

K etchikan, Alaska
He was a trip, the Chief Counsel of Great Northern Timber and Energy. That's what all the lawyers in his stable said.

Richard D'Amato wore his hair longer than the norm for an international corporation's chief lawyer and he really didn't give a damn. It was lustrous black hair, constantly hand-brushed as he spoke--a habit his mother had been unable to break him of. His blue-brown eyes twinkled with glee when he had an opponent on the ropes and bleeding. And of course he had been blessed with perfect teeth, God's gift to the public; all smiles when the cameras rolled but all scowls and curses behind closed doors.

D'Amato was medium height, medium weight, and extremely litigious. He would litigate a case at the drop of a hat rather than simply pay a claim and write it off as a cost of doing business as most timber and energy companies did. "No fight, no pay," he told his staff; in other words, make the claimants earn every cent they hacked off of the corporation. "We don't pay claims," he repeated to any errant claims manager talking settlement. "We go to court and we stall, we prevaricate, we make things up, we hire expert witnesses to drag things out for years. We make sure that claimants and their lawyers slink away sorry they ever filed papers in court."

As the Chief Corporation Counsel at Great Northern Timber and Energy, Richard D'Amato's duties boiled down to three recurring tasks. First, there were the forestry, gas, and mineral leases around the world. The company had 23,000 such leases and they produced everything from bauxite to crude oil to timber. All around the world, a battalion of 301 lawyers maintained order--as best they could-- among the lessors and lessees.

Second task: the ongoing problems with ranchers, farmers, and "squatters," as D'Amato referred to them--people who were legally living on one of GNTE's leased properties. A hundred and fifty years ago these people might have been called "mountain men," and ranged from fleeing felons to people who were just fed up with the human race and so they had headed for remote places. Ordinarily they were self-sufficient, hard as nails, and difficult to uproot.

The third duty--which consumed 75% of his time--was "claims made." Claims made ranged from personal injuries where a chain saw had kicked back and someone lost an arm to exactly the kind of claim Jesse Osako was evidently about to bring. These were claims for property damage (bad enough), personal injury (worse), and death (even worse), where the claim postulated injury based on changes Great Northern Timber and Energy had made to the leased lands by logging or mining or both.

And there was always the possibility of the type of claim that made D'Amato lose sleep. These were the political/legal claims by tree huggers that could literally put Great Northern out of business if some politician got a wild hair and voided a lease on the scale of the Tongass Forest, where millions of acres were involved. These problems put Great Northern Timber and Energy at great risk. Which is why the head lawyer was willing to go to such great lengths over the Osako case: from such relatively inconspicuous beginnings could major cases grow, cases resulting in lease forfeits and cancellations that could cost GNTE millions of dollar, maybe even billions.

Arthur Andrews entered the office of Richard D'Amato without knocking as his meeting with the Chief Counsel was set for eight a.m. and the lawyer expected absolutely punctuality. If you were on time, there was no need to knock.

"Mr. D'Amato," said Andrews, extending his hand across the massive desk of petrified wood that had been hacked and dragged out of the Petrified Forest of Northern Arizona.

"Art," said D'Amato, "did you have to shoot anybody?"

It was a joke, the lawyer's way of saying he would stop at nothing to protect corporate gold stored away in corporate vaults.

"Not yet. Didn't even have a gun with me," said Andrews, ever the literalist.

"Huh," the lawyer muttered, seeing that the comment had been lost on his underling. "So tell me what we know."

"We know the cutback caused by erosion has destroyed sixty-five riverside dwellings and injured a dozen or so. Three dead, including an old woman, an infant, and an Iraq war vet in a wheelchair."

D'Amato smiled. "I heard they don't float so good."

"Infants?"

"Wheelchairs."

"Oh."

"So this lady lawyer, this Christine Susmann, what did she see and do?"

"Pictures. Took lots of pictures. Walked upstream a mile or so, downstream a mile or so, more pictures."

"I don't like the sound of that. So who is she?"

"We've turned her life into a fairly thick file. She's an Afghanistan war veteran, a lawyer--of course--a mother of two, one kid sick, and married to some dummy who supplies sand and gravel for contractors."

"Sand and gravel? What's she doing married to a guy like that?'

"They were married before she went to law school. Love, I guess."

"Love, hell, she doesn't want to pay alimony to the bum. That's my analysis."

"You may be right. She had two other people with her. Some black guy with tape measures, a movie camera and a still camera. Plus there was a kid hanging off a pair of those arm crutches."

"Arm crutches? What's his story?"

"He must be her son. I don't think he has anything to do with our mess."

"Mess it is. What's our next indicated step?"

"I say we slip the Jap ten grand and see if he goes away."

D'Amato thumped his dense desk with a fist. "Damn you people! When are you gonna hear me? We don't pay diddly. Not even go-away money. No, no, no!"

Andrews leaned back in his chair. "Okay. I was just thinking out loud. Do we go after this guy? Does he have an accident? What?"

The lawyer looked out his large window at the million dollar view of Alaska pine running up the surrounding mountains. He said, slowly, "I think we have an act of God. I like that. Act of God. Let's say a tree kills him."

"That's worked before."

"Or a fire on his fishing boat. Now that's hard to unravel if the damn boat sinks."

"We can do it."

"Do it, then. We'll nip this thing in the bud before it goes any further."

"All right, sir. Consider it done."

"I will when I read the obit in the paper. Ball's in your court, Andrews."

"I'm on it, sir. You won't be disappointed."

"That, I like."

Alone again, D'Amato took a tour of Christine Susmann's website and cringed. There it was, in fourteen point all-caps bold: PUBLIC POLICY LAW. "What the hell--" the Chief Counsel sputtered. Then he read on. When he had absorbed her website, he had her sized up. She was a real threat.

He decided then and there to give her a special kind of attention.

29

F ollowing Winona's testimony, Christine called to the witness stand Miss Georgia Lundquist from CSI of the Chicago PD. Lundquist was a svelte black woman, no more than five feet tall, with huge eyes and a nice smile. Like all police employees, she looked over at the jury and gave a small smile, which they returned.

"State your name," Christine began.

"Georgia Z. Lundquist."

"Occupation?"

Crime scene investigation, Chicago PD."

"What do crime scene investigators do?"

The tech gave a half-smile. "Visit crime scenes and investigate."

Christine returned the smile. "Of course. But can you tell us how you approach a crime scene, such as the one in this case?"

"Well, when we arrive on a crime scene, the uniforms will have ordinarily taped it off."

"Meaning what?"

"You know, the yellow crime scene tape that says 'Crime Scene, Do Not Cross.'"

"Of course. Continue, please."

"We then take photographs. Of everything. If it's a shooting scene we look for bullets, shell casings, blood, and so forth, as you might expect. Then we mark and photograph the physical objects."

"And if it's a rape scene, such as we have here?"

"We're looking for transfer evidence, primarily."

"What is transfer evidence?"

"Generally speaking, that would be ejaculate and other bodily fluids on the sheets, bedclothes, victim's clothes--that sort of thing."

"Fingerprints?"

"Yes, we dust for prints. That's a long, arduous process and we usually have one team member dedicated to that and that alone."

"Did you have a dedicated fingerprint tech on this case?"

"Me."

"You were the duster?"

"Yes, ma'am."

"Did your fingerprint dusting locate any prints?"

"Many. Mostly from the room's occupant. As you might expect, they were everywhere."

"What about others?"

"I located one on the headboard just under the shelf that runs across the headboard."

"One what?" Christine asked.

"A palm print. I found a palm print that matched a palm print taken from one of the defendants in this case."

"Okay, when was his palm print taken?"

"When he was arrested and booked into County. Palm prints are always taken in felony cases. Just to be sure we have them if necessary."

"What did this headboard print tell you?"

"I did the match-up on it, which is assisted by computer. The scores were in the ninety-ninth percentile."

"So the proof that it was a palm print from the defendant is far beyond a reasonable doubt?"

"I wouldn't know about that. I don't know what percent a reasonable doubt is."

Christine had made her point, so she didn't bother following up.

The palm print was strong evidence, stronger than seventy percent, say, and would be compelling inside the jury room.

"Now. Tell us which defendant matched up with that palm print."

The CSI tech reviewed her file notes. "Name of Noah Adams. Permanent address Anchorage, Alaska. Local address is Theta Kappa Alpha fraternity, Chicago."

"Which places him inside the room, perhaps on the bed, when the crime was committed."

"Objection!" Adams' lawyer called out. "It does not place Mr. Adams at the scene of anything."

"Sustained. Counsel, please rephrase."

"Withdrawn. Thank you, Ms. Lundquist. That is all I have."

Cross-examination by Adams' lawyer went nowhere. After all, the computer match and the whys of the match, including all points of similarity, had been talked about in depth by the CSI, which only further embedded the truth of what she was saying in the jury's mind.

Christine made very few notes while the cross-examination was underway, and it was only when it fizzled out that she asked to excuse the witness, which the court granted.

They took the morning break and Christine went into the hallway to look for her next witness. Winona accompanied her. They tracked down the DNA analyst in the ladies' restroom, where she was carefully applying a light slip of lipstick. With her ring finger she smoothed out her work and then washed her hands.

"Well," she said, shaking Winona's hand. "Haven't seen you for ages."

"Right on, Betsy. It's been at least since last Friday, right? She testified in one of my pre-assignment cases, Chris," Winona explained. "Meet Elizabeth O'Reilly. That's *Doctor* Elizabeth O'Reilly, incidentally."

"I know that," said Christine. "I hired her, and I read her CV. Thanks for coming--what should I call you?"

"Everyone calls me Betsy. At least until we get in there." She laughed, waving generally in the direction of the courtroom.

"Betsy, do you have everything you need from me?" asked Christine.

"I do. My workup is always from my lab, so there's really nothing else you can give me by the time the prosecutor is involved."

"Fine. Then shall we go on inside?"

"Judge Duchamps, is it? She's easy enough to work with. You can probably ask her to take judicial notice of my expertise and then you won't need to waste time proving who I am and whether I'm qualified to do what I do."

"Duly noted. We'll do it that way, if possible. If not, I have your curriculum vitae."

"Then let's do it."

30

Winona located Jeb Franklin at the TKA house. He was the fraternity brother whose room was the scene of the rape. She spoke with him and advised him that he was under investigation as a possible accomplice in the sexual assault of Bussie Speers. He said he knew nothing about it, but agreed to accompany Winona to speak with Christine.

They arrived at Christine's office after six o'clock that night. Christine was waiting. She surveyed the young man and considered how he might be able to help.

Jeb Franklin was tall and bookwormish looking, with thick eyeglass lenses and a gaunt appearance. His hair was medium length and attempted the latest spiky look, but it fell flat--literally--in an unflattering manner.

Jeb said he was a grad student now, getting his master's in biology. He already had an undergrad in biology and was working toward becoming a Ph.D. botanist with an interest in space exploration and identification of possible alien life forms.

Christine asked, "Do you recall the night Bussie was raped in your room?"

"My room?" he exclaimed and cringed away from Christine's desk. "How could you possibly think it was my room?"

"Have you seen the nude pictures? Everyone on the Internet with a prurient mindset certainly has."

"Well, I don't have a prurient mindset, so the answer is no."

"Detective Lindsey, please show Mr. Franklin a few of the photographs with the sharp focus in the background."

Winona passed several 8x12 color blowups to Jeb Franklin. The boy's face turned white and sweat popped out on his skin. "Oh, my God."

"Yes, tell us what you see there," Christine said.

"It's my moth--my mother. That's my mother back there!"

"Yes, we thought so." Christine asked, "Now do you recall this incident in your room?"

"I--I do."

"What can you tell us about it?"

"I can tell who was there."

"Who?"

"The five boys you arrested."

"Including the dead ones?"

"Yes, them too."

"And including the ones in the courtroom where you're going to give testimony tomorrow?"

"Ye--ye--yes. I remember it."

"Good. We'll see you Friday morning at nine o'clock a.m. in the courtroom of Judge Agatha Duchamps. In fact, Detective Lindsey, would you be able to bring the witness to court Friday?"

"Happy to."

"See you then, Mr. Franklin."

31

A s a Marine sniper and extensively trained soldier, Arthur Andrews had become a jack of all trades, more or less.

Wiring the fishing boat was simple. The boat was moored with several others just ten miles north of Totem Park, north of Ketchikan, Alaska. From where he lived beside the half-mile-wide channel called the Tongass Narrows, at the wheel of his Toyota truck, Jesse Osako could reach the boat in about forty-five minutes by road.

At this time of night there was no one around.

From the bank, using his headlights, Andrews could make out *Jessie's Midlife* at the end of a fifteen-foot ramp. The entrance onto the ramp was fenced. Andrews climbed out of his truck and slipped on latex gloves. Andrews walked out onto the pier and approached the fenced ramp behind which the vessel was moored. *Jesse's Midlife* was a midwater trawler used to net pelagic fish such as tuna and mackerel. Jesse, a retired pharmacist who had sold his pharmacy in Vallejo, California, and moved north to Ketchikan's environs, had paid $225,000 for the boat with $75,000 down and the remainder yet on the books. The boat provided his livelihood and was all he had left after Milee drowned in the swift-running river where their home had nestled east of the Narrows.

Andrews nipped the ramp chain with a bolt cutter and the lock fell into his hand. He pocketed the lock and stepped onto the boat, which all but ignored his weight, and made his way forward.

The cabin door swung open freely; Andrews made his way forward still, and down a small passageway to the engine room.

Twin diesels were mounted side-by-side in a configuration that Andrews recognized. Andrews had brought along a common forestry firefighting tool used as a fire starter. It was known as a driptorch. It contained a mixture of gasoline and diesel, at a mixture of 30% and 70% respectively. The fire it would start would appear to be nothing more than a common engine fire followed by an explosion. He attached a timing device to the wick stem and set the detonation for noon that day. Jesse would be far out to sea by then and salvage of the boat would be all but impossible as the polystyrene resins in the fiberglass would quickly burn it down to the waterline and sink it in a mile of water.

Andrews hurried out, refastened the chain and lock—minus one chain link—and sped away in his vehicle.

By 5:30 that morning Jesse was onboard, idling the engines to warm them, and had his coffee brewing in the galley. His nets were electro-mechanical, so his need for any other crew was limited to two men, both old-timers on the Ketchikan fishing industry who had moved north to escape civilization--or the civilization they thought Ketchikan represented. By 5:45 the two crewmen were onboard at their duties and had cast off. Jesse got the all clear and backed the boat away from its dock and turned for open waters.

By ten o'clock they were fishing the mainland shoreline, which they just could make out on the horizon. The net had returned twice with a good catch of tuna and they were making a third pass.

At 12:03 p.m. a fire broke out in the engine room. Fuel began dumping out of the severed fuel lines, adding to the blaze. The resins in the deck and sides ignited, the hull lit up like a blowtorch and within minutes the boat was burning stem to stern. The dense black smoke caused three sets of lungs to spasm and all ability to inhale and exhale was lost.

At 12:16 p.m. the remaining metal emblements of *Jesse's Midlife* lay on the ocean floor where air pockets continued to release and bubble to the surface. The bodies of the three fishermen had been consumed in the fire and would never be found.

The black smoke had been spotted from the shore. Coast Guard cutters arrived on the scene hours later. A debris field a quarter mile long had streamed away from the wreckage and recovery of floating debris for further inquiry was undertaken. But no human remains appeared, not even by the next morning, when the cutter finally departed the scene of the sinking.

Next-of-kin were notified.

32

P ati Moran was the corporate designate sent by Horizon Wireless with its phone records for a cell phone owned by Noah Adams of Anchorage.

She was a heavy, mouth-breathing woman who had a heart of gold, which she proved as she went over the phone records with Christine a page at a time, explaining where voice calls had been made and where texts or photos had been dispatched by the phone.

Then she reached into an attaché case and extracted a folder dated the weekend of Chicago University's homecoming last semester. On the sleeve was the tag: Noah Adams.

As the jurors watched and waited, the folder's contents were marked one by one. Four folders with duplicate contents were passed to the defense table, one folder per lawyer. Eyes quickly scanned, fluttered and opened wide in horror.

"Now, Ms. Moran, this photograph marked State's one-twenty-two--tell us what this is?" Christine asked.

"That is a photograph texted from the cell phone of Noah Adams of Anchorage. The cell relay tower is in Chicago."

"Do we know whose number it went to?"

"We know the receiving number, but we don't know the identity on the other end."

"But you have no doubt this photograph was texted to that number--over the Internet."

"No doubt. Yes, it was."

"If I told you the receiving number was the text number of a website called Ex-Girlfriends.com, would that surprise you?"

"No. We see that kind of thing all the time."

"Now, if I asked you the same questions about the remaining thirty-seven photographs, would your answers be essentially the same?"

"They would be exactly the same."

"Your Honor," said Christine, "the State moves to enter these items into evidence and asks the court's permission to pass them to the jury."

"They are admitted--without objection," the judge ordered. "You may pass."

With that, Christine passed the thirty-eight photographs to the front row juror on the left-hand side.

The juror saw the first photo and looked at the ceiling. "My God," she moaned.

She reviewed several more and then began passing them along to her fellow jurors. One by one the jurors were exposed to the original nude pictures of Bussie Speers posed and arranged--always with her face in the frame--on someone's bed. That last part would be brought up soon enough so the jury would know the usual occupant of the bed.

"Your Honor, could we recess for maybe fifteen minutes while the jury continues to pass the photos around?"

The judge nodded. "Let's make it thirty minutes. Restrooms are available as well."

Everyone in the courtroom stood as the judge stepped down.

Everyone except the jurors. They were still passing the photographs.

Shock was displayed on all their faces. Shock and horror.

But still they passed the photos around.

UPON RETURNING to the office after trial, Christine received word from Nathan Osako that his father, Jesse, had perished at sea. From what could be pieced together, Jesse's fishing boat had caught fire. The fiberglass boat had quickly gone to the bottom, which onlookers from the shore had been able to judge by the appearance and disappearance of black smoke in a relatively short period of time. Nathan wanted to know what Christine could do to help, as he was extremely bitter and suspicious.

Christine had an idea, but she decided not to discuss it with him. She said only that she wanted to track down a few things on her own and that she would get back to him.

Her office made arrangements to send flowers to Nathan's home.

For her part, Christine had already guessed what she was going to learn.

And she meant to stop it before it could enter her own home and destroy any more of her loved ones.

33

The box ad cost $72.00 per week. Christine took it out for two days. The following day, the ad appeared in the Chicago University newspaper, *CU Rag:*

Did you attend a party with Noah Adams?
Were you date-raped?
Please call this number to speak with attorneys
who will sue to help you recover money damages
for the crime.
312-XXX-XXXX

THE FIRST DAY the ad ran, Christine's staff fielded eleven calls from young women claiming to be victims. Then began the arduous task of interviewing them, culling out the opportunists, and investigating the remaining five for corroborating witnesses about party attendance, dates, and Noah Adams' involvement as the girls' date. The second day produced four more calls. Again, the process was repeated.

In the end, Christine had the names of three witnesses she would add to her witness list. The defense attorneys objected to the additions, a hearing was held prior to court and the judge allowed the additions predicated on the State's producing the witnesses for thirty minutes of defense interviews prior to testifying. When it was all said and done, Christine had three live, very believable young women whom she would call to testify in her case in chief.

34

Thursday afternoon, Christine called Steve Emel to the witness stand.

He was sworn, took his seat, and sat blinking and wide-eyed. There was no eye contact with the jury, all of whom were leaned away from the witness. Looks of disgust were on the faces of more than a few, and they sat with their arms folded in front of them as if rejecting Emel and his co-defendants' sadism.

After eliciting his name and address and the fact that he was a final-semester senior, Christine approached the subject of the toga party. He admitted he had been there and then described in very detailed language the sexual assault of Bussie Speers.

"Was your cell phone used to take pictures of the nude victim?"

"No, ma'am."

"Now, I obtained your cell phone records, correct?"

"Correct."

"And you and I reviewed those records, correct?"

"Correct."

"Were any instances of your texting pictures of the victim located in your records?"

"No."

"Did you yourself sexually assault Bussie Speers?"

"Yes."

"Why?"

"I was drunk. Everyone else was doing it. They were waiting for me to perform. Peer pressure, I guess."

"Tell the jury why Bussie was assaulted."

"Noah said if we ruined her by posting pictures of her on the Internet that we'd own her. Nobody else would want her, he said. Then we could use her anytime we wanted."

"Define 'use her.'"

"You know, have sex with her."

"In other words, the entire scheme was so that you and your fraternity brothers could have a sex slave?"

"Yes."

He then went on to describe the roles that had been played by the other defendants. He described what he had witnessed them do and recalled parts of each one's statements at the time of the assault.

After several more confirmatory questions regarding time, place, actors, and events, Christine turned the witness over for cross-examination.

First up to the plate was Noah Adams' attorney, Jameison Knoell. He was a public defender, senior in tenure to the other PDs in the office, and had a violent sneer on his face as he approached the podium.

"Mr. Emel," Knoell began, "everything you've testified to today was bought and paid for by the district attorney, isn't that true?"

"Objection!" Christine said. "Improper question."

"No," said Judge Duchamps, "it's probably not improper. Stretching, perhaps, but this is cross-examination."

"Answer the question, please," said Knoell.

"Nobody paid me anything," said Emel.

"But it's true that your time in prison has been greatly reduced in exchange for your testimony today, correct?"

"I guess so."

"You guess? Well, was it reduced or wasn't it reduced?"

"It was reduced."

"By how much?"

"It's not how much, it's a cap."

"And what is that cap?"

"She said the most time I'll have to serve is ten years."

"Ten years in prison?"

"Right."

"What else did she say?"

"Just that she would recommend and agree to a lighter sentence in return for my cooperation."

"What else did she say?"

"She said she wanted to nail Noah Adams the worst."

"Why Noah Adams? Why nail him the worst?" Knoell asked.

"Because he was the one who invented the scheme of us having female sex slaves."

"Anything else she said?"

"She said you'd try to get me to lie."

"Why?"

"She said you were an experienced and devious attorney who was often able to get witnesses to lie on the stand."

Chuckles erupted from the jury. Knoell evidently hadn't heard the old axiom about cross-examination, the one that said you never want to ask the final question, the one you don't already know the answer to. But he'd done it anyway and now he had been made somewhat of a joke.

But Knoell had been around the block so many times that nothing flustered him. So he came roaring back and thoroughly discredited Emel with a new line of questions regarding Emel's participation in the date rapes of other young women at other times and places. Christine was surprised; she hadn't been aware Emel was such an experienced pervert and she kicked herself for not digging deeper into his history.

Lesson learned. She tried to rehabilitate the witness after two more attacks came from two more attorneys. But by then the witness lay incinerated and smoldering, burned to the ground by the defense.

But it didn't really matter all that much. She had managed to get the full story in front of the jury. She had managed to get facts into evidence that would overcome the defendants' motions for directed verdict after the State had rested its case.

The case would definitely make it to the jury now, for decision and verdict.

35

J eb Franklin was on the stand, perspiring and angry. It was his room where the assault had taken place, and he knew that because he had been there.

"What do you mean, you were there?" Christine asked.

Franklin was a geek, and pictures of his room and his bed had been admitted into evidence and passed to the jury.

"I wasn't inside the room, but at one point I opened the door to my room. Then someone kicked it shut in my face."

"Who kicked it shut?" Christine asked.

"I believe it was Noah Adams."

"You saw Noah Adams do that?"

"I saw his foot kick backwards, heard the thump on the door, then it slammed in my face."

"So your room was hijacked that night of Homecoming Weekend at CU?"

"Essentially, yes. I wasn't allowed inside."

"Did you consent to the use of your room?"

"God, no. I knew what was going on in there and I wanted it stopped!"

Christine asked, "What was going on in there?"

"Well, I opened the door and stuck my head in. The girl was nude and people were snapping pictures with their cell phones. When I saw her, she was on her back with her legs spread. Then they rolled her over, and the door slammed shut."

"Who did you see in there?"

"The three guys sitting at that table and my two dead fraternity brothers."

Christine took a deep breath. "Let the record show that the witness has identified as being in his room and participating in the taking of pictures the defendants Noah Adams, Hanley Miscont, Steven Emel, Parks Swansong and Jordan Weeks."

"The record may so reflect," the judge said. "Please proceed."

"What was said by any of the defendants?"

Franklin looked over at the jury. "You sure you want me to say?"

"I'm sure."

"Someone shouted, 'Get the fuck out, Frankie Beans.'"

"Frankie Beans?"

"You know, franks and beans. It was my handle."

"Your handle?"

"My nickname."

"Now, do you recall looking at these nude photographs in my office?" Christine asked.

"I do."

"And do you recall looking at State's Exhibit 444 and telling me that was your mother back there?"

"I do."

"What did you mean by 'that's my mother back there'?"

"Here," he said, holding out his hand for the photograph. "The girl is on her side here, and these hands are groping her. But see the headboard of my bed? The heart-shaped picture frame?"

"I do."

"Well, you can make out my mother's picture in that frame. I've had that since I was eleven. It goes everywhere with me."

"So that's the mother you were referring to?"

"I don't have any other mothers, so yes."

Christine continued, "So we definitely know the assault took place in your room?"

"Yes."

"Which proves your story that you witnessed who was there?"

"Objection!" one of the defense attorneys cried. "It proves nothing of the kind. The photograph and his mother don't prove who was there at all!"

"Sustained," the judge replied.

Christine withdrew the question. The inference had been made to the jury and now they knew why she had taken the time to go into that line of questioning at all. While technically the picture of his mother didn't prove who was there, in reality it did.

She disengaged and cross-examination followed.

Jeb Franklin was a truthful witness and the cross-examination proved that. The more the defense attorneys asked, the more they wished they hadn't.

Then they threw up their hands and it all came to a halt.

The State rested. The defense attorneys argued to the judge for a directed verdict. A directed verdict said, basically, that even if the facts presented by the State were taken as true, the State's case still didn't prove enough to go to the jury for decision. In other words, they were asking the court to dismiss the case. Judge Duchamps wasted no time in her ruling.

Directed verdicts were denied.

Now it was the defense attorneys' turn, beginning first thing Monday morning.

36

"**M**om, check out my Bulls sweatshirt!" cried Jamie as he burst through the front door on his crutches. He was wearing a red and black hoodie and smiling for what seemed like the first time since Sonny's death.

"Hey, guys," Christine said to Jamie and Ed, who had followed the teenager inside.

"Wow, what a place!" Ed said from the foyer, looking around at the living area off to his left. "Looks just like my parents' home."

Christine took his jacket and hung it in the hall closet. "What does your dad do?"

"He's a judge now. Downstate. Before that he was defense counsel for the railroads crisscrossing the southern Midwest. If there was railroad litigation in Kentucky, Tennessee, Missouri, Indiana, or southern Illinois during the seventies and eighties, chances are my dad was involved somehow."

"Is he still sitting on the bench?"

"He is. He just came off the chief judgeship for our county and now he's back with a full civil calendar. Exactly where he likes to be. He calls it his sweet spot."

"Well, hey, come on in the kitchen--Jamie's already in there destroying the pies I baked--and we'll have a cup. Coffee okay?"

"Sure. Or hot chocolate. I can go either way."

"The hot chocolate does sound good. Let's."

"All right."

The two adults and Jamie settled around the kitchen table. The centerpiece consisted of spring wildflowers from the hothouse out back.

"You grow these yourself?" Ed asked.

"Uh-huh. I love wildflowers. Ever since we lived in Flagstaff and I worked for Thaddeus. We used to hike into the Inner Basin and find early spring wildflowers. They're at the center of my soul, Ed."

"Mom's soul has lots of stuff at its center," Jamie added. "Like her kids, her airplane, her clients, our dad."

Silence fell over the small group.

"Well, yes, there is that," Christine finally said. "Your dad will always have a special place inside me."

"As well he should," said Ed. "We can never stop loving people just because they're gone. That's not how people are built."

"Mom sure isn't. She still talks about him like he just went out back to cut firewood."

"Jamie, I--"

"It's true, Mom. It's like you're afraid Janny or me will forget him. We never will."

"Okay, thanks for that," said Christine. "Now, tell me about the Bulls. Who were they playing?"

"Miami Heat. Second game of the finals," Jamie said. "It was an exciting game down to the last two minutes, then Chicago pulled away by eight points and it looked like a sure thing. Suddenly Miami makes two three pointers and the lead is down to two. Derrick Rose drives to the basket for two and then makes a steal and sinks a three pointer. After that it was all over."

"Pretty much," said Ed. "Add in about six time-outs in between all that and you've pretty well got the whole game."

"Where did you sit?"

"Ed has us on the front row. I mean on the floor. It was amazing. And look, I got two Bulls' autographs on my program."

Jamie unfolded the program for his mother to see.

"Wow, amazing," said Christine.

"I know. I'm taking it up and putting it on my corkboard. Later, you guys. And thanks again, Ed."

"You're certainly welcome, Jamie. Let's do it again soon."

"You've got it!"

Jamie left his cup half-full of hot chocolate and Christine took it to the sink. She ran water into it and slowly said, "That was very nice of you, Ed. He's really hurting for that kind of male attention."

"Sure he is. All boys are at that age. But you know what's really cool? Jamie is great company. That kid knows everything, and if there's something he doesn't know he'll definitely have an opinion about it anyway."

They both laughed. Christine sat down one chair away from her guest.

They both stared at the wildflowers.

"So," he finally said, "is it too early to take you to dinner?"

"If that's all it is, is dinner, I think it would be just fine."

"Great. How about next Saturday? Just you and me?"

"Done. Two friends out enjoying a meal. That's about all I can offer right now."

"Of course. And I certainly wouldn't dream of asking for anything but friendship anyway. I'm not like that."

"I figured you weren't. Hey, how about some music?"

She walked to the built-in sound panel beneath the eastern windows. Soon light rock was streaming from Sirius XM.

"Oh, that," he said. "I love that song! Who is it?"

"You're kidding, right?"

"No, I'm music illiterate."

"That's Journey," Christine said with a smile. "With the new guy from the Philippines. He took over for Steve Perry."

"Okay, you're certainly up on it."

"I've seen them three times in concert."

"Who else do you like?"

"Really? Keith Urban. He's very sweet. And plays lead about as well as anybody."

"What modern groups?"

"I don't keep up that much anymore. I know Janny likes Pink and wants to buy Pink this and that all the time. Now, who do you like?"

"There's that Sixties group. ARE or something."

"REO Speedwagon?"

"Hey, let's dance. You'll be amazed how good I am. I know, we can twist."

"Does anyone even do that any more?"

"We do," he said, and he was up, twisting.

Christine joined him. Halfway through the song they were both laughing so hard they had to sit down.

"Whew!" she cried, still laughing. She playfully punched Ed in the shoulder and he took her hand. Briefly, but he took it. At first she was shocked and didn't pull away. But moments later she gently withdrew her hand and took a drink of hot chocolate.

"Twisting," she finally said. "I've never even tried that before. But it's easy. What other dances do you know?"

"Slow dance. That's about it. We'll go dancing sometime if you like to dance."

"I don't know if I do or not. Sonny and I never went dancing."

"Well, here's your chance to start with a novice. I've never taken anyone out dancing. It could be a first for us."

"Could be," Christine said quietly.

"Anyway, it's time for me to hustle off home. Charlie needs a can of dog food."

"I'm assuming Charlie is a dog?"

"He's my English Setter. Beautiful dog."

"Do you hunt him?"

"No, I don't kill stuff. Do you hunt?"

"No, I don't hunt."

"All right, well, thanks for the hot chocolate and the twist. It's been grand."

"Grand indeed. And thanks again for Jamie."

"Hey, that was my pleasure. What a great kid."

"Thank you."

"Goodnight, Chris."

"Good night."

He leaned and gave her a hug and patted her twice on the back.

"Later," he said. Then he left.

37

M onday morning dawned bright and sunny and Christine hurried across up one block and over two, anxious to get things done. Winona accompanied her and they made plans as they walked.

As it turned out, they wouldn't need those plans at all.

Hanley Miscont III had finally succeeded in driving his attorney Albert Adelman stark raving mad. He was insisting on testifying "to clear my name," and Adelman was using every piece of logic he could think of to dissuade his young client. But then Miscont reminded Adelman that he, Miscont, was paying Adelman's bill but that didn't mean he was turning over his future to the lawyer. It was only about money, and he made that clear.

So, against his lawyer's wishes, Miscont took the witness stand.

After his name and Chicago address were given, Adelman asked his client what he recalled about that Homecoming Weekend party.

"The truth? The truth was that I spent the weekend in Edmunson Library studying for final exams."

"You're saying you didn't attend the party?"

"That's right."

"Did you know about the party?"

"Well, the library closed at midnight and they kicked all of us out. So I went with some other kids to Denny's and we had a midnight breakfast."

"Give us the names of those other kids," Adelman said.

"Uh--I can't."

"Why can't you?"

"I didn't know their names, to tell you the truth. They were just kids in my study group."

"From your Calculus IV class?"

"That's right."

"If I produced a class roster with those names on it, would you be able to pick out the names of the students you were with at Denny's?"

"No."

"Why not?"

"We never gave last names," Miscont said. "Just first."

"So you can't identify possible corroborating witnesses."

"By name? No. But if you brought them into court and stood them in front of me, I could tell you."

"But I couldn't do that without names in order to subpoena them, could I?"

"Hey, that's what I thought I was paying you for. You were supposed to get the names and stuff that you needed. You never told me to do it."

"We haven't had this conversation before, have we?"

Now Adelman was covering himself against possible malpractice claims later. He wanted to make a record that his client's claim to alibi witnesses had never been made known to him until that very moment in court.

"No, we haven't had this conversation," Miscont said.

"In fact, you have never mentioned to me before that you had alibi witnesses, did you?"

"No. But you didn't ask me, either."

Christine was happy to just sit back and allow young Miscont to hang himself. So far, he was doing a pretty fair job of it. Arguing with your own lawyer in front of the jury is never a good idea. Inside she smiled, But her exterior was icy, cold, and filled with obvious disdain for the witness who was feigning innocence.

Adelman limped ahead. "So we've established that you were with a group of people. Now--"

"Objection!" Christine was on her feet. "No such thing has been established. Object to the form of the question as it assumes facts not in evidence."

"Sustained, counsel. Mr. Adelman, you haven't proven that your client was with a group of people. You've only proven that that is his claim and that you are, well, surprised by that claim. Please rephrase your question."

Bingo. Damage done, thought Christine. *But whoa, we haven't even started yet. It's going to be my turn to go after this son of a bitch and then--*

"Let me rephrase," Adelman said. "You say you were with a group of people."

"Yes."

"But you don't have names, even though you had spent a semester with them in a classroom setting?"

"That's right."

"So--what happened after breakfast?"

"Well, it was about one-thirty when we finished. I drove around for an hour or so before returning to the fraternity house."

"The TKA fraternity house."

"That's right. Then I parked my car and went in the front entrance. Our parking is in front."

"What happened next?"

"I saw a girl naked on a couch in our family room. She was passed out."

"What did you do?"

"I hunted down a blanket and covered her up," Miscont said.

"You covered her up?"

"Yes, sure."

"Did you touch her?"

"Maybe on the shoulder, when I pulled the blanket up to her chin."

"Anything else?"

"No, that's my whole point. I was her protector, not her attacker. I don't get where Emel gets off saying I did anything to this helpless girl."

"Right."

"Or Franks and Beans. I mean, Jeb Franklin. He couldn't have seen me there, because I wasn't there."

"What did you do next?"

"Went upstairs and went to bed."

"Had you been drinking that night?" Adelman asked.

"Yeah."

"What did you have to drink?"

"Coffee."

"At Denny's?"

"Yeah."

"That is all. Do you have anything else you wish to say?"

"Only that I'm very ashamed of what happened at my fraternity. I never would have joined that group if I had known this kind of stuff was going on. And if I found out, I would have moved out. I can't condone that kind of behavior."

"So it violates your moral sense?"

"It violates my morals, yes."

"Thank you. That is all."

Hanley Miscont III stood as if to step down, but the judge reminded him that cross-examination would follow first.

Christine strode up to the podium.

"Violates your sense of morality?" she echoed. "What sense is that, Mr. Miscont?"

"You know, I hate stuff like what they say happened."

"So Jeb Franklin is wrong when he says he saw you there with the nude girl in his bedroom?"

"Yes, he's wrong."

"And Steven Emel is wrong when he says you were there?"

"Yes."

"And you say that instead, you were out with a study group but you don't know anyone's name from that group?"

"That's right."

"And you actually expect this jury to believe you?" Christine asked sharply.

"Objection!" Adelman shouted.

"Sustained. Counsel, you know better."

"Sorry, Judge, I'm just having trouble trying to make sense of what the witness is saying."

Adelman yelped, "Objection!"

"Counsel, you are admonished," the judge said. "There will be time for closing arguments. But that time isn't now. Please continue."

Christine then asked, "Mr. Miscont, could I see your cell phone?"

The witness patted his inner suit pocket. Then he withdrew his cell phone and presented it to Christine.

"What's the password?" she asked.

"Trustfund, all one word."

"Of course it would be. Excuse me."

Christine pressed the button marked PHOTOS and scrolled right for a few seconds. Then she said, "Oh, here we are. Your Honor, I am going to ask the clerk to mark this cell phone as State's Exhibit before we proceed."

"You can't do that!" cried the witness. "That's private property."

"No, when you come into court," said the judge, "nothing is private anymore. Not once you take the witness stand. The clerk will mark the cell phone."

Christine continued. "Now. This is your cell phone?"

Meekly, Miscont said, "Yes."

"And this picture right here, from this set of pictures--would you tell the jury what's depicted in that picture?"

"A naked girl."

"What? Let's let the jury hear that."

"I said, it's a naked girl."

"And these other photos, one-two-three--" She counted until she had reached thirty-three and then stopped. "These other thirty-three photos. What are these pictures of?"

"A naked girl."

"Same girl?"

"Same girl."

"Who is the girl?"

"I don't know her name."

"Does the name Bussie Speers ring a bell?"

"Yeah, I guess that's her."

Christine held the phone closer to Miscont. "Did you take these pictures?"

"No, someone texted them to me."

"Who was that?"

"I don't remember."

"Well, let's check out your text history, going back—let's see, to the Homecoming Weekend period of text messages. Nope, I don't see any texts on here of this naked girl's picture. So let me ask again, where did these pictures come from?"

"I. Don't. Know."

"Isn't it a fact that you snapped these the night you participated in the rape of Bussie Speers?"

Miscont looked around Christine, at his lawyer. "Can't you object or something? Shouldn't we be objecting?" he asked Adelman.

Adelman sadly shook his head and looked away.

"Again," Christine pressed, "isn't it true you took these pictures? And let me advise you, you are under oath and the penalties for perjury in Illinois are very severe."

"Yes. I guess I took them."

"You guess you did."

"All right, yes, I took them. But I didn't rape her."

"Of course you didn't. Who else was present when you took the photographs?"

"Noah, Steven, Jordan, and Parks."

"Did they rape her?"

"I don't know."

"Did they penetrate this girl with their penises?"

"I guess."

"And yet you didn't?"

"No," Miscont said stubbornly. "It violated my morals."

Christine turned to the judge. "That's all, Your Honor, except I would move the cell phone into evidence."

"Admitted," said the judge. "Counsel? Mr. Adelman? Any re-direct?"

"Nothing, Your Honor," Adelman replied.

Christine sat down at the counsel table. When no one was watching, Winona reached over and gave her arm a squeeze.

"Beautiful," she whispered. "I dig your chops, kiddo."

"Thanks. Try not to gloat."

"I'll try."

Adelman and counsel for Adams and Emel stood and rested the defense case.

"Counsel for the State? Anything further?" the judge asked.

"The State would move to call three witnesses," Christine replied. "Their names are Ciroc Boxer, Andrea Boxer, and Emily Darkmane."

"What is the purpose?"

"These are impeachment witnesses, Your Honor."

"Impeachment of whom?"

"Noah Adams."

"But Noah Adams hasn't testified."

"No, but he's claimed he's innocent by pleading not guilty. I would impeach that claim, Your Honor," Christine said.

"Very well. But keep it brief, please. I would like to get this case to the jury today."

"Will do, Your Honor."

Christine then proceeded to call the three CU students. Each of them testified to events in their own lives similar to what had happened to Bussie Speers. In each case, the girls had gone to a party with Noah Adams and had awakened with no memory hours later. Then their pictures had shown up on the Internet. Following that,

Adams had pressed them for sexual favors. All three had submitted to him.

The witnesses were previously unrevealed, though the defense attorneys, pursuant to the judge's requirement, had been allowed thirty minutes to question them prior to their testifying. Cross-examination did nothing to void their testimony or any part of it.

By the time Adams' own attorney had completed cross, the stories were well cemented in the jurors' minds: two sisters, Boxer and Boxer, had attended a party at Adams' invitation. The next day, after they had awakened nude and doped up, their pictures had been published worldwide. They had been shocked and horrified.

The third young woman, Emily Darkmane, gave the same story.

38

The next morning, Christine and Winona met early for coffee. They discussed the pros and cons of going ahead with further testimony or saying they had no more impeachment testimony. They were considering whether to call a group of TKA fraternity brothers who could testify, variously, that one had seen Noah Adams leave the toga party and head up the stairs after the ceremonial kissing of the ring. Another could testify he woke up in the family room as Noah Adams carried a nude girl down the stairs and laid her on one of the couches there. Adams had winked at the other boy and motioned for him to go back to sleep. Then he had held a finger up to his lips, as in "quiet," and the boy understood he was to tell no one what he had seen.

The third potential witness was Helen Ondermoor, who wanted to testify that she had been Noah's date for the party but that he had abandoned her to the fraternity at large for dances and conversation after he took a call on his cell phone and left the basement. She had no idea where he'd gone, but she had been very angry and had gone straight back to her sorority and cried with her roommate until three a.m.

"From my point of view, it would be piling on at this point to present these other witnesses," Winona said. "We don't want to make the jury start feeling sorry for him."

"I doubt that will happen," said Christine. She blew across her coffee and pulled a loose lock of dark hair away from her forehead.

"You never know. Right now, it's in your pocket."

"Probably right. I always have to remind myself we're not killing snakes here, we're just putting bad guys in jail. We don't need blood. We only need a boot on their throats. We have that now, on all of them, I'm guessing."

"Right. So let's close and make final arguments and give it to the jury."

AN HOUR LATER, Christine was making her closing argument. She talked about Winona's testimony and her care in talking to all of the fraternity brothers. She talked about CSI and the palm prints. She talked about Pati Moran and the Horizon cell phone records, complete with all the photographs that had been texted by Noah Adams. Then she went into the photographs contained on Steven Emel's phone, and she talked about Emel's testimony.

But the worst of it all, probably, was the cell phone brought into court by Hanley Miscont III. It definitely put him in the room and clearly identified him as one of those who had taken the nude girl's picture.

The testimony of the CSI tech about DNA reports was gone over, plus the hospital rape exam, and how it had come back positive.

Christine wrapped up the testimony review by going back over Jeb Franklin's ID of his room from the photograph containing the picture of his mother, and his testimony placing the five defendants inside his bedroom with the nude girl.

With great trepidation she then approached how the victim of the rape had shot two of the defendants to death. Word had come back through the bailiff that one of the jurors had casually asked about what would happen to Bussie since shooting the two fraternity broth-ers. Christine knew she had to cover the issue.

"Bussie pulled that trigger in a moment of complete and utter mental overload. No, she wasn't acting sanely, and who could blame her? These evil people had just destroyed her life and she knew there was no coming back from it. At least that's how she perceived her own predicament."

She paused for water and then began again.

"Even her own father and mother had had to review the photographs of their daughter, posed with hands and fingers doing all sorts of obscene things to her body. Yes, she pulled the trigger, but it was really the boys who were acting through her. They had injected themselves so deeply into her thought processes that she was no longer thinking at all when the shots rang out several months ago."

She paused and took another swallow of water from the glass she had brought to the podium.

"So I urge you to set aside any acts by Bussie. She was placed in the horrible position of having nude, obscene photographs of herself viewed by a courtroom full of strangers. She was placed there by the defendants themselves, both living and dead. When she came into court that day, she was at the end of her rope. No, the rope wasn't even in her hands any longer. She had fallen away from the tip end of sanity and was free-falling through madness itself. As I urge you to see it, these defendants set loose the instrumentality that killed two of them. They set it loose on themselves, jointly and severally. So for this, please forgive her. Find it in your hearts to forgive her, as you return a verdict of guilty on all Criminal Sexual Assault charges and guilty on the conspiracy charges. Conspiracy to commit sexual assault."

Christine mopped her eyes. She scanned her notes.

Then she continued. "One final thing. There's the crime of admin-istration of a controlled substance to another without their consent. A very serious crime against Steven Emel. While the State has made an agreement to cap the time served by Emel at ten years on the rape and conspiracy charges, there is no agreement on the administration of controlled substance charge. So please, find him guilty on that one too and I promise you I will see to it that the court sentences him to an additional ten years minimum, consecutive time, on that charge alone."

By twelve o'clock, the defense attorneys had had their say, and the judge was prepared to read jury instructions, but first they took a shortened lunch break of forty-five minutes.

Court reconvened at one. The judge then read jury instructions to the jurors and went over forms of verdict until two-fifteen. The jury then filed out to deliberate. Christine watched them go, looking for any clues as to their tendencies, and saw nothing that would help alleviate the butterflies in the pit of her stomach.

Then she turned to John and Bussie Speers. They had been seated in the row of chairs directly behind Christine and Winona's table for closing arguments. Christine had referred to Bussie several times, taking pains to point her out yet again to the jury so they would have a mental impression of her sweet face as they went inside the locked jury room to deliberate about her and about her attackers.

Christine and Winona gave the young woman hugs.

"Thank you," she managed to say, tears filling her eyes, which she had blotted continuously during Christine's closing argument. "How could those defense lawyers suggest maybe I was going along with what happened that night? I wasn't even conscious!"

"Well, that's their job," her father told her. He passed his arm through hers and held her against him. "No one on the jury believed them. I was watching."

"What do you think, Christine?" said Bussie. "Did anyone buy it?"

Christine made a flick of her fingers as if brushing off a bothersome fly. "Not a chance. Your eyes are closed in all the pictures. Clearly you weren't cooperating."

Thirty minutes later, a burly sheriff's deputy came into the courtroom holding a folder full of documents. He approached John Speers.

"That them?" asked Speers.

"Yessir," said the deputy. "I'm ready to lay the lumber to them."

"What are we doing?" said Christine. "What's up?"

"Indictments," said the deputy.

"I went before the grand jury two days ago," said the district attorney. "These three young men were indicted on charges of conspiracy to commit murder and various accomplice crimes."

"For whose murder?" Christine asked.

"For the murder of Sonny Susmann."

Christine's eyes filled with tears and immediately spilled over. At last, movement toward seeing justice done for Sonny!

"I wanted to wait until they had a conviction first, so they would be felons already when I served the indictments. They'll never get out of jail again. Not in their lifetimes."

"Hurray!" cried Winona. "It's about damn time! Congratulations, Chris. You deserved to be here to see these served on them, sister lady."

"Yes, I do want to see the looks on their faces," said Christine. "Sonny and I have waited a long enough time for this. At last, we'll see those goofy smirks wiped off their faces."

"They weren't smirking this morning," Bussie said. "They couldn't even look at me while you were talking about me."

Two hours later, the bailiff entered the courtroom and spoke in the monotone of a courtroom deputy long-accustomed to jury verdicts. "They've got a verdict. They just knocked on the door and said they were finished deliberating."

The judge was notified and, on her order, the jury was brought back into the courtroom. Everyone remained standing, and Judge Agatha Duchamps again resumed the elevated platform.

"Who is the foreperson?" she asked.

"I am," said a diminutive lady in a green blazer.

"What say you?" asked the judge. "Please read the verdict."

"We, the duly impaneled jury in this case, do find unanimously that the defendants are guilty of Aggravated Criminal Sexual Assault."

She then went into the other crimes, all guilty findings. The last one was the administration of a controlled substance: guilty as to Steven Emel only. He was the only one who had been charged.

"Ladies and gentlemen, the court thanks you for your service. The jury is excused. Defendants are remanded to the custody of the sheriff for sentencing on June 10. Court stands in recess."

The defendants rose up at the counsel table, varying degrees of shock registering on their faces. At which point the deputy with the paperwork walked up to them, named each name, and handed each defendant his own indictments.

"What the hell?" cried Albert Adelman.

"Murder?" said Xavier Delfino. "Where did this come from?" he asked Hanley Miscont III, who only shook his head and stared at the floor. Then three huge apes wearing deputy sheriff uniforms took them away.

Christine and Winona shook the family's hands and received thanks and blessings. The lawyer and the detective then hugged each other and cried together.

"Tears of joy, tears of sorrow," Christine whispered to Winona.

"God bless you, girl," said Winona. "But trust me, it will get better."

Christine then approached John Speers.

"I want to talk to you," she said.

"I think I know what it's about. Is tomorrow at nine o'clock soon enough?"

"Your office?"

"No, your office."

"See you then."

39

"Now that the rape case is concluded, I want to defend Bussie."

John Speers looked across Christine's desk and he slowly nodded. "I see. I thought that might be what you wanted to say to me."

She smiled. "How could I not? In a way, it's a continuation. It started with the rape trial against her assailants to her shooting two of them. It makes perfect sense to me."

He scratched his head. "I don't know, though. Do you see any conflict of interest?"

She pushed away from her desk and looked out her east windows at the lake.

"Maybe. Maybe not. But I'm willing to duke it out in court. My guess? I don't think the special prosecutor is going to even object."

"What if the judge objects?"

"Who did she draw?" Christine asked.

"Sandrajane Curtens."

"Old Hang-Em-High."

"Yes, a plea bargain will be extremely difficult to get with that lady on the stand."

"My first impulse is to move for a change of judge."

"On what grounds?"

"About a year ago Sandrajane sanctioned me," Christine said. "She made me pay a thousand dollar fine for contempt."

"What was the contempt?"

"I called a witness a son of a bitch."

"In open court? Why on earth?"

She spread her hands. "Because he was behaving like a son of a bitch. Believe me, it was worth every dollar."

"Good grief, Christine."

"My point being, I think I can successfully argue that she's prejudiced against me and should recuse herself. I think I've got enough."

"You just might. You called a witness a son of a bitch? I'm going to have to think about that."

"What about my request? Do I get the case?"

He slowly nodded. "I know Bussie wants you."

"Who's she got right now?"

"Jack Tavers of Andrews Greeley."

"No, she doesn't want Jack. He's a great guy, but he's not going to get it done right."

"And you will?"

"I will."

"Okay, say we decide to go with you. How much of a fee are we talking about?"

She smiled. "Who said anything about a fee? I want the case, not the money."

"My kind of defense lawyer."

"Well, think it over, John."

"You know what? Let's do it. I'll call Jack and explain."

"And pick up the file from him."

"Will do. I'll have it back to you by five o'clock."

She stood and extended her hand. "Successful summit, John. We have a knack for doing business together."

"Let's hope our one-and-oh record continues."

"It will. I can all but promise you that. This case is very personal to me. Bussie is very dear to me. I'll extricate her from this mess."

"Is that a promise?"

She smiled. "You know lawyers can't make promises. But this time I will. I'll get her out of the murder charges. That's my promise to you."

"It doesn't get any better than that."

"No, it doesn't."

"Let's do it."

"I'm on it, John. Now just get me the file. And tell Bussie I'm coming out to your place to see her."

"Done and done."

40

J ames Macpherson of XFBI was sixty years old, an asthmatic married to an inhaler, and built like an Olympic diver. He was tall, lithe, and worked out two hours every day. As ex-FBI he was licensed to conceal carry and his weapon of choice was the Sig Sauer, which he had also carried while working as an active FBI agent.

Ordinarily he was an intense, OCD kind of person, but today he was beyond intense. He was a bloodhound with a blood spoor.

Macpherson had identified the man following Christine Susmann as a low-level thug masquerading as a risk management employee of Great Northern Timber and Energy. The thug's name was Arthur Andrews and he had no idea Macpherson was on to him.

XFBI had been running parallel surveillance of Christine wherever she drove around Chicago. One car a half block behind, switching off with a parallel car coming across every second block while car one turned away and ran parallel a block away. It was the oldest--and most productive--game of cat-and-mouse on the books, something taught in the FBI Academy's 101 course on tailing a suspect. Between Macpherson's own car and Bob Drewers' parallel car, they had pinpointed the target, traced the car rental to Arthur

Andrews and traced him back to Ketchikan, Alaska, where he reported to work at Great Northern Timber and Energy.

At one o'clock, after the Great Northern Timber and Energy quarry had tailed Christine to lunch and then back to the office, three XFBI cars suddenly pulled one ahead, one behind and one beside. They forced him to the curb and two agents jumped out and approached the driver. Agent Macpherson rapped on the man's window. The driver lowered it.

"Who are you and why did you force me off the road?" Andrews demanded to know. He was wearing silverized sunglasses that Macpherson snatched from his face in one easy move. The man began to resist, but Macpherson pulled his suit coat away from his gun and let Andrews take a look.

"You really don't want to argue with me," Macpherson growled.

"Who the hell are you?" The guy was still belligerent.

"We're your worst nightmare. Now: why are you following Ms. Susmann?"

"Screw off, mate. I don't have the foggiest what you even mean."

"Let's assume that's true. Let's assume you've just been acciden-tally tailing our lady. Be advised: this shit stops here and now, Mr. Andrews. Or you aren't making it back to Alaska."

"Sure, sure, now--"

Macpherson reached inside the car and grabbed the man by the hair. He slammed his face against his steering wheel and blood shot out of his nose.

"I said, it stops now. Now you get your ass out of Chicago by six o'clock or I'm going to surface again and you're not going to like my attitude. Got it?"

"Uh-uh-uh," the man said, trying to stanch the flow of blood with napkins from his coffee stop. He tore them into two strips, rolled them and jammed them in his nostrils.

"I said, got it?"

"I. Got. It."

"Don't test us, friend. Just hie your ass outta town."

"I'm done here."

"I'll say."

Then the man added something he would later regret. "But your girl wants to watch her back. I'm only saying."

"We'll see. My guess? When she finds out about you, you're the one who wants to watch your back. Friend, I shit you not."

"Fine. We'll call it a stalemate."

"Call it whatever you want. But go."

Macpherson backed away from the rental car, never for a second taking his eyes off Arthur Andrews.

But Macpherson wasn't done. He continued to surveil the man until he was wheels-up and gone.

Then Macpherson reported the contact to Christine. Name, address, employer--all of it was transmitted to her by text message.

At the other end of the line, Christine saw the text and it made the hair on the back of her neck stand up. The guy had said she'd better watch her back. Her heart fell.

Again. They were coming again.

This time she wouldn't wait.

This wasn't going to happen.

41

J uly 4th was a national holiday, of course, and a first date for Christine. It had been almost eight months since Sonny had died, and she felt like she was ready to re-emerge.

Ed picked her up at seven o'clock sharp. He was wearing a pink shirt under a dark green blazer, dark gray slacks, and penny loafers without socks. On his wrist was a Rolex Submariner.

She was wearing a soft summer dress with pale blue Salvatore Ferragamo cap toe pumps, a pale blue belt, and a small evening bag with pale blue piping, a thick gold necklace, and her wedding ring. Her long dark hair had been styled that afternoon by Charles Lord at Taylor Reese Salon after she left the office at noon--Saturday hours.

"Great wheels," Christine said when he opened the door to his Lincoln Navigator for her. "I wouldn't mind having one of these myself."

"You should get one. They're heavy and they're comfortable on the road."

"I think I will," she mused. "So. Where are we off to?"

"I thought we'd hit Ditka's for a steak, followed by some dancing at McJohn's 501 Club."

"Sounds great. But Ditka's on July 4th, really?"

"Reservations six weeks ago."

"For tonight? You must have been pretty sure of yourself."

"Hey, I knew *someone* would go with me. Lucky for me, it was you."

They headed east on the Kennedy. It was still very light out and silver slivers of jet aircraft could be seen coming and going from O'Hare, off to their right as they neared the O'Hare Airport Terminals exits.

"So," he said after a comfortable silence. "How are you and the kids getting along?"

"So-so. Mostly good days at this point. Janny can still cry in her sleep occasionally, but it seems like even that's tapering off."

"Good to hear. I worry about those guys."

"You worry about my kids?"

"Sure. Especially the little one. She's an angel and she should never have had to see what she did."

"Oh, I agree. But her therapist keeps reminding me how resilient kids are. You know. She has new friends this summer and she's taking English riding lessons, so she's keeping busy."

"And Jamie boy. How's he?"

"Believe it or not, he got some kind of temporary patent on his software. Some kind of one-year protection. A junior patent--I don't know what you call it."

"Good for Jamie! What a bright young man."

"He is. So he's well and happy. He especially likes the attention you've been giving him. And I can't thank you enough, Ed. You've really stood in the gap with him."

"Hey, who could resist? The kid's IQ must be about two hundred. Half the time I don't have a clue what he's talking about. Software, advanced calculus. In middle school, yet."

"I know. Some of his courses are college credit. Go figure."

"I can't. Anyway, how are you doing?"

"I'm pretty good, all things considered. As you know, the practice is under control, I'm working with Bussie, and we're getting some good help lined up for her."

"No, I'm not asking about the law practice, Christine. I'm asking about you. About Christine."

"Pretty good. I haven't been seeing anyone, but that shouldn't surprise anybody. It's only been eight months. Aren't you supposed to wait a year or something, according to Emily Post?"

"Who gives a damn? I'm just glad you would come out and eat with me tonight. In fact, I'm delighted."

She turned and studied his profile. What wasn't to like? Then she said, "Yes, me too. I'm glad I came out with you too."

Parking off Michigan Avenue was valet at Ditka's. Ed helped Christine out of the SUV and they went inside.

"Have you been here before?" he asked after they were seated.

"No. First time here. What down is it and what yard line are we on?" she asked in joking reference to the football memorabilia taking up every inch of wall space. They were across from a row of huge coaches' portraits, and Christine recognized Vince Lombardi but none of the others.

He laughed. "Well, it's first down and we're on the fifty."

The waiter approached. "Appetizer? Refreshments?"

"Coach's Pot Roast Nachos--you'll love this, Chris. And something to drink?"

"Glass of wine," she said to the waiter. "Don't bring a bottle."

"Two glasses of your best," Ed said. "With the nachos."

"Sounds great," Christine agreed. "What do you recommend for the entree?"

"I love the Kick-Ass Paddle Steak. You might really enjoy the Full-back Filet Mignon."

"I could do that. I haven't eaten since my protein drink at breakfast."

"So," she said easily, "what's this about dancing? Do I even know how nowadays?"

"I hope so. You were going to teach me."

"Hey, I doubt that. So tell me about yourself. Where did you grow up, that kind of stuff."

"I think I told you once my father was--is--a judge. He'll retire next month after more than twenty years on the bench."

"Was he a good dad?"

"The best. I only hope someday I can be half as good to my children."

"So you're planning on having children?"

"Definitely. I don't want to miss that."

"And your mom, what is she like?"

"My mom got into home rehabs. She read some books and started buying fixer-uppers, doing lots of the work herself, thanks to the staff at Home Depot, and then making five or ten thousand on the flip. As time went by that spread got better and better. She finally opened her own construction company and built commercial office space out of big old abandoned buildings in mid-size towns in the southern Midwest. She's still doing that, although Dad's announced he wants to travel."

"Siblings?"

"One sister. She lives in Saint Louis. She's a nun."

"Oh, I didn't know anything about your religious background."

He shook his head violently. "Oh, no. Hers, not mine. Notice I didn't go into the priesthood. My riches are stored up on earth, not in heaven."

"Uh, I think you have that backwards."

"Well, I'm young. We'll see how that works. Now what about you, Christine? Folks still alive?"

"I'm from a small town downstate, Orbit. My parents are physicians."

"Did you like growing up in a small town?"

"Definitely. That's why we moved our kids to Barrington when we came up to Chicago."

"And you came up here because?"

"My boss, Thaddeus Murfee, opened a practice in Chicago. I came with him. And Sonny too, of course."

"Oh, yes, Thaddeus does medical malpractice, birth-defect cases?"

"That's his mainstay," Christine said with a nod. "But he actually does much more than just med-mal. He's very busy. Someone even told me he was thinking of running for some political office. But I'll believe that when I see it. He tries to maintain a very low profile, so politics would be a complete one-eighty for him."

"You were a paralegal at first?"

"Yep. Then law school at the University of Chicago."

"Wow, that's impressive. Ranked in the top three in the country."

"We all say it's number one in the country. But, hey, that's what we're supposed to say, right?"

"Yes. Then you started practicing how long ago?"

"Not long. I went overseas first and that's--"

"That's when you got hurt?"

"Yes. Lost these two fingers. Came back pissed off at the world and decided to try something new. So law school seemed like the right thing."

"Do you enjoy law?"

"Sure. I was JAG in the military, you know?"

"I know. Been there, done that."

"You were JAG?" She knew the answer, but there was no point in letting him know about the extensive background study.

"Yes," Ed said. "I was a prosecutor and I did some defense work too."

"I think I remember that from your resume. Except you were a captain and I was an NCO. How about that."

"And now you're my boss. The worm has definitely turned."

She laughed. Their wine arrived, followed shortly by the nachos appetizer. They began nibbling and sipping. Fifteen minutes later, Christine felt the wine begin to loosen her up. Another ten minutes and she had drained her glass.

"That was delicious vino. Can I get a second?"

It was ordered and arrived minutes later.

"I've set the bottle aside, sir," said the waiter. Ed winked at him and smiled.

After a long, sumptuous meal, they decided to walk up to Michigan Avenue and stroll around. Thirty minutes later they took a cab to McJohn's 501 Club. The place was near Lake Michigan and featured a huge dance floor that looked out over the water. Inside, the music was deafening.

"This is the wrong place," Ed shouted into her ear. "Let's find something quiet."

They went back outside and hailed another cab.

"Do you know of any quiet dance spots?" Ed asked the cabbie.

The man smiled in the rearview. "I know just the place for a quiet night out. Something cool and groovy, light jazz, dim lights?"

"You read my mind."

"C'mon on downtown. Let me show you."

Two blocks off Wacker they pulled up in front of a façade of black marble with small gold lettering that said, simply, "Sharon's."

After paying and tipping the cab driver, Ed took Christine by the arm and they went inside.

A three-piece jazz combo was softly playing. A dozen couples were dancing, and small candlelit tables circled the floor.

"Exactly," Ed told the headwaiter at the door. "Someplace dark," he said and smiled at Christine, who returned the smile.

They danced. And they talked. And they danced some more and talked some more.

Three glasses of champagne and a dozen dances later and Christine all but fell into her chair.

"Whoo!" she exclaimed. "I'd better slow down."

"Not to worry," Ed smiled. "I don't have any grand designs on you. I'll get you home safe and sound, so let your hair down all you want."

"Thanks for that. Where do you live, downtown?"

"Actually, I do. I've got a rehabbed condo off LaSalle."

"Can we go there? I'd like to see where you live and you can make me a coffee and sober me up."

"Done."

They found another cab; the drive was less than ten minutes. Ed paid the driver and they went inside a clean, well-lighted lobby with two security guards on duty, both of whom smiled at Ed and nodded as Christine and Ed headed for the elevators.

The condo was two bedrooms, two baths, with a great view of a building across the street.

"This is about it," he said. "Probably not the view you were expecting, but, hey. Downtown Chicago is pricey."

"I guess it is," she said. "Now, about that coffee?"

He made coffee and they sat together on the blue leather couch. Shoes were removed, belts loosened, and they leaned back. Christine dreamily listened to the jazz playing over the sound system, then excused herself and disappeared inside the downstairs bathroom. She leaned across the sink and studied her dark eyes in the mirror.

"No, you don't," she told herself. "No, you don't."

An hour later Ed brought her another coffee and bent to place it on the table at her side. Without a word she reached out and touched him on the cheek.

"I want to, but I can't," she whispered.

"I know."

"I mean, I'm still wearing his ring."

"I know you are. We'll be friends. Someday you'll be ready to remove it."

"Thank you."

Two hours later they had retrieved his car and she was home. He softly kissed her on the mouth when they reached her front door and paused under the porch light.

"Good night," he said, and walked away.

"I liked that," she called after him.

He threw his head back and laughed.

Then he was gone.

42

Christine pulled off the freeway, steered the motorcycle along the backcountry road for one mile, then pulled off at the T-intersection with Maple Manor Road. With a screwdriver from the Harley's saddlebags she removed the bike's license plate from the rear mount. Illinois only required one plate for motorcycles, so the task was a quick one. She kicked it into neutral, clamped the caliper brake, and hit the starter. Then she dropped it into low and turned back onto the secondary highway. Eight miles later, she turned off to their house.

At the front door she rang insistently until Bussie answered. The girl had said her parents would both be gone that Thursday afternoon, but she didn't know why Christine had asked.

"Come in, Ms. Susmann," said Bussie.

Christine was wearing jeans, a black HD jacket, and was carrying two black helmets.

"What's that for?" Bussie asked.

"Do you take any medications?"

"Yes, they have me on a mood stabilizer. And I still use some stupid acne lotion. It's prescription."

"Go get them. And bring your backpack. Stuff it with your favorite things."

"Why?"

"We're preparing the defense of your case, okay? You're going to need to trust me on this."

The girl's face brightened. There was hope after all. "Okay, be right back."

Ten minutes later she reappeared. She was wearing jeans and a sweatshirt, and was carrying an overstuffed backpack.

"Ready?"

"Yes."

"Here, put this on before we go out."

The girl slipped the helmet on her head.

"Now put both arms through the backpack. That's it. Good."

Christine led the young defendant outside. She mounted the motorcycle.

"Get on, please."

The girl climbed on behind Christine and automatically encircled Christine's waist with her arms.

"Hang on!"

Had they been watching--which they weren't--any neighbor would have been clueless as to the identities of the two riders. Likewise, the license plate on the back would never be traced since it was now tucked away inside the bike's saddlebag.

Eastbound on I-90, they turned off at the O'Hare Airport Terminals off-ramp.

Christine wound around three roads until they reached Terminal Two. There she parked the bike and led Bussie through the terminal to the General Aviation terminal. They made their way through until they came to the doorway leading out to the tarmac. Christine showed her aircraft owner's card and the door was opened. She led the way to the waiting Gulfstream.

Once aboard, they strapped in and removed the motorcycle helmets.

"What are we doing?" Bussie wanted to know.

"Taking a trip."

"Where are we going?"

"I told you. We're going to prepare your defense."

"Oh. Okay, cool."

"Just sit back and plug in the iPod on the seat beside you. It has all your favorite music already loaded."

"My favorite music? How do you know my favorite music?"

"A little bird hacked your iTunes account. It's all there, waiting for you to pop on the headset and lean back."

"Wow."

"You're welcome."

"I mean really. This is way too much."

Christine reached across the aisle and patted the girl's arm. "No, for you, it's not too much. Now let me make some calls on my air phone while you listen to your sounds. Okay?"

The girl plugged the buds in her ears. "Okay."

After three hours had passed and the plane had gone 1500 of the 5,000 miles, the girl removed the ear buds.

"How much longer?"

Christine smiled at her. "Hungry?"

"Starving."

Christine motioned to the cabin attendant. He arrived and took orders for two chicken sandwiches, tossed salads, milk for Bussie and hot coffee for Christine. They wolfed down the sandwiches. Strawberry pie was served with strawberry ice cream.

"Whose plane is this?" Bussie asked.

"Mine. Do you like it?"

"Do you mean you own it?"

"I do."

"Holy shit."

"I know. That's what I said my first time aboard."

"How much longer will we be flying?"

"About nine hours. The food will make you sleepy. Your chair fully reclines into a flat single bed. Just put it back and Herman will bring you a pillow and blanket. So get some shuteye. You're going to need it."

"Where are we going?"

"Where they speak Portuguese."

"Rio?" Bussie asked, wide-eyed.

"Southern hemisphere, let's call it."

"Okay."

At six a.m. they touched down on a runway five hundred miles beyond Rio.

It was a small airport with a short runway, and the pilots had called ahead to make sure they could bring the heavy Gulfstream in there. They were assured the runway was modern and able to support even the larger commercial craft. In fact Linhas Aereas Brasileira flights came and went once daily.

A jeep with driver was waiting to take them into the large town.

Two streets over from the main thoroughfare, they found them-selves on an ancient brick road. The driver pulled over in front of a walled house. The property line was actually on the sidewalk, and on each side of the entrance were walls. The left hand side was under a roof and the right hand side was all patio, walled in, of course, as was the style.

Christine punched a series of numbers into the door's keypad and led the girl inside.

An older woman and an older gentleman, who, Bussie would learn, were there to take care of her, greeted them. They took her backpack and led her to a large room with a canopied double bed, sliding doors that looked out on a pool and Jacuzzi, and a flat screen mounted on the wall opposite the head of the bed. A MacBook was plugged in and waiting, as well.

"Here?" Bussie asked Christine. "I'll be staying in here while we prepare?"

"Yes, this is your room while we prepare your defense."

"How long will I be here?"

"What do you say we go outside by the pool and talk about that?"

They were served the country's version of coffee, with real cream fresh that morning, and they talked. The old woman watched them from the kitchen window. She saw the young girl cry and saw the woman hand her a handkerchief. The girl wiped her eyes and the talking continued. Then the girl began nodding as the woman talked on and on. The girl smiled, then stood up and kicked off her shoes and stepped onto the top step leading into the pool. The water came up to her ankles and she bent to feel it with her hand. She cupped a little water in her hand and passed it over her face. She smiled again. Then she laughed.

Over the next three days a steady stream of people appeared at the front door of the home, went inside, and reemerged two or three hours later, their wallets and purses bulging with American dollars. During that time the girl's hair changed color. It was cut in the latest South American style--undercut and meticulously fashioned. A banker arrived with a signature card for her new account. Credit cards were prepared in her new name. An army of language teachers began teaching her the rudiments of Portuguese.

Christine directed everything from the office in her home. Her home--it was titled in the name of a company that was owned by a company that was owned by another company. In the end, it was all owned by Christine but soon would no longer be.

A lawyer came. He transferred the deed of the property from the closest company's name to the name of Alessandra Alegria. That girl was born the same year as the girl once named Bussie. Same month and day, as well. A new birth certificate was produced. Driver's licensing was easy; it was a country where bribery was a fact of everyday commerce. The MVD officer was only too happy to oblige with a license. Then there arrived a bright new car that exactly matched the social status and taste of the new Alessandra.

"You wanted to attend medical school?" Christine asked Alessandra on their third day in Alessandra's new home. "Here is your admission to the 2018 class at the School of Medicine at UFBa. This medical school was founded in 1829 and is the best med school in South America. You'll finish your undergrad first, but admission is guaranteed."

"How is it guaranteed?"

"Let's just a say a donor funded a new microbiology lab in return for a seat in the 2018 class."

"Isn't that like cheating?"

"Not if you continue the 3.8 GPA that you had at Chicago University, it isn't. It's just a little added bonus to the school. Besides, I've always wanted my name on some building somewhere in the world. Now I have it."

"What do I do for friends?"

"Start over. Call no one. Ever. Not even your parents. I'll make arrangements for visits with them in neutral places. They can never know where you actually live."

"But aren't I giving up a lot?"

"Darling girl, that old life was over. You were looking at a lifetime in prison for a murder that looked like first degree. Maybe we could have pled it down, but you still would have served twenty years in prison for a crime you never wanted to commit. Trust me on this."

"I do trust you, Christine."

"I know, Alessandra."

"That sounds so strange."

"It won't. Women change their names every day when they marry. Some of them several times before they get it right."

"I know."

"Now, I have my own kids at home waiting for me. They need me and your defense is done."

"So I won't be going back to court?"

"Well, duh. Hello?"

"Just kidding. I love you, Christine. My dad said I could trust you. Does he know about this?"

"Not yet. He'll know you're well and okay, but he'll know about none of this."

"What about his house? Or his job?"

"He'll most likely be voted out of office. But that's okay. I need an experienced criminal attorney in my office. Who knows? My representation of you would then extend to him. He could know all about you and no one could pry it out of him. Same attorney-client privilege. As for his house, we can fix that. It's only money."

"And what about when they ask you about me?"

"I'll simply say, 'Sorry, attorney-client privilege.'"

"So they can't make you tell?"

"Privileged information. No, they can't. Only you can give yourself up."

"Will anyone come looking for me?"

"Doubtful. The only one would be the special prosecutor appointed to your case. And she won't really give a damn as it's not a career job for her. No, you're safe now. I wouldn't leave you here if you weren't."

"How do I earn money?"

"Have you looked at your bank account?"

"Not really."

"Let's just say you won the lottery."

"I love you, Christine."

"I know you do, Bussie. I know you do. Now let's have a hug and I'm off."

"Goodbye."

"Goodbye, Alessandra."

43

Some call it industrial espionage. Some call it commercial spying. But in Christine's case it was relying on what she knew: if there's a buyer, there's going to be a willing seller. The trick is to find him. Or, as in this case, her.

Her name was Zamora Winthers and she was the executive secretary to Richard D'Amato, Chief Counsel of Great Northern Timber and Energy.

Christine paid Winthers $50,000 and in return got the text messages D'Amato had traded with the Risk Management team at Great Northern Timber and Energy during the time period covered by Jesse Osako's problems. The recipient of the emails was Arthur Andrews, who was an Iraq War veteran, honorably discharged from his duties as a Marine sniper, and an employee assigned to no manager in Risk. Which meant, to Christine, that the guy was D'Amato's plant and was available to troubleshoot whatever problems D'Amato ran into.

The emails were replete with code for murder.

"Chicago is out to take away our Tongass leases," said one text.

Okay, thought Christine, *what if Chicago is a reference to me?*

"What response?"

"Falling tree," was the terse reply from D'Amato to Andrews.

She was jolted beyond anything she had expected. They were coming for her. *Falling tree* simply meant a mishap was to befall her. Or her kids, or all three of them. She recalled that after she'd gotten notice of Jesse's death from his son, Nathan, she had had very strong suspicions. Now they were confirmed. Great Northern Timber and Energy had very likely gone gunning for Jesse Osako. Now they would be coming for her, if she knew her corporations and their scorched earth policies.

Is this guy another Jackie Barre? she wondered. *Is this how private practice is actually going to be?*

She was standing at her desk, reading page after page of text exchanges. Suddenly she felt woozy. She thrust out a hand to steady herself. Still swaying, she turned and sat--dropped--onto the desk. Closing her eyes, she considered what was bothering her. Then she knew. She had watched Thaddeus Murfee in his law practice and often was right there beside him. She had been terribly abused in Russia and she had seen her husband murdered during the Bussie Speers prosecution. *Well, welcome to the real world,* she thought. *This is how it goes.*

Which meant it was time for her to send her own message to Great Northern Timber and Energy. She wanted to alarm D'Amato as much as he had alarmed her.

Two days later she had her new identification: credit card, driver's license (South Dakota), and passport. It was her own picture, taken in a south Chicago back room where a genius engraver plied his trade. The bundle ran five grand--a steal. She made arrangements for the jet to deliver the kids to her sister Rosalind for two weeks at the beach. She told Roz only that she had business to attend to and that she was to forget Christine had ever even told her that much.

Then she caught a train to Saint Louis. No ID required, no record of the trip. From there she went to Mobile, Alabama. In Mobile she bought round-trip airfare on Alaska Airlines to Fairbanks. Under her new identity, of course.

Zamora provided Arthur Andrews' personnel file--with photograph--for another ten thousand. Cost meant nothing to Christine at this point. She was protecting her family and she was willing to spend every dime she had to do that.

At Ketchikan she bought a "previously owned" Lincoln Navigator for $12,500 cash. The used car dealer was elated. He gladly processed the title exchange with the help of Christine's throwaway ID. The car would be abandoned in Ketchikan; the ID would be abandoned in Mobile, where the phony persona would disappear like smoke in air.

She picked up a .40 caliber Glock at a Saturday morning gun show. ID, but no background, no waiting. Complete with three magazines, loaded, no extra charge. A gunsmith in the back of a bait and gun store supplied her with a noise suppressor for $5,000 cash. With the gun silenced, her payback would go unheard by all but the intended victim.

Arthur Andrews lived in a double-wide at the Lazy Tongass Mobile Home Park. Unit 11.

She had no doubt he would be armed. A retired Marine sniper-- he would be armed to the teeth and very dangerous.

The exterior door was aluminum frame, the top half a screen with a sliding window, the bottom half aluminum sheeting. It was across this aluminum sheeting that she dragged a fork from Sally's diner and--who would believe it?--meowed like a cat. She did this several times until a light inside flicked on.

Immediately she walked twenty feet directly across from the door and sat down in the wet grass, her back against the neighboring unit's exterior wall. Her knees were drawn up and she held the gun in a two-hand grip, muzzle pointed at the door. Dressed in black jeans and black turtleneck, she wouldn't be visible to the Marine even for a second, not with the interior light ruining his night vision.

Sure enough, he opened the inside door, pushed open the outside door and peered out into the night, a 1911 semi-auto profile in his free hand. "What the hell?" he cursed into the night.

She only had two fingers and a thumb on her right hand. But the first finger was the middle one and she applied it to the trigger of the

Glock: squeeze-squeeze-squeeze, just like the Army had taught her to shoot.

Her first round caught him directly in the heart and knocked him back inside. The exterior door, on its hydraulic hinge, started to close.

She leapt from her position and went inside and closed the door.

Even wearing latex gloves it was easy enough to continue the conversation with Robert D'Amato at Great Northern Timber and Energy on Andrews' cellphone.

She thumb-typed:

Chicago wouldn't agree to the plan.

You will be next.

Rethink.

She carefully placed the cellphone in Andrews' outstretched hand. She pressed his thumb several times on the keyboard.

With his thumb he involuntarily pressed SEND.

His work there was done. But he stayed anyway.

She left.

Driving south on the Tongass Highway, she tossed the gun into the Narrows. Another mile and she tossed the suppressor into the same waters. Now she had a chance at a lawsuit that was only about law and not about trying to kill each other. Maybe. Either way, she was ready.

In Ketchikan North she stopped at the all-night McDonald's. She had to admit, she was starving. Big Mac, fries, strawberry shake. She ate on the far right of the drive-up window after she had pulled ahead twenty yards. There was no traffic on the highway; Ketchikan was a small place and only the occasional semi pulled by, heading up the grade.

After she'd parked the Navigator back behind the restaurant, she grasped her travel bag and pulled. Then she locked the vehicle and gave it a friendly pat. Inside Mickey D's she used the pay phone. Yellow Cab would have someone there within ten minutes.

Outside the restaurant, she found a cement table and chairs still damp with dew. She plopped down anyway and stifled a yawn.

She stretched and peered into the dark Alaska sky. She saw

herself clearly for the first time since Sonny's death. She was the she-wolf come around to protect her young. She was Sergeant Susmann of the United States Army taking on a force ten times her size and strength and returning from battle with a Silver Star. She was the fierce and brilliant lawyer who could walk into any courtroom and lay anyone low.

And she was a mother and a friend.

The wedding ring was then removed from her left hand.

She was back.

THE END

ALSO BY JOHN ELLSWORTH

THADDEUS MURFEE SERIES

Thaddeus Murfee

The Defendants

Beyond a Reasonable Death

Attorney at Large

Chase, the Bad Baby

Defending Turquoise

The Mental Case

Unspeakable Prayers

The Girl Who Wrote The New York Times Bestseller

The Trial Lawyer (A Small Death)

The Near Death Experience

THE JUSTICE SERIES

Flagstaff Station (Book 1 New Series)

SISTERS IN LAW SERIES

Frat Party: Sisters In Law

Hellfire: Sisters In Law

MICHAEL GRESHAM SERIES

Lies She Never Told Me

Michael Gresham: The Lawyer

Secrets Girls Keep

The Law Partners

Carlos the Ant

Sakharov the Bear

ANNIE'S VERDICT

DEAD LAWYER ON AISLE 11

30 DAYS OF JUSTIS

THE FIFTH JUSTICE

PSYCHOLOGICAL THRILLERS

THE EMPTY PLACE AT THE TABLE

ABOUT THE AUTHOR

For thirty years John defended criminal clients across the United States. He defended cases ranging from shoplifting to First Degree Murder to RICO to Tax Evasion, and has gone to jury trial on hundreds. His first book, *The Defendants*, was published in January, 2014. John is presently at work on his 25th thriller.

Reception to John's books has been phenomenal; more than 2,000,000 have been downloaded in 60 months. All are Amazon best-sellers. He is an Amazon All-Star every month and is a *U.S.A Today* bestseller.

John Ellsworth lives in Arizona in the mountains and in Cali-fornia on the beach. He has three dogs that ignore him but worship his wife, and bark day and night until another home must be abandoned in yet another move.

johnellsworthbooks.com
johnellsworthbooks@gmail.com

AFTERWORD

Much of what happens in this book happens via the office of the Cook County, Illinois, District Attorney's Office. As an Illinois attorney, I am only too acutely aware that the prosecutors in Illinois are actually called States Attorneys. But for the sake of easy cognition, I have referred to them throughout as the "District Attorney." That seems to happen in most of my books and I mention it here only because in this book it is so pervasive.

The Cook County Criminal Court commonly known as the California Court is real. It is located on California Street in Cook County and is responsible for the yearly processing of an overwhelmingly number of criminal cases. The people who work there, from the cafeteria employees to the judges to the administrative and clerical officials are all incredibly helpful people as well as knowledgable beyond the call. How they manage to maintain such order and reason in the midst of a criminal calendar that would make most municipalities turn around, is beyond me. Hats off to you all.

CPSIA information can be obtained
at www.ICGtesting.com
Printed in the USA
BVHW041817210620
582013BV00013B/435